Advance Praise for Soul Designers

"An exciting debut novel! *Soul Designers* blends meaningful threads of faith into an all-new dystopian society as Dona Watson crafts intrigue and humanity with a thoughtful pen. Whether you're a long-time spec fan, or just getting started—*Soul Designers* is a story of hope that's a wonderful addition to any fiction lover's shelf." – Joanne Bischof, Christy Award-winning author of *The Lady and the Lionheart*

"A magnificent tale of what it means to be human. Set in a futuristic society, Dona Watson's *Soul Designers*, explores a world populated by humans and genetics—the flaw being that the gens have been purposely engineered without souls. As such, they cannot enter heaven when they die. Watson puts her characters right in the heart of the moral struggle between faith and science. This is a book with a killer premise and riveting characters, and I highly recommend it!" – USA Today bestselling author Merrie Destefano, author of *Valiant, Shade,* and *Afterlife*

"Dona Watson's *Soul Designers* is a futuristic thriller that explores intriguing ideas. I applaud the originality. It really kept me guessing!" – Kerry Nietz, award-winning author of *Lost Bits* and *Frayed*

"I was quickly drawn into the world Watson set up as a very believable but scary possibility; what if the wrong people gained control of our souls through genetic manipulation? Her description of the differences between the haves vs.

have-nots, her skillful handling of the technical aspects, the eternal implications, and how Jack fought back despite his faith struggle kept me turning the pages late into the night to a very satisfying ending. Recommended!" – Beverly Nault, award-winning author or *Fresh Start Summer* and *The Kaleidoscope*

"Dona Watson has penned a thoughtful tale of a society in which the very nature of salvation and the soul is up for grabs—and the dark consequences such a line of reasoning sparks. Join Jack as he searches for the truth about what happens to his father and struggles to bring the plight of the gens to the attention of the only person in the world who can relieve the oppression they face." – Steve Rzasa, awarding-winning author of the *Mercury Hale* series and *Deception Fleet*

SOUL
DESIGNERS

DONA WATSON

Copyright © 2023 by Dona Watson
Runewood Press

Cover by Kirk DouPonce, Fiction-Artist.com

ISBN 979-8-9876320-0-0 (paperback)

ISBN 979-8-9876320-1-7 (ebook)

For my mom and dad,
who never stopped believing in me.

Chapter 1
August 2261, New Santiago

J ack Metcalfe stumbled and wiped blood from the corner of his mouth, the officers' laughter fading as they walked on. He scooped up the pieces of the handheld Orichi computer scattered on the ground and cradled the broken device in his hands. Six months of savings, now shattered.

Quiet hung in the air. Any nearby gens had probably fled for the safety of homes or darkness. Gens. That's what they called his people, as if they weren't human. It didn't matter that he was half-human and half-gen. His dad was genetically engineered and that was enough to lower his standing in both camps.

Dad. The man who had abandoned his mother when she needed him most. With disgust, Jack pushed the thought aside, stuffed down the black hole his mind reserved just for that. His father didn't deserve to be called "Dad."

Jack leaned against the cold wall of a two-story apartment building and looked up into the dusky sky. Soon this day would be over. With a deep breath, he brushed the dirt off his worn pants, straightened his slightly too-small jacket and staggered toward the tiny, run-down hovel he called home. Curtains fluttered as gens peeked out like mice making sure the cat was gone. When the police patrolled the gens' quarter, they took what they wanted and the gens typically trembled in fear.

Once home, Jack let himself in and ducked under the low doorway. As the door clicked shut behind him, his mother, Eva, rushed in, concern etched on her face.

"Oh, Jack." She tipped his chin to one side with a fingertip and examined a gash across his right eyebrow. "They found you again, didn't they?" She shook her head. "Have a seat in the kitchen and let's get you cleaned up."

He laid the shattered pieces of his handheld on the kitchen table and inspected the remains as he took a seat. Maybe it could still be salvaged, or at least maybe he could still save the day's inventory logs from work. Over the years, he'd had to get good at fixing broken things.

Eva bustled in, torn bandages and a jar of antiseptic in hand. With a damp cloth, she dabbed at the dried blood trailing down his temple. His gaze lifted to a cracked mirror hanging on the wall. Against his pale skin, the blood stood out like a neon sign advertising the hatred of others. Sometimes he wished for the gens' reddish-tinted skin and black hair. Then the blood they drew wouldn't be so obvious. His fair complexion, blond hair, and tall stature guaranteed exclusion from the gens' humble society. But his bright golden eyes left him despised by humans.

Ethan, his adopted brother who had been taken in by Eva when he was just an orphaned toddler, walked into the room, studied Jack, and grabbed one of the few glasses they owned from the cupboard. "What happened to you?" He turned on the faucet and waited a few seconds for the water to run clear.

Jack shrugged. "The usual."

"Sit still," his mother commanded. "I'm almost done."

"I'd think by now you'd find a different route home." Disdain colored Ethan's voice.

"It wouldn't matter." Jack tipped his head to one side as his mother applied an adhesive bandage above his eyebrow. "They'd find me anyway."

She placed the first aid supplies on one corner of the tiny kitchen counter and uncovered a bowl resting on the back of the well-worn stove. Jack gently pushed aside the various electronic components and she placed the food in front of him. Beans again. He stifled a sigh and instead shot her a slight grin. At least there was enough to fill his stomach. He shoveled a spoonful into his mouth and chewed, forcing a swallow.

She poured a glass of water for each of them and sat across from him in one of the three creaky wooden chairs. "How was work?"

Jack swallowed. "Nothing exciting. Just the same old stuff."

Ethan snorted. "Listen to you. You sit in an air-conditioned office and play with your computers while I'm out picking up garbage in the gutters. You should be grateful."

Jack took another bite, choosing not to answer. He didn't disagree but any reply would stir up the old argument with his brother—and that would just grieve their mother.

Eva cast a warning glare toward Ethan. "Jack, did you see Robert today about your application?"

Muttering, Ethan placed the glass in the sink and stomped out.

As his footfalls faded, Jack shook his head. "No. He was out." Robert might have gotten him the job as a favor to their mother, but that didn't mean Jack saw him often. He had little to no reason to frequent Robert's office and his half-brother obviously had no desire to associate with a low class half-sibling. But Eva didn't need to know that. "I tried to make an appointment but his schedule was full. His secretary said to come back later."

"Again?" Her thin shoulders slumped. "That's what they said yesterday. And the day before."

"Don't worry, Mom. He knows we need the extra income this job would bring, just to make ends meet."

The back door creaked open and a young woman poked her head into the room, puffing a breath of air through platinum blonde bangs. The rest of her hair was dyed black, matching the black straight hair built into the gens' DNA. Amber and Jack had been close, if unlikely, friends ever since they had met as teens at a rally for gens' rights.

Amber eyed the bandage on Jack's forehead and her smile morphed into a frown. "Are you okay?"

He gently fingered the wounded area and nodded.

Amber's gaze fell to the table and hardened with anger. "Oh Jack. Not your handheld. Who was it this time?"

"It doesn't matter." Amber didn't need to know the police had knocked it from his hand and beat him up. She'd just get herself in trouble.

"Jack! You have to stand up for yourself." Amber plunked down in the remaining chair.

Eva scooped up Jack's empty bowl and rinsed it in the sink. "I'll leave you two alone. I need to finish the laundry."

Amber watched her with compassionate eyes but made sure she was out of range before speaking. When she did, her voice was quiet. "I spoke with Ryan today. It sounds like he might be willing to pull some strings and see if he can get you that appointment." Although Ryan's position in the government administration offices was new, Amber's friend had been very helpful so far.

Jack nodded. "That would be good." There was more at risk here than just a promotion for Jack. The outcome could determine the future for all gens. If he could get access to the main databanks, he just might be able to find out how to gain a soul for the gens. *Just because they can genetically engineer people doesn't give them the right to withhold the one gene that grants us a soul*, he thought.

"Oh, just a minute. I have a call." Amber reached up to tap the tiny communicator barely visible in her ear.

Jack took advantage of the interruption to fetch a few tools from his room. When he returned, Amber's face had drained of all color and her jaw hung slack. She stared into his eyes with a distraught expression. His heart skipped a beat.

"What's wrong?"

She paused a few moments before answering. "They just found Ryan's body in an alley near his apartment."

Chapter 2

Jack cursed and looked to one side. The kid had been only eighteen, but even then, a great computer programmer. Genuinely talented and extremely loyal to his friends.

"So now what do we do?" Amber's voice was soft.

"We have to warn the others." Jack paced as far as the small kitchen would allow, two steps in each direction. Suddenly the air in the tiny room felt stifling. Besides, it was time to leave for their meeting with the other loyalists.

Jack shrugged on his jacket, grabbed a hat, and headed out the back door, Amber close behind. Outside, night had fallen and with it the temperature. The buildings and pavement of Gen Town still radiated the heat of the day, but cool dampness hung in the evening air over hushed streets, most residents already home for the night, safe from the roving gangs. Though the population was poor and hungry, so were the thugs.

Jack hunched his shoulders and tugged his cap down as far as it would go over his blonde hair lest it shine like a beacon in the night. Amber glanced behind them, her eyes bright and cautious. Jack wasn't exactly sure why she, a human, chose to be friends with a half-breed like him, but he was glad she did.

The two kept to the shadows until they reached The Down and Dirty, a rundown bar favored by gens. This time it only took one pull to wrench open the weather-beaten door.

Inside the dimly lit room, a couple of familiar faces glanced up. It pained Jack to see the hopelessness in their eyes as they tried to drink their pain away. Pete, the owner, bartender, and sympathizer to the gens' cause met Jack's gaze and tipped his head toward the back. Amber and Jack headed that way through the thick cigarette smoke. Health inspectors would never come to this neighborhood to enforce the no smoking laws. No one really cared if the gens killed themselves or not.

On the far side of the room, a shadow-filled hallway led to a door. Jack tapped lightly then opened it, glad to see two of their group already there, both gens. "Demir, Adwin."

Demir, the heavier of the two, broke into a tight smile. "Jack! Good to see you." His eyes flicked to the bandage on Jack's forehead. "Trouble today?"

Jack jerked a nod. "Who else is coming tonight?" He pulled up a chair and seated himself at a round table with seven chairs.

Just then, the door opened and a tall young man entered. His red hair, freckles, green eyes and fine clothing marked him as an outsider but Jack was willing to take all the help he could get to further their cause. The young man shook hands all around. When he came to Amber, his eyes lit up.

She offered a half-smile in return. "Hey, Kennan."

He pulled out a chair for her, then seated himself nearby.

Jack opened his mouth to speak, but just then the door opened again. He paused for a moment while Rochelle rushed in and grabbed a seat.

"Ok," Jack said. "Shall we get started? I think we're all here."

Several eyed the conspicuously empty seventh chair.

Jack paused and took a deep breath. "Ryan won't be joining us." He met every eye now focused on him. "He was found murdered today in the alley near his house."

Shock registered on each face and time seemed to stop. The only sound was a soft gasp as Rochelle covered her mouth with her fingertips. Kennan found his voice first.

"What happened?" he asked quietly.

"We don't know yet. Amber?" Jack tipped his head her direction.

The young woman nodded. "My brother called with the news. I don't know how he found out. But that's all he knew."

Adwin sighed and shook his head slowly. "Now what?"

"We lay low." Jack traced the table's wood grain pattern with his fingertip. "I'll keep trying to work my way into a position at the Ministry of Religion. I think that's where we'll find the answers. The priests are the ones holding the secrets."

"Yeah," Kennan said with disgust. "The only reason they grant a soul every year to one 'lucky' gen is to assuage their own consciences."

Murmurs of assent echoed around the table.

"It's not right that they refuse us the right to an afterlife just because we're gens." His eyes glinted with anger.

Jack held up his hand. "Yes, we all agree that they have no right to withhold an eternal soul from the gens. But before we get carried away here, let's focus on the issue at hand."

"Do we know yet who the priests have chosen for this year's honor?" Amber asked.

Jack shook his head. "They keep that information pretty well under wraps until it's announced publicly. I'm hoping that if I can see my brother, I can get him to give me a position in his office. Maybe once I'm in, I'll have access to information like that."

"So now what?" Demir's gruff voice rumbled through his broad chest.

"Well, I'll keep trying to work my way in. The rest of you, lay low—at least until this blows over. I don't want anyone else getting hurt. Meanwhile, keep your eyes and ears open and see if there are others around you who might support our cause." Jack's eyes met Amber's. "Amber and I will try to discover what happened to Ryan. If we can identify who killed him, I'll let you know."

Amber nodded. "I'll see what I can find out."

"Any questions?" Jack scanned the now-somber faces, gaining a couple of head shakes in reply. "Okay, then. I think that's it. If any of you come across anything on the streets, at work, or anywhere else, please try to get word to Amber or me."

One by one, the allies pushed away from the table and filed out without the usual chitchat. Jack and Amber left together and headed back the way they had come through the night. With no streetlights, Gen Town could be very dark after sunset.

"Maybe I should walk you home." Jack glanced sideways at his friend.

Amber's eyebrows creased together. "And have you stopped by the police for being in the human quarter after dark without a pass? I don't think so."

Jack frowned, hating to admit that she was probably right. "They probably wouldn't even see me," he said, even though he didn't truly believe that himself.

The two walked the rest of the way in silence, each lost in their own thoughts. When they reached the edge of the gen quarter, Amber turned toward Jack.

"That's far enough. Thanks for keeping me company."

"Are you sure you don't want me to walk you home?"

Her face half in shadow, Amber shot him a smile in the dim light and gave a playful nudge. "Go home and try to get some rest." She then shoved her hands in the pockets of her black jacket and stepped into the brighter glow of the human quarter, her steps quick.

Watching her go, Jack breathed a prayer to the gods for her safety. After a few moments, he turned toward home, plunging back into the darkness of the gen quarter.

Chapter 3

J ack rubbed his eyes. He had been at this for hours and still wasn't finished with the handheld. He slid the case back together and flipped the switch. The device whirred to life, but only for an instant as the screen flickered and then went blank. With a sigh, he turned it back off. A higher-quality model would have been sturdier, but a twenty-year-old, bottom-of-the-line unit was all he could afford.

Opening the case, he re-checked the electronic connections and tried again. After a characteristic whirr, the screen's backlight came on, glowed softly, and the main menu appeared. With relief, Jack turned the device off and replaced the plastic outer case.

His mind drifted to the insurgents. He hadn't said anything at the meeting for fear of being called a traitor, but he wondered nonetheless if, by some miracle, he might be the one granted a soul this year. As a half-breed, he had never received the final treatment that would grant him an afterlife. Without a soul, there was no chance of reaching heaven, no matter how much he devoted himself to God.

But more importantly, in the process of gaining a soul, he might discover the priests' secret as to how it was done. Then he could share the information with the gens and change their futures forever too. He allowed himself a wistful smile.

Jack placed the final screw in place and tested the device once again. Satisfied it now functioned properly, he tumbled into bed.

It seemed he had barely closed his eyes when the alarm clamored for him to wake up a couple of hours later. With a groan, Jack sat up on the edge of the bed, a short pallet with a sagging mattress cast off by some unknown human many years before. The night's sleep had been far too short.

He stumbled to the tiny bathroom, flipped on the single dim light, and squeezed inside the room. Standing in front of the chipped porcelain sink stained with orange streaks of rust, he twisted the wobbly handle and scooped both hands full of cold water and splashed it on his face. A shiver ran down his spine as the cold jolted him awake. Jack finished his morning routine, grabbed an apple, and headed out the door, relieved he hadn't run into Ethan before he left. Arguments between the two came too easily these days and he suspected his brother avoided contact with him as much as he did his brother.

Jack headed toward the public administration offices, the night sky giving way to the soft glow of dawn. With most humans still at home or in bed, the streets lay quiet. But if he hurried, he might reach work before his supervisor Justin did. Unbeknownst to most, Justin was also a relative—his mother's brother. Jack liked to remind himself that this man was a near relative, just because he knew that it irked the obnoxious man. To Justin, it was a great embarrassment to have a half-breed in the family. For that reason, Justin took his anger out on Jack as often as possible.

But this morning, Jack didn't feel up to the battle. If he could just get to work before Justin, that would spare him at least some of the man's ire. No matter how early Justin arrived, he expected Jack to already be in place and hard at work. If he wasn't, there'd be hell to pay.

With a firm grip on his handheld, Jack trudged down the sidewalk, his head pounding with fatigue. One car and then another passed by with a soft purr, destinations programmed into the Artificial Neural Network and their owners probably reading the morning news or going over notes before reaching the office. For a brief moment, Jack imagined how nice it would be to have one of the vehicles at his disposal. But then he pushed the thought out of his mind. It was virtually impossible for any nonhuman to have the privilege of owning a vehicle that operated on the ANN. Just too expensive.

Eventually, Jack reached his destination. He climbed the front steps of the grand building two at a time, its classic Corinthian columns only shadows on the periphery of his vision. He had seen it so many times its grandeur no longer awed him.

Once inside, he followed the corridors, turning one way and then another, burrowing ever deeper into the warren of offices until he finally reached the narrow shelf that served as his workstation.

Hopefully, Justin wasn't in yet. Jack remembered the last time he had arrived after Justin. He'd spent all morning sorting through dusty, no, filthy boxes. Then, when he had returned, he had no chair and his personal Orichi had disappeared into Justin's office. It hadn't been easy to get the device back.

Seconds later, Justin poked his head around the corner, a characteristic frown on his face. Seeing Jack seated at his station, the man walked away without a word. Jack breathed a sigh of relief and turned to the work of the day. He fired up his Orichi handheld and logged onto the network, navigating to where financial summaries were stored. Time to dredge through the numbers, looking for discrepancies or errors that if discovered by the public might pose a public relations disaster for the government. Jack recorded on his computer any data that looked even slightly out of kilter, then double-checked them against another database. Without his handheld, he would have had to copy the figures down by hand.

Jack suspected that there was truly no reason for his job to exist. The system probably already had redundancies built in that would flag such information. However, he also knew that the only reason he had the job was because his mother had begged and pleaded with her brother to find him a job in administration, fearing that his human characteristics would single him out for lethal abuse in a manual labor job like Ethan's. At first, his uncle had been skeptical. Sometimes the humans forgot gens could be intelligent—even though some were engineered with superior intellect that allowed them to perform tasks the humans found distasteful but still required a close eye to detail.

Yes, Jack was sure Justin, who refused to be called Uncle, had created this job, not because he was convinced Jack was smart enough to work in his office, but to quiet Eva.

Jack settled into the relative quiet of a normal workday until Justin summoned him. Jack walked into his uncle's office—and straight into an ambush.

"What have you done?" Justin's face was red with anger, fleshy jowls jiggling with indignation.

"Is there a problem, sir?"

"Why didn't you review the reports from the governor's celebration?"

Jack folded his hands behind him. "I'm currently reviewing the last three years, as you requested."

"What about the two years before that?"

Jack stood in silence. It wouldn't do any good to remind him that he had done exactly that the year before and then again six months ago.

Justin leaned back in his chair and growled, "I want you to go to the archives and get the actual reports. The database might be wrong." He sat in silence for a few seconds, probably waiting for a protest, Jack thought. But he wasn't about to give the man such satisfaction.

Pressing his lips into a fine line and frowning in a look of frustration, Justin leaned forward. "You have got to be the most worthless creature ever! Can't you ever do anything right?" He paused, but Jack knew from past experience the man wasn't finished yet. "Your idiot mother should never have borne such a carcass of a being."

At the insult against his mother, Jack fumed inside. It was one thing to impugn him, but when Justin attacked his mother...well, that was too much. Jack feared that one of these days he would lose control and punch his fist into the man's face. But not only would he have to pay for such an act, but he'd lose his job and then his mother would suffer too. So he clenched his jaw and stared the man down. It was all he dared to do for now.

After several moments, Justin barked, "Well? What are you waiting for? Get out of here! You'll never get it done standing there looking like an idiot."

Jack jerked a nod and turned to leave. Passing through the doorway of Justin's office, he heard the man call out behind him, "And I want those other reports finished by the end of the day."

As he walked away, Jack rolled his eyes. It would take hours to finish all these reports. Hours he would never be reimbursed for. Gens didn't get overtime.

Rather than taking the lift, Jack headed for the back stairs. He might not be allowed into the lift anyways if any humans were present.

He pushed the door open and stepped into the stairwell. The cool air soothed him and he rolled his shoulders against the tension there. The shuffle of his shoes on each step was, blessedly, the only sound to be heard.

Two floors down, he stepped into the lowest basement. The massive room extended far beneath the large government building and then some. Sensor-activated lights blazed on, making the room starkly clinical in appearance. Here was one area that modern technology had never reached. Why should it? No one ever needed to come here. Everything was logged into the network database. Jack was tempted to get the report online instead and not bother with the paper files, but everyone knew that when a file was copied manually onto another device, the file carried a meta tag showing where it had been downloaded from. Knowing Justin, he might examine the file and check the tag; it wouldn't be the first time he had done so. And if that happened...well, Jack couldn't risk another suspension without pay.

He walked for what seemed forever, passing old equipment and furniture abandoned long ago. For the hundredth time, he wished the humans would let the gens use what was considered to be a pile of garbage, but that would never do, would it? *Let's not make the laborers too comfortable*, he thought sarcastically.

Finally, he reached an old terminal that tied into the same database he could have accessed from his office. He dragged over an old office chair and plopped down into it, causing a cloud of dust to puff up and fill his nostrils until he sneezed.

He quickly located the files he needed and transferred them onto his handheld and headed back toward the stairs. Along the way, he decided that this would be a good time to check in at his half-brother's office. Robert's secretary did say, after all, to "come back tomorrow." He'd have to hurry though. It wouldn't be long before Justin looked to see if he was back yet—if he hadn't checked already.

After jogging to a neighboring building and climbing ten flights of stairs, Jack finally reached the receptionist's office and placed himself in front of her desk, trying not to gasp for air.

A beautiful redhead sat primly behind her desk, half turned away from Jack. Her red suit had to have cost a fortune. Of course, Robert Bradley's secretaries were always drop-dead gorgeous. Nothing but the best for him. Much like the other priests.

When Miss Beautiful turned and looked up, recognition dawned on her face and she frowned, releasing a deep breath.

"You again?"

"I'd like to make an appointment with Robert."

The young woman just looked at him, tapping her blood-red fingernails on her desk in a staccato rhythm. They had been a different color yesterday and probably would be again tomorrow to match whatever color she wore. Those little whatchamacallit devices made it so easy to change one's nail color in seconds. She didn't respond but regarded him with green eyes, her expression not changing one bit.

"You said to come back today," he prompted.

"Yeah. Right." She looked down and stabbed a stylus at a panel built into her desk, bringing up her boss's schedule. "He's still out of town, but he'll be back tonight. How about nine o'clock tomorrow morning?"

Jack could hardly believe his ears. He had half-expected to never be admitted. Even though tomorrow morning he should be as good as chained to his desk at nine, he'd deal with the fallout later.

"Yes," he agreed, trying not to sound overly eager. "I'll be here."

Without a word, Miss Beautiful turned back to her work, effectively dismissing Jack from sight. Ignoring her disdain, he turned back toward the stairs, heart soaring. Jack made his way back to the office as quickly as possible, but when he stepped out of the stairwell, Justin pounced.

"Where have you been?" His uncle scowled.

"I went to the archives like you told me to."

"It shouldn't have taken that long." Justin resumed walking and called over his shoulder, "If you want to keep this job, you'd better get busy. I'm not paying a lazy half-breed who leaves a job undone. You're lucky to be here."

Ah, yes. Once again he has to remind me of how thankful I should be to work for such a wonderful man, Jack thought.

Finally, hours after everyone else had gone for the day, Jack finished his assigned tasks. Grateful to have reached the end of a long day, he disconnected from the network, scooped up his Orichi, and headed for the door.

Once outside, he scanned the area in front of the administration building for Amber, hoping she had been able to uncover some useful information during the course of the day. With the flexible schedule of a college student, she often could find information that he simply didn't have the time to dig for. Hopefully she hadn't been waiting long.

Starting down the steps, Jack scanned the crowd, determined not to be roughed up like the night before. He touched his aching forehead and winced. No, he definitely didn't want to go through that again tonight.

Scanning to one side and then the other, he finally spotted Amber leaning against one of the marble blocks that bordered each side of the steps. She flashed him a grim smile.

Jack walked over to join her and leaned against the wall next to her. They stood in silence for a few moments before Jack spoke, his voice low, lips barely moving lest someone was spying on them.

"Did you find out anything about Ryan?"

"Mm-hm." She stared straight ahead.

Jack waited while Amber collected her thoughts.

With a deep sigh, she half turned toward him. "Apparently he left work and never made it home. When he didn't show, his brother went looking for him. He's the one who found Ryan in the alleyway." She paused, playing with the zipper pull on her leather jacket. "I never found out what he wanted to tell me."

Jack felt his eyebrows rise. "He had information for you?"

Amber jerked a nod. "A couple of days ago, he sent me a message to meet him today in the university library. He said he had something he wanted to tell me in person. But he never got the chance." She quickly dabbed at the corner of her eye.

"I'm sorry, Amber. He was a good friend, wasn't he?" Jack looked sideways at the young woman as a tear spilled down her cheek.

"Yeah." She shoved her hands in her pockets. "Thanks."

"You wanna walk?" Jack tipped his head toward the street.

Amber nodded and they headed down the steps side-by-side. Maybe good news would help her feel better.

"I got an appointment with Robert scheduled for tomorrow."

Amber's eyes grew wide. "Seriously?"

It was Jack's turn to nod. He tried to keep a silly grin off his face.

"I can't believe it," she said. "Maybe there's hope after all."

Then a new thought occurred to Jack. "Ryan knew I was trying to set up this appointment. Maybe he hacked into the system and set it up."

"Hm." Amber looked at him sideways with a thoughtful expression. "I dunno about that, but...yeah, maybe," she whispered.

The two walked the streets of New Santiago, heading back toward the gen quarter. To Jack it seemed a subdued mood hung over the city as if its people were waiting for something to happen. Jack hoped it was true. The city could use a change.

"We need to tell the others," Amber said.

"Hm?"

Amber's voice shook Jack from his thoughts.

"Tell them what?"

"Ryan did tell me one thing before he was..."

Her voice cracked with emotion and Jack wrapped his arm around her shoulders. She rested the side of her head on his shoulder as they walked, her face turned just far enough that he couldn't see. She sniffed and he didn't need to see the tears on her face to know they were there.

"I know he was looking at the administration's computer network structure. He said he had found something. Some kind of hidden directory."

Amber and Jack continued to move through the city and into the gen quarter. When Jack opened his front door, he nearly tripped over a letter that had been shoved underneath. A crisp white envelope with nothing but his name scrawled on the front, barely legible. He slid a finger under the flap, pried open the envelope, and pulled out a letter.

"It's from Ryan."

Amber's eyes grew round and she peeked over Jack's shoulder. "What's it say?"

Jack read the message aloud.

I think someone's after me. In case something happens to me, I want to make sure you know what I've found so far. There's a hidden computer directory. Also found inconsistencies so I sent sniffer bots to look for hidden files. Also found a backdoor. Cracked the password but haven't had the chance yet to dig around much. But it looks like there's a hidden structure, maybe a secret organization inside the government? Files documenting the organization's activities go back years. It looks like someone very high up has been keeping big secrets for a very long time.

Many records seem to profile people from all walks of life. There are also memos and procedures. It's going to take a long time to plow through it all.

A string of numbers and letters were scrawled in the margin as if written in haste.

Jack met Amber's glance and said, "We're going to have to be very careful. I think someone got wise to Ryan's digging."

Chapter 4

T he next morning, Jack arrived early at work and dug into his tasks with gusto, his thoughts focused on the upcoming appointment with Robert. If he made enough progress on his tasks, Justin might not miss him while he was gone—in the guise of an extended break, of course.

Soon it was time to leave. Jack scooped up his handheld, not daring to leave it behind, then rushed downstairs and outside, turning toward the offices of the Ministry of Religion. He arrived out of breath and tried to breathe evenly as he stood in front of Miss Beautiful's desk.

After several moments of not being recognized, Jack cleared his throat. Still no response.

"Excuse me."

The woman glanced up and without a word, waved him toward an empty chair. Ignoring her dismissal, Jack stood firm.

"Can you please tell Robert I'm here?"

"*Father* Robert," she said, accentuating the first word, "will let me know when he's ready for you. You can wait over there." She gestured again toward the chair.

Jack doubted this was the complete truth. In fact, he doubted Robert was even aware he was waiting. Reluctantly, Jack took a seat, hoping against hope that Uncle Justin wasn't looking for him.

After twenty excruciating minutes, the inner door opened. Robert was three years older than Jack and yet miles apart from his half-brother. They shared a mother in Eva, but Robert had been raised by his father, who had passed away some years back. Robert's blue eyes settled on Jack and he raised one eyebrow.

"What are you doing here?"

Jack stood to his feet. "We have an appointment."

"Is that right?" Robert looked to his assistant.

She nodded, eyes wide with sincerity. "Yes, Father. That's correct. I put it on your calendar."

Jack wondered where the prissy, arrogant Miss Beautiful had disappeared to and who had installed this respectful young woman in her place.

"All right, then." Father Robert gestured into his office, holding one hand out as if to guide this errant member of his flock to safety. Inside, Jack knew it was all for show. All to impress the lovely young woman and show how gracious and benevolent the priest could be to his poor half-breed brother who apparently had been handed such a terrible lot in life. But Jack didn't buy the act for a minute. If this man truly cared about the poor and disadvantaged, he'd never let their mother live in such poverty.

In contrast to his mother's hovel, the inside of Robert's office gleamed. Rich wood grain paneling, elegant built-in bookshelves laden with heady theological works. Plush carpeting. Once inside, Robert closed the door behind him and sat behind a massive desk carved of dark mahogany and polished to a high shine. Now that the door was closed, the smile slipped from Robert's face.

"What do you want, Jack?" A tone of impatience crept into his half-brother's voice.

"I want to talk to you about a job application."

Robert raised his eyebrows skeptically. "Don't you have a job?"

Jack bit back the words he wanted to say, *You know I do*, and instead tried to slip a mask of sincerity on his face. "Yes, I do. But it doesn't pay enough."

"You shouldn't need much."

"True. *I* don't need much, but Mom needs to eat too." Jack boiled inside to think that Robert could care so little about his own mother. "Don't you care what happens to her?"

Robert sighed and scowled. "Yes, of course, I do."

He's such a good liar. Jack struggled to keep a grip on his emotions.

"What do you want from me?" Robert pressed.

"I filed an application here with the Ministry for a position in network administration."

Robert seemed surprised. "You have the skills for that?"

Jack nodded. "I thought maybe you could put in a good word for me."

Robert studied Jack for a moment. "Maybe. I'll see what I can do."

Inside, Jack still seethed but he tried for a voice of sincerity. "Thank you. I would greatly appreciate it."

"If that's all...?" Robert looked down, shuffling through the papers on his desk.

Jack rose. "I'll just let myself out now."

"Mm-hm." Robert never looked up.

Jack left the Ministry offices and practically ran all the way back toward his almost-a-cubbyhole stub of a counter in Justin's office. No sooner had he stepped through the doorway, than his uncle pounced, scowling.

"Well, if it isn't Jack the Slacker." He chuckled at his own joke, then turned serious. "Where have you been, boy?"

Jack caught his breath. He hadn't thought of what he would say if confronted. Time to think fast.

"I was...delayed."

Justin opened his mouth to reply just as a call came through on his earbud.

"Don't let it happen again. Now get back to work," he snapped as he reached up to tap the earbud.

Jack slowly exhaled in relief and returned to his little corner. There he spent the remainder of the day going through the motions of work, his mind jumping from the possibilities of the new job, to helping the insurgents, to being able to provide for his mother, to wondering if Robert would remember his promise, and back again. After leaving work, he absentmindedly plodded home.

Once there, Eva placed another bowl of beans in front of him. He could feel her studying him.

"How was your day, Jack?"

"Good." He took a bite and swallowed. "I saw Robert today."

Eva shot him a glance, eyebrows raised.

"He didn't make any promises, but said he'd see what he could do."

A few more bites and the bowl was empty. Jack thanked his mother for the food and pushed away from the table, then retired to his pallet and fired up the Orichi. He tried to lose himself in sketching out various scenarios the insurgents could try, activities they could attempt in an effort to win their freedom. But down inside, he knew they could protest all they wanted, harass the officials as much as possible, but their freedom ultimately hinged on one thing: finding the secret of souls. And that kept bringing him back to the job at the Ministry offices. As a network administrator, he should be able to continue Ryan's work. It was the only lead they had.

Late the next day, a message flashed up on Jack's handheld.

> *You have been granted an interview for the position of network administrator. Report to the Ministry of Religion's administration offices tomorrow at 10:00.*

To get the time off, Jack had to show the memo to his uncle.

"Huh," Justin grunted in reply. "You really think you have a chance? I'm surprised they're even considering you." He regarded Jack skeptically. "I'll bet they don't know you're a half-breed."

Jack looked off to one side, biting the inside of his cheek lest he say something he'd regret. Justin still had the power to write him up and any black marks on his record would virtually guarantee he'd never get that job. In fact, he was surprised Justin hadn't done that yet.

"Yeah, I'm sure that's it." His uncle smirked. "Once they find out, they'll kick you out and you'll come crawling back here to me, asking for your job back."

Jack clenched his jaw and returned to his corner.

The next day, Jack retraced his steps back to the Ministry of Religion. Heart pounding, he walked to the elevator and punched the Up button.

"You," a voice growled behind Jack. "Where do you think you're going?"

Jack spun around to find a security guard standing behind him, hands on his hips. The man's paunch hung over the belt of his dark blue one-piece uniform, stretched tight around his middle. A small-caliber gun hung from one side of his belt, a club from the other. This looked like the kind of arrogant fool who could be trouble. Jack wasn't afraid of the man; however, he knew he would need to tread carefully. He opened his mouth to reply, then closed it, swallowed, and tried again.

"I have an appointment at the administration offices."

The man scowled. "Let's see some proof."

Jack turned his handheld toward the guard, who read the memo, then turned his eyes back on Jack.

"All right. Everything appears to be in order. Off with you."

Jack turned back toward the elevator, then felt a hand on his shoulder. The man gripped Jack's shoulder tightly and spun him around.

"But you're not taking the elevator." He shoved Jack off toward the back of the lobby. "The stairs are that way."

Well, it was worth a shot, Jack thought to himself.

He found the stairs and climbed up to the third floor, emerging from the stairwell into a utilitarian hallway. He followed it until it dumped him out into a plush lobby. To one side, opposite the main lobby doors—the ones he would have preferred to use—ran a polished granite counter, flecks of silver sparkling from the depths of the gray slate, slick and cool under his fingers. He reported in with the receptionist and before long, a woman strode in, all business in her pressed slacks, low heels and modest blouse. Wavy blonde hair just brushed her shoulders and softly framed her face, but when her eyes met his, doubt flickered and her smile faded, replaced with a stern look. Jack's golden eyes had betrayed him yet again.

"Jack?" she addressed him with a forced smile.

"Yes, ma'am."

"I'm Vanessa. This way, please."

Jack returned the greeting and followed Vanessa through a broad wooden door further into the Ministry's building. Once they reached her office, Vanessa took a seat behind her desk and gestured toward an upholstered chair opposite her, facing the desk. She referenced a fairly new handheld in front of her.

"I'm the manager of the Information Technology department. You're looking for a job in network administration?" She leaned forward, her back ramrod straight, hands folded on the desk in front of her.

Jack nodded, trying to gauge the woman's mood and respond appropriately.

"What makes you think you would fit in here?" Her words were more a statement than a question.

Jack met her gaze directly, determined not to cower at her condescension. If he was going to fail this interview, he might as well do it while maintaining his self-respect.

Jack ran through his list of qualifications, citing the work he had done for his uncle at the public administration offices. He told her about the equipment he had worked on and the technology he had learned on his own. She listened with a slight frown. When he finished, silence reigned for a painful minute. Then she spoke.

"I want you to know that I had another person in mind for this job. Someone who has proven himself to me already. Proven he could do this job efficiently and professionally." Her eyes bored into his. Jack forced himself to not look away. "But a directive has come from above assuring me that you are perfect for this job. A directive that I dare not disobey."

Jack gulped. He could hardly believe his ears.

Vanessa sighed deeply, threw up her hands and leaned back in her chair. "If you want the job, be here tomorrow morning at eight."

Jack nodded. "Yes, ma'am. I'll be here."

"Fine then. I'll see you tomorrow."

"Thank you, ma'am." Jack stood and let himself out.

Jack drifted to his office in a daze. Maybe the gods had smiled on him after all. And yet, he couldn't lose the lump in his throat, somewhat terrified at the prospect that faced him—working his way through the main computers looking for the files that Ryan had found. The ones that had gotten him killed. If an expert like Ryan couldn't dig without detection through the files and directories familiar to him, how could Jack expect to succeed?

And yet, the prospect of facing Justin, of telling him that he had gotten the job, made Jack smile. He looked forward to not having to endure the man every day.

His mind drifted to the tasks his new job would demand of him. True, he had a basic skill base that would provide a good foundation, but there were many things he still had to learn in order to perform the job well. That in itself would take all of his time and then some. How long would it take him to learn those things before he could pick up where Ryan left off?

Jack's feet carried him to the door leading to the department where he worked. He found Justin hunched over his desk, eyes glued to the computer screen, fingers hovering over the keys. Though he always appeared to be busy, Jack wondered what exactly the man ever produced. It seemed the only things accomplished in the office came from his support staff.

Jack rapped his knuckles on the doorframe and Justin looked up, his impassive expression turning into a scowl when his eyes met Jack's.

"What d'you want?"

"I got the job." Jack tried to refuse the smile that threatened to spread across his face.

Justin sat up straight, eyebrows raised. "What?!"

"I got the job," Jack said more emphatically.

Justin stared at him, his mouth clamped shut, lips pressed into a thin line.

"I start tomorrow morning."

Jack's uncle shook his head as if to rid himself of the disbelief he was surely feeling. Then the ever-present scowl settled on his face once again. "Hmph. I wonder how long it will take before they discover their mistake. Before they discover what a worthless loser they hired. I suppose then you'll be back, looking for your old job." He paused. "Don't expect it to be waiting for you."

At Justin's words, the old anger rose up inside Jack but he clenched his jaw and swallowed it back down once again. No sense mouthing off and burning his bridges. After all, Justin still had some amount of pull and could probably find a way to make his life difficult, even from a distance. Instead, Jack looked at him with as earnest of an expression as he could manage. And yet, he couldn't help but make a slight jab.

"Thank you, *Uncle*, for the job. I really appreciate the kindness you've shown."

Justin's face turned red and he rose to his feet, but Jack spun on his heel and walked away. Heading toward the hallway, he heard the man spit out behind him, "I'm not your uncle!" The words echoed across the office and turned a few heads in curiosity.

At that, Jack allowed himself a smile. Let the man make a fool of himself. A couple of employees watched him leave, apparently startled by the uproar. Jack tipped his head their direction and stepped out of the office, downstairs, and out into the open air. With the prospect of a new job ahead, the trees somehow seemed greener, the skies bluer. He filled his lungs with fresh air and descended the steps of the administration building, leaving it behind and, hopefully, stepping into another life.

Jack pushed open his front door and stepped inside. Two steps into the room and his mom poked her head around the corner, face scrunched up in concern.

"You're early. Is everything okay?"

"Yeah, Mom. Everything's okay." Jack smiled and stepped farther into the room and wrapped his arms around her in a hug. She tentatively returned the gesture. He released her and leaned back, looking into her eyes. "I got the job."

Eva's jaw dropped and she gasped, eyes round with surprise. "Oh, Jack! That's wonderful!" She pulled him into her arms for another hug. "Praise be to God. I knew he'd take care of us."

Her hair tickled his chin and he inhaled a whiff of that special, comforting fragrance that was his mom. She trusted everything to her God. He looked around the cramped room at their tattered furniture and the scratched table in the corner. To him, it didn't look like God cared—if there even was a God. But his mom's faith could not be shaken. It was just one more thing about her that he loved, even if he didn't share her faith.

Jack reached into his pocket, pulled out a coin, tossed it into the air and caught it again. "I found this on the way home. Let's go celebrate. I'll bet we can get a couple of sausages down on the corner."

Eyes sparkling, Jack's mother scooped up the small bag she took with her everywhere. Jack remembered when years ago she had pieced it together from fabric scraps she had rescued from who knows where. The pink roses had since faded until it had almost gained an antique effect. He pulled open the door and gestured grandly toward the outside like a high-class gentleman.

"After you, madam."

She rubbed a calloused hand on his arm affectionately. "Thank you, Son."

Jack and Eva walked down the short path and onto the street. Strolling to the corner, they approached a vendor standing behind his cart.

"Afternoon," the gen rumbled in a deep bass voice.

"Manny! How ya doin'?" Jack shoved a hand into his pocket and fished out the coin. "We'll take two sausage rolls."

Manny jerked a nod. "Comin' right up." He lifted a door on the top of the cart, plunged a pair of tongs into the rising steam, and pulled out two links. With practiced hands, he wedged them inside buns and Jack placed the coin in his hand. Manny examined the coin, eyebrows raised.

"Come into some extra today?"

"Found it on the way home." Jack couldn't help but smile at his good fortune.

Manny grunted, withdrew the change from his pocket, and handed it to Jack, who pocketed the change, then with his mom, walked a short distance away to perch on the edge of a half wall. When Jack's mom bit into her sandwich, she rolled her eyes in delight.

"Mm, this is so good."

Jack's heart warmed to see his mother smile, something that didn't happen often enough these days.

Shifting his gaze down the street, Jack's eye caught on a beggar limping down the cracked sidewalk toward them. His coat little more than a network of spiderweb-thin threads, feet bare, his face wrinkled and baked a deep red from constant exposure to the elements. Jack's mother followed his line of sight, and when she saw the old gen, compassion filled her eyes. As he drew near, she stood and brushed a few crumbs from her threadbare skirt.

"Sir, wait," she called out and moved to break her sandwich in half. Jack shook his head. Needy creatures of any race always broke her heart.

"Mom." He placed his hand over hers, holding them still. "I'll take care of it."

She pressed her lips together in a thin smile, then spoke softly. "Thank you, Son."

The beggar stopped his shuffle and turned hopeful eyes toward Jack.

He tipped his head toward the vendor. "Come on. Let's get you something to eat."

The old gen's face broke into a wide grin, revealing decayed, yellowed teeth.

Jack paid Manny for another sausage sandwich and the beggar bowed several times in thanks.

"Thank you, sir. Thank you. May the gods smile on you for your kindness." He clutched the sandwich in dirty fingers. "I'll say a prayer for you today at the shrine."

Jack knew he would. He could see in his mind's eye the old gen at the Grove shrine outside of town, bowed in prayer before the standing stone honoring the gens' nature gods. He wondered if it had changed much in the past several years.

He hadn't been out there in ages. Returning back to his seat on the wall, he looked sideways at his mom.

"When we're finished, would you like to walk up to the park?"

His mother shot him a look of apprehension, eyebrows drawn together. "But will we have enough time to get home before dark?"

Jack nodded. "It's a long ways until dusk. We'll be fine."

Their sandwiches gone, Jack stood and offered an arm to his mom. She brushed the crumbs off her faded yellow skirt and slipped her hand into the crook of his elbow, a smile on her face.

"This was such a good idea." She settled the straps of the flowered bag onto her shoulder and held it tight against her side, nestled under her arm.

Jack so wanted her to feel special. Perhaps a little lighthearted conversation could distract her for a bit from the squalor of the rugged district. They picked their way around piles of trash and where sections of the sidewalk were missing; little puffs of dust rose with each step.

Within twenty minutes, they crossed the border into the human quarter, the sidewalks here level and intact, the gutters swept clean of trash. Three blocks later, a beautiful park came into view. Magnificent oak trees reached gnarled branches outward to form cool shadows beneath, the perimeter framed by colorful displays of flowers genetically designed to bloom profusely year-round and old boxwoods trimmed into swirling arabesques. Paved walkways cut through a lush green lawn, all leading to the center of the park where a large, white gazebo awaited the next party or concert.

Jack's mother sighed and gently ran her fingertips along the edges of the fragrant flowers. They passed the next hour in quiet contentment, walking through pockets of shade and finally coming to rest on an iron bench.

"I think this is my favorite place. I used to come here often when I was a little girl. And then your dad and I spent many happy hours here." Her voice was so quiet, Jack strained to hear. He nodded, afraid to break the spell of peace resting on the glade and on his mom's face. And so they sat, side-by-side, and simply listened to the birds calling out to each other.

After a time, the sun crept lower in the sky, the air cooling as it went. Jack hated for the evening to end, but they had to be back in Gen Town by dark.

"Mom, we have to go."

She nodded. "I suppose so." She took a deep breath of the clear, late-afternoon air. "I wish we could stay here forever."

Jack offered her his elbow once again and they strolled toward the edge of the park. When they reached the sidewalk running around the perimeter, she turned and glanced back over her shoulder one more time at the oasis of beauty.

They returned home in silence, reaching their street just as the sun began to cast long shadows along the ground. Once inside, she placed the worn bag in her room.

"Are you hungry?" she called from around the corner. She breezed back into the front room, her face bearing the most peaceful look Jack had seen in a great while. "I picked up some bread this morning and I can make a pot of rice."

"That sounds fine."

Jack retrieved his Orichi and settled on the narrow couch, making sure not to sit on the torn cushion where pieces of flattened fluff the color of dirty snow poked out. He fired up the device and navigated to a project he was working on—designing an inexpensive type of secure neural darknet that the gens could use to communicate without being detected by the human's global system.

Meanwhile, thoughts of the new job he was to start in the morning lurked in the back of his head, threatening to rise up into full-blown anxiety. What if he couldn't do the job after all? What if he was caught? What if...

Jack shook his head to clear his mind and refocused on the project at hand. The basic design of the system was in place, but the anti-detection measures—that was the stickler.

With his thoughts targeted on the project, Jack barely tasted dinner, and before he realized it, the hour had grown quite late.

Just as well, he thought. *My nerves are so tight, I probably couldn't have slept anyways.*

———◁O▷———

Jack woke early, went through his morning routine, and headed out the door in plenty of time to reach the Ministry offices early. Once there, he climbed the stairs. He went straight to his new boss's office, only to find she wasn't there yet.

He shifted his Orichi from one hand to the other and wiped sweaty palms on his pant legs. Sitting in Vanessa's guest chair, he self-consciously shot a glance out the doorway. There seemed to be a steady stream of people in the hallway and each one glanced in as they passed by.

Word must be out there's a new employee, Jack thought. Some glanced at him curiously, others with looks of disdain. At least he would know who might be helpful and who to avoid.

Before long, his new boss stepped through the doorway, a satchel slung on her shoulder big enough for a tablet and room to spare.

"Good. You're early." She pulled open the doors of a tall wooden cabinet and plunked her bag onto a deep shelf inside. Turning to Jack, she regarded him for a moment, her expression unreadable. Then she marched back toward the door, her voice crisp. "Come with me. I'll show you around."

She led him through a maze of cubicles, past various departments and meeting rooms, then pointed out a room where the servers were located. Finally, they reached an empty cubicle.

"Here's your home away from home." She lifted one corner of her mouth in a wry smile. "I think you'll find you spend more time here than you ever thought you would. Get settled and I'll send someone around to take it from here."

Alone in his cubicle, Jack lowered himself into a squeaky desk chair. Compared to his little shelf in the administration building, his new workstation was a castle. A wide desk supported a state-of-the-art computer, two large monitors, and everything else a top-notch network administrator could need. He leaned back and ran his fingertips along the metal edge of the desk topped in a light gray veneer. He had just begun to inspect the contents of a few drawers to one side when he heard a shuffle behind him.

Jack spun his chair about to find a young man about his own age standing in the doorway. His black hair was shaggy enough to match his rumpled clothes. When his eyes met Jack's, he raised his eyebrows. Jack sighed at the common response to seeing his bright golden eyes. Then the young man blinked and his doubtful expression disappeared, replaced with a forced smile.

"Name's Keto. You must be the new guy."

Jack stood and held out his hand, but, ignoring the proffered handshake, Keto brushed past him and sat in Jack's chair facing the desk.

"Vanessa said to show you your duties so listen up. I've got deadlines of my own."

Oh joy. This should be fun.

Jack's handheld caught Keto's eye. "That your slate?"

"Yeah." Jack knew what he must be thinking—piece of junk—and he prepared to defend himself, but Keto just pushed it aside and reached for the keyboard.

With an admonition to "pay attention," Keto outlined the hierarchy of the network within a few minutes, his hands flying across the keyboard, showing Jack the general layout of the computer system. Then he described the day-to-day operation of the network and told him what he would need to do to maintain the system hardware and software and how to keep up the network logs while tracking the nature and resolution of problems as they arose. Then Keto showed Jack how to log in to the network in order to monitor the data traffic coming through their node but explained that he wouldn't need to bother with it just yet, so "just be aware of how it works."

"For now, your primary responsibility will be to inspect the types of data that come through here," Keto clipped. "That way you'll know if there's an anomaly. That'll probably be a hacker. Got it?"

Jack nodded. He had hardly had a chance to get a word in and before he knew it, Keto was gone, the desk chair spinning slightly from his rapid departure.

Jack spent the rest of the day sifting through data transmissions, trying to get a feel for normal traffic flows. He barely had time to think about his real reason for being there. He had plenty to learn first.

Chapter 5

Over the next two weeks, Jack learned his job and the insurgents laid low. Except for Kennan.

Jack waited for Amber on a bench in front of the Ministry of Religion by the large water fountain. Water bubbled up from the top and down into three tiered basins before spilling over into a large koi pond. Sunshine played on the water's surface, illuminating the tops of sparkling ripples that flowed outward from the fountain to nudge floating lily pads. Jack closed his eyes and soaked in the sun's rays, the gurgling of the water soothing his jittery nerves.

"I thought I might find you here." A voice cut into his reverie. "Do you always come here at lunch?"

Jack opened his eyes to see Amber, thumbs shoved in the front pockets of her skinny black pants. A matching tank top exposed most of the red rose tattoo on her left shoulder. An oversized black leather bag hung suspended from the other. "Only for the last week or so. It's peaceful."

Amber sat beside him and watched the water tumble down into the pond. "Kennan wants me to give you a message." The musical water helped mask her quiet voice lest prying ears hovered nearby.

"Again? Can't he take a hint?"

She cracked a wry smile.

"Let me guess. He wants to storm the Ministry offices and kidnap the pope."

Amber snorted a laugh. "Not quite. But he still wants to know what our next course of action is and when we're going to meet again."

"Actually, I've been thinking about that." Jack leaned forward, elbows on his knees. "Things have been going pretty good at the new job."

"It's been, what, two weeks already?"

Jack nodded. "I've been busy learning how the system works." He cast a glance around to see if anyone else was within hearing range. "I think I've found a way into the central data array."

Amber arched her eyebrows.

"The computers here are actually off-site secondaries hardwired all the way to the main computer. They function as nodes that monitor both sides of a heavily encrypted firewall between regional government offices and the central data array."

"Okay..." She looked doubtful—or confused. Jack couldn't tell which.

"Amber, don't you see? This is perfect. My job is to monitor the traffic passing through the firewall. That gives me access to the servers on both sides." He laid a hand on her black-clad knee. "Somewhere in there is the info we're looking for."

A look of realization crossed her face. "So now what?"

"Well, now comes the hard part. I need to find the data." He sighed and studied the ground. "Somewhere out there is the secret that got Ryan killed. The secret that condemns us to a life of hopelessness. I *will* find it."

"But what about everyone else? They need something to do or the group will fall apart."

Jack nodded. "Tell Kennan to spread the word down through the usual channels that we'll meet again next week—Monday night, as usual. That will give him something to do."

Jack said goodbye and headed back to work. He gave a slight tug to the door leading to the IT offices. The door unexpectedly flew open and out stumbled Vanessa. Startled, she squeaked in surprise, eyes wide.

Jack caught her by the arm and held her upright for just a moment until she regained her balance.

"Uh, thank you." Vanessa tugged on the hem of her pullover, readjusting it around her waist.

"Are you okay?"

She pushed a stray lock of blonde hair behind one ear, her cheeks blushing. "Yes. Yes, I'm fine. Thank you." She started to walk away, then looked back. "Oh! Jack! I almost forgot. We need to talk. Let's go to my office." She turned and walked back through the door.

Full of trepidation, Jack's mind raced, wondering what she could possibly want. What he might have done wrong.

Once they reached her office, she directed him to have a seat.

"I understand Keto has been showing you the normal operation procedures for the network. Have you been keeping the data traffic logs current?"

Jack nodded, even though the man had done little more than point him in the right direction and let him figure it out by himself.

"Good. The next thing I want you to do is learn how to actually monitor the data traffic flow using our proprietary software." She settled behind her desk and leaned back.

Jack reflected on how it seemed his golden eyes no longer made her uncomfortable. That was good. He needed her to trust him. But with that thought a pang of guilt shot through his mind. He didn't want to deceive her but he had a job to do. *I have to keep the main objective in mind here—to help the gens.*

Vanessa continued her directions. "It shouldn't be too difficult. I believe packet sniffers are already set up to flag suspicious activity. As you're getting started, I want to make sure you're comfortable managing both incoming and outgoing network intrusion detection."

After asking if he had any questions, Vanessa promised to send Keto over to show him what to do.

Over the next couple of weeks, Jack continued learning the system and even earned an occasional grudging "good job" here and there from Keto.

Whenever Jack got a few minutes, he explored the file directories at the satellite government offices, looking for the hidden directory Ryan had found and hoping he was hiding his tracks well enough to not arouse attention.

After one particularly exhausting day, Jack scooped up his handheld and headed home. He walked in the door and put his things down. Hearing the clang of a spoon against a pot, he strolled into the kitchen. As he entered the room, his mother looked up, met his eyes, and turned back to her pan on the stove.

Jack looked over her shoulder. "Mmm. Is that chicken soup? It smells great!"

She nodded and Jack paused for a moment. It wasn't like her to be so quiet. "Mom? Is everything okay?"

Jack's mother turned her face toward him, a slight frown creasing her forehead. "That's exactly what Robert asked me."

Jack remembered his last conversation with his brother and his apparent lack of concern for their mother. "Robert? When did you talk to him?"

She banged the spoon on the edge of the pot, knocking a few drops of soup back into the pan. "I didn't actually speak with him." She moved to the sink and rinsed her hands. "He sent a note. He wanted to know how I was doing and whether your new job was working out okay."

Jack sat in one of the wooden chairs and leaned forward, fingers interlaced in front of him on the table's rough surface.

"I got to thinking about it." Eva turned around and leaned back against the counter, arms crossed. "I haven't heard from him in years."

Jack opened his mouth to reply, but she held up her hand. "Let me finish before you say anything." She glared at him a moment before continuing. "Because I haven't heard from him in so long, it's unlikely he really cares about how I'm doing, which means that he's really asking about you."

It felt as if a rock dropped into Jack's stomach and his mind filled with dread.

"Why would he be asking about you?" Her expression unchanged, she waited silently. "I hate to be suspicious, but that's not like him."

Jack's mind raced. Surely Robert had no idea he was searching for hidden files. How could he? Jack leaned back in his chair and prodded himself to think quick, to come up with something that sounded reasonable without divulging to his mom the dangerous truth that he was a spy. "Maybe he hadn't thought of us for a while and then when I met with him, he's been wondering what happened."

She tipped her head and raised her eyebrows in that expression that moms were so good at. Probably something they mastered when humans first started walking the earth, he thought wryly.

The back door squeaked open and in walked Amber, a pleasant smile on her face.

"'Evening!" She slowed and looked from Jack to his mom and back again, a look of concerned curiosity on her face.

"Hello, Amber." Eva's voice came out a bit forced but pleasant. "We were just sitting down for a bowl of soup if you'd like to join us."

"That'd be great. Thanks." Amber slowly seated herself at the rickety table.

Jack's mom pulled four chipped stoneware bowls from the cupboard and ladled steaming soup into them.

"Here, let me help you." Amber took the bowls as they were filled and placed them on the table. An awkward silence lay in the room. When Jack's mom turned toward the stove, Amber looked at Jack, eyebrows raised. He replied with a shrug of his shoulders.

Before long, the stomp of boots outside announced Ethan's arrival. He tromped into the kitchen, nodded a greeting to Jack and Amber, then planted a kiss on his mom's cheek, peering into the pot.

"Hello, Ethan." Eva's voice was soft and caring toward her youngest.

"Smells great!" Ethan reached to pull out a chair, but she shooed him away.

"No you don't. Go wash up first."

With a sigh, Ethan headed for the bathroom. Once he returned, he joined the others already seated and the four began to eat.

Jack focused on his dinner, trying to act like he normally would, but he found himself avoiding Eva's eyes nonetheless. His thoughts centered on Robert's missive, which did nothing to lessen his feelings of unease. He worried about what it could mean, but even more so, he worried about what it might mean for his mom. He hoped she wasn't getting pulled into something she knew nothing about. He could only imagine what Robert would do if Jack's clandestine activities were discovered. Whatever his reaction, it wouldn't be good.

After a quiet dinner and after the table was cleared, Ethan went out to meet friends. Jack's mother shot him one last warning look and left him and Amber alone in the kitchen.

Amber leaned across the table toward Jack and whispered, "What's going on? What's wrong with your mom?"

Jack looked up at the ceiling and took a deep breath. "She got a letter from Robert." His hushed voice matched hers.

"Your brother?" Amber raised her eyebrows.

"He was inquiring as to our...welfare."

"Huh. Do you believe him?"

Jack shook his head. "No. We haven't heard from him in a couple of years. Then when I met with him a few weeks ago, it was obvious he hadn't had a change of heart." He ran a hand through his short, blond hair and leaned back. "Him contacting Mom to ask how I'm doing is a bit suspicious."

"So what're you gonna to do?"

He shrugged his shoulders. "Keep going, I guess. I still haven't found the files Ryan referred to but there are still a lot of directories to search through. At least I can access both sides of the firewall. If there's something hidden in there, I'll find it..."

Jack's voice trailed off as Mother walked through the doorway and a sinking feeling grew in his stomach. Eva's eyes grew wide with alarm and she searched first Jack's then Amber's face as if to read what was in their minds.

"Please tell me," her voice trembled, "that I didn't hear that correctly." She clasped her hands tightly together and her eyebrows pinched together with worry. "Jack...what are you into? What are you looking for?"

"Mom, you don't need to get involved in this."

"What do you mean?" Then her jaw dropped and she shook her head slowly from side to side. "No...it couldn't be..."

"Couldn't be what, Mom?"

"I heard whispers in the market. Rumors that a group of gens were banding together against the humans. To find the key to souls..." She lowered herself into a chair. "Jack, please tell me you're not involved in that."

Jack returned her gaze with silence and she covered her mouth with her hands, then took a deep breath and folded her hands in front of her.

"Jack, this is treason. You realize that, don't you?"

"Mom..."

"Is that why Robert's looking over our shoulders? Does he know?"

Jack paused a moment. "I don't think so."

"But surely he suspects something or he wouldn't have sent the note." She cast her gaze to Amber. "Did you know about this?"

Jack's friend nodded her head and a quiet moan escaped Eva.

"Would you two stop and think about this?" Her eyes filled with tears and she clutched Jack's arm, her fingers grasping so tightly it almost hurt. Her voice turned desperate. "It's not too late. Both of you." She extended a hand to Amber. "Whatever you're doing, just walk away."

Her pleas were met with stony silence and the tears spilled down her cheeks. "Jack, I already lost your dad. I don't want to lose you too."

Just then, the back door banged open and Ethan strolled in. He took one look at his mother and then his eyes drilled into Jack's.

"What's going on?" His voice was hard, demanding.

Eva sat back and closed her eyes, hands in her lap. Ethan put a strong hand on her shoulder.

"Mom? What's the matter?" When she didn't answer, he turned to Jack. "What have you done?"

Before he could answer, Amber stood.

"I need to get going," she said, her voice small and hushed. She slipped away, but when she neared the door, Eva jumped to her feet and hurried after her.

"Amber! Wait."

The door had yet to creak open and Eva's muted voice could barely be heard around the corner.

"You don't have to be involved in this, you know. I don't want anything to happen to you."

Amber's reply was too soft to understand, but Jack easily understood the meaning behind Ethan's glare—the young man would protect their mother at any cost. Jack met Ethan's eyes without blinking, willing his brother to know he felt the same way.

The back door squealed shut and Eva rushed through the kitchen into the front of the house, lips pressed grimly into a thin line. Jack jumped to his feet and moved the other direction toward the back door, leaving Ethan standing alone in the kitchen scowling, hands on his hips.

———◆———

Jack wandered the neighborhood until his feet carried him to the doorway of The Down and Dirty. He pushed the door open and stepped inside the dimly lit room and up to the bar. Pete wiped a spill off the scratched wooden surface, his friendly smile comforting.

"Hey Jack! How's it goin'?"

Jack grunted in reply.

"That good, huh? What'll ya have? Sounds like you need a good stiff drink tonight."

Jack shook his head. "No, I don't need anything to dull my senses. Just give me a tea."

Pete poured the drink and placed it in front of Jack. It looked pretty weak, but Jack knew times were tough for everyone, even Pete. He ran his finger around the top rim of the glass. A spill of liquid smoothed the way as he traced the edge full circle.

Jack sat in companionable silence for an hour or so, then placed a few coins on the counter. With a nod at Pete, he wandered out into the now-dark town. Thinking of the last time he was beaten, Jack quickened his steps and headed for home, hands in his pockets.

When he reached the tiny house, he saw it too was dark. Jack let himself in, taking care to keep the front door from slamming shut. But he could do nothing about the squeak of the hinges and he winced as they announced his arrival. Inside, a lamp on the side table cast a yellow glow about the room.

He paced across the tiny room, stepping with caution to avoid the creaky spots in the floor. Retrieving his handheld from the side table where he had left it earlier, he settled himself on the couch and woke the device. No sooner had he put stylus to screen, than a shuffle at the doorway to his mother's room caught his attention.

"I didn't wake you, did I?"

Eva shook her head. "I couldn't sleep if I tried." She seated herself on the couch next to her son. "Jack..."

He placed a hand on her knee. "I know what you're going to say, Mom."

Her eyes flashed angry. "Do you? I'm not sure about that. I don't know exactly what you're involved in, but I know that whatever it is, you are putting our entire family—you, me, and Ethan...and Amber—in danger."

Jack took a deep breath. It was clear he'd never escape from this conversation without accounting for his actions. "Okay. Let me explain."

She leaned back and crossed her arms in that this-had-better-be-good posture.

"It's like this." He gathered his courage and sought for the right words that would help her understand. "I just want to help."

She raised her eyebrows.

"The gens. Their lives. Or lack thereof, that is. Mom, they have no future." He blurted these words out and the rest came in a rush. "You know that. They live, they die, and then what? Nothing. They fade away into nothing." He paused and lowered his voice, remembering Ethan asleep in the other room. "What about Ethan?" He lowered his voice into a low whisper, aware of the despair in his voice, but not caring about it at this point. "What about me? What about all your friends here?" He gestured in a wide half-circle to the town outside. "You have the promise of an afterlife with your God. We don't. Maybe there is a God, like you say. But I don't see how there can be when he doesn't even give us the chance to be with him if we die. I look around me and see...the gens don't have any hope. They live to work and then they die. So what?"

Jack's mom sat in shocked silence.

"You know I'm right. Why should I serve a God if I have no chance of ever meeting him? Why should I not risk everything if it means giving my friends—all the gens—a hope and a future? Something to live for."

She bit her lip and looked down into her lap.

"All most gens have now is heavy labor, abuse, and death. That's not much more than the hell your church warns people about."

"You're right." Her reply came barely loud enough to hear. "I don't like to think about it, but I know you're right." She raised her chin, the expression in her green eyes soft now, resigned. "So what do we do?"

Jack wrapped his arms around her and held her close. "Mom, I didn't say anything because I didn't want to put you in danger."

"I see that now." She leaned back and looked him in the eyes. "But it's too late to worry about that now, isn't it?"

Chapter 6

O ver the next couple of hours, Jack told his mother everything. The gens, the insurgents, Ryan, Amber's involvement, and his spying at work. When he finished, she sat motionless for several moments, buried in thought. Then she spoke soft and low.

"You're the leader in all this, aren't you?"

Jack nodded. She absorbed this information for a moment then continued.

"I want to help. What can I do?"

Jack allowed himself a slight smile. His ever-selfless mother.

"For now, just sit tight and we'll play along with Robert as if nothing is going on."

"What about Ethan?" Her forehead wrinkled in concern.

"I'd rather not drag him into this just yet. I'd like to have a better plan in place first. Also, I want to make sure he'll support us when things get tough."

"Okay," she nodded. "Just promise me you'll be careful."

Jack kissed his mom on the forehead as he rose to go to bed. "Of course. I'll do my best."

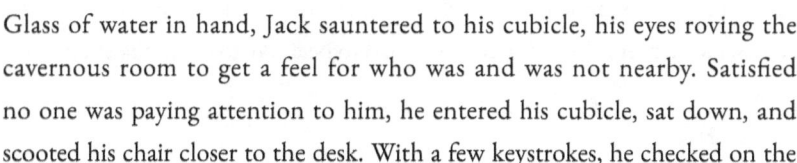

Glass of water in hand, Jack sauntered to his cubicle, his eyes roving the cavernous room to get a feel for who was and was not nearby. Satisfied no one was paying attention to him, he entered his cubicle, sat down, and scooted his chair closer to the desk. With a few keystrokes, he checked on the network-monitoring program. Satisfied all was well, he pushed it to one side of the screen and brought up a new window. He typed in the commands to open a new directory. With one more glance over his shoulder, he turned back to his work and brought up the lean little program he had written. He checked the results of the previous day's search.

There it is. His script had earmarked one particular directory that needed further investigating. He typed in a few commands to open the directory in question.

Access not granted.

Jack puffed a breath of air out his mouth. Encrypted. He needed a password. Just then a moment of realization washed over him and he dug through his pockets until he found the worn note Ryan had written. Jack reviewed the random string of characters in the margin. Could this be it?

Jack typed in the string, sent the command, then sat up in surprise. It worked! The password opened the directory, and there, in one long list, appeared a list of files.

Heart racing, Jack's fingers hovered over the keys, then he deliberately pushed one key at a time until he had entered the command to open the first file. *Access not granted.* He tried the other files as well, all with the same result. The files were all encrypted. Hoping against hope, Jack tried Ryan's password again, but to no avail. Not that he expected it to work. That would be too easy.

But even if he couldn't open them—yet—he knew he was in the right place, just from the names of the files. They all looked to represent some reference to laboratories, trial results, and genetics. This had to be it.

Deep in thought, Jack typed the commands to reduce the size of the window and push it to the screen's background. He brought up the monitoring window he was supposed to be checking on and absent-mindedly watched the names of the files being scanned scroll by. In reality, his mind tugged and pried on the issue at hand, trying to think of a solution. There was no way he was likely to stumble across another set of passwords. There had to be a way to break the encryption codes.

"Jack?"

He jumped as a sudden voice behind him broke his concentration. Jack spun his chair around to find Keto leaning against the frame of the cubicle's entrance. Jack gulped. How long had he been standing there? What had he seen?

"Hey, Keto." Jack was surprised to hear his voice sounded steady.

Keto's eyes shifted from Jack's face to the computer screen. It took all of Jack's will to not follow his gaze and see what was on the screen behind him.

"What's up?" Jack's voice pulled Keto's attention back to him. The programmer hesitated as he regarded Jack.

"I'm going to get lunch and wondered if you wanted anything."

Surprise swept over Jack and he stilled his facial muscles while forcibly keeping his mouth closed lest his jaw drop. Meanwhile, his mind raced as to how to cover his tracks. One simple keystroke and his secret work would be revealed on the screen behind him for all the world to see.

"Mind if I come along?"

"That's fine. You ready?"

"Almost." Jack placed one hand on his desk, preparing to spin back around. "Give me a minute and I'll be right there."

"Sure. I'll meet you in the lobby." Keto turned and headed in the general direction of the restroom.

Jack calmed his nerves and turned back to his screen, quickly bringing up and then closing the incriminating window. He whooshed a sigh of relief, scooped up his Orichi and headed down the stairs for the lobby.

In his panic, he hadn't thought about it until now. Keto had actually invited him to lunch. It was a bittersweet thought that maybe he was starting to be accepted by the same people he had to deceive. Many gens would give anything to be in his place—working in an office and actually starting to earn the respect of his coworkers. It was a rare opportunity, but one he could not fully enjoy.

◆O◆

Two days later, Jack sat at his desk checking the logs as he had been instructed to when something caught the corner of his eye. He glanced up to see Vanessa entering his cubicle.

"Hello, Jack."

He returned the greeting but noted that though her voice was soft and on the surface all looked well, he had a growing suspicion that something wasn't right and it felt as if something like a rock dropped into his stomach.

"You know, Jack, you've become one of my best workers."

He decided to ignore the undertones of where this conversation could be going and instead smiled broadly. "Thank you, Vanessa. That's kind of you to say so."

"But," she inspected her nails and then glanced back up, "reports have been brought to my attention that you have been accessing off-limits files. When I saw that, I just knew they couldn't be right so I looked for myself."

Jack shifted in his chair and licked his lips. The rocks in his stomach grew heavier.

"Unfortunately, it looks like there might be some truth to the allegations after all." She crossed her arms and slumped a bit. "Please tell me, Jack, if there's a good explanation as to why you would have been trying to access top-secret files." Jack searched for words but couldn't find any. When he didn't answer, Vanessa's face grew sad. "What is it, Jack? What is so important that you would risk everything for it?"

Jack held his tongue, figuring that at this point, anything he said would only make things worse.

Vanessa hung her head and sighed. She looked to one side over the tops of the cubicles and beckoned with her hand.

Jack stood hesitantly, afraid of what he might find. There, a police detective headed their way, three officers in tow. When they reached Jack's workspace, Vanessa backed out of the way and let the men pass. The detective, his jaw clenched tight and distaste reflected in his eyes, grabbed Jack by the arm, spun him around, and cuffed his hands together behind his back.

Without a word, they dragged Jack from his cubicle, and as he passed by, his eyes met Vanessa's. Her face was sad, almost tired. Jack regretted having had to deceive her. It hurt to have betrayed the trust of what could have been a true friend. He shot her what he hoped was an apologetic smile, then hung his head and focused on the floor, avoiding the curious stares of his coworkers, their whispers hot in his ears.

Turning toward the outer doors, Jack saw Keto standing off to one side, arms crossed, his expression unreadable. He wondered if Keto's hard expression was the frown of a man angry at seeing a friend's betrayal or if it was the hardened glare of the one who had turned him in.

Once out in the hallway, the detective grasped Jack's arm and propelled him down the hall toward the office's elevator. After a brief wait, the doors opened and Jack stepped inside. He shook his head at the irony. The first and probably only time he was allowed to take the elevator was because he was under arrest and accompanied by human officers. Reaching the ground floor, they propelled Jack to a boxy transport vehicle waiting outside. Opening a side door, they shoved Jack toward the opening. He lifted his foot to step inside, but snagged the sole of his shoe on the bottom of the doorframe. With his hands securely fastened behind him, he stumbled, hit his head on the side of the doorway, and fell half inside of the vehicle. His other foot slid out from under him, raking his shin on the edge of the frame. The officer behind him whipped out his baton and struck Jack on the ribs.

"Get up, gen!" The way he spat out the word "gen" made it sound profane.

Jack grunted, the pain from the baton radiating across his back and his shin burning. He struggled to his feet, lowered his head, and ducked inside, sliding onto a bench seat. The officers climbed in the front, punched in the coordinates for their destination, and the vehicle lurched into motion. After about ten kilometers, they pulled up to the back of the local intelligence offices. The officers hauled Jack from the back of the vehicle and into the building, where he was pushed into the first empty cell they came to. The door clanged shut behind him and, in shock, he stood in the middle of the barren cell, bereft of furniture or fixtures of any kind. The odor of disinfectant over sweat and urine overcame Jack's sense of smell and he wrinkled his nose in disgust.

His hands still secured behind him, Jack lowered himself to the floor, first to one knee and then down onto his backside. Pushing with his heels, he scooted backwards until he reached the wall. The bands around his wrists cut into Jack's skin and his side throbbed.

Jack wondered how long he'd have to wait. He had heard stories of what happened to prisoners at the intelligence offices, but those stories were mostly unconfirmed since the prisoners were rarely seen again. He leaned his head back in despair, wondering if he would ever see his mother again. Or Amber. Or...

Jack shook his head to clear his thoughts, determined to not let fear get the best of him. Even in prison, he still had a mission, even if that mission was simply to not give away his friends and compatriots to the government.

Jack was uncertain how long he sat there in the glow of the artificial lighting. He did know it had been several hours when they finally came for him. The security alarm beeped as the guard unlocked the door.

"Get up," he growled.

Jack struggled to his feet, striving to keep his balance. The guard shoved him down the hallway and into a small room. The lighting overhead cast a bluish-white glow over a rectangular table in the middle of the floor. Bare walls painted stark white further lent to the barrenness of the room.

"Sit." The man shoved Jack into a chair on one side of the table, then stepped aside, arms crossed.

Jack shifted in the chair and glanced to his right, where the guard stood glaring.

After several minutes, the detective who had arrested Jack entered and sat across from him at the table. He leaned forward on the table, hands folded in front of him, and stared at Jack. Clean-shaven, he wore his neatly trimmed dark gray hair swept to one side. A heavy brow accentuated dark circles under his eyes, giving him a brooding look. The long sleeves of his dark blue button-down shirt were rolled halfway to his elbows, both its fine weave and the fact he was not in uniform a testament to his privileged station.

"So, they tell me you've been poking around in places you don't belong." The hard edge in his voice only made its quietness more menacing.

Jack returned the man's stare and kept his mouth closed. He knew that no matter what he said, it wouldn't help.

The officer took a deep breath and shook his head. "You know it's not going to do you or your friends any good if you don't cooperate."

Jack looked down at the steel tabletop, straining against the bonds that held his hands behind him. He figured that his aching shoulders and numb arms would not be the worst of his worries before this was finished. Either way, he knew that a lot of pain and abuse was in his near future, so he decided that under no circumstances would he say anything that would betray his friends or the insurgents.

The officer grunted. "All right. Let's make this easy. Here's what I want. First I want you to tell me what you were looking for, and then I want you to tell me about your friends and what their pathetic little plans are."

Jack looked up in surprise. They didn't know? *Maybe there's hope after all,* he thought.

The officer raised his eyebrows. "Well?"

"It's like this, sir." Jack willed calmness into his voice. "If you don't know, I'm not going to tell you."

The man clenched his jaw and shot a glance at the guard.

Before he knew what had happened, the guard had kicked the legs out from under Jack's chair and he crashed forward. His jaw smashed into the metal table and then the table edge raked his cheek and ear on the way to the floor. He crashed onto his side, head smacking on the hard concrete. Sparks of pain shot through Jack's vision and his head throbbed. He heard the legs of the officer's chair scrape backward and the man stood, glaring down at Jack.

"I repeat, what were you looking for?"

With some difficulty, Jack rolled over onto his back and lay there, eyes closed, gasping for air.

The agent leaned over, hands on his knees.

"Jack Metcalfe. Are you paying attention? I don't think you fully appreciate the seriousness of your situation. Why are you digging into top-secret files? I need to know what your friends are up to and I think you know what that is. And you're going to tell me."

Suddenly the ridiculousness of the situation struck Jack and he began to chuckle. Here he was, the scum of the earth, according to these officers, and yet he was the one with the information—and thus the one with the power. And he would remain able to hold something over their heads as long as he kept that information to himself. They could abuse him all they wanted, but he knew it was unlikely they would kill him until either he gave them what they wanted or until they gained the information from another source. The more he thought about it, the funnier it seemed.

He opened his eyes and in his morbid mirth, he found strength, a resolve stronger than it had been a few minutes previous. He couldn't keep the smirk off his face as he looked up.

"What's so funny?" The agent frowned, his forehead wrinkled with angry frustration.

"You," Jack wheezed, his breath still coming in gasps, pain still radiating through his side and head. "You think you're on the good side. You think you're one of the good guys. But you're not." He shook his head. "They're using you. The system that you're working for is corrupt. They walk on anyone standing in their path in order to get where they want to be. And if you're in their way, they'll walk on you too."

The agent drew back his foot and kicked him in the ribs. Jack cried out in pain but never stopped laughing. Even to him, his laughter sounded maniacal.

"You've lost it." The resolve in the agent's calm exterior cracked. The man spit on Jack, and for the first time, he raised his voice. "You have no idea what you're up against."

"Oh, I think I do." Jack's laughter subsided. "But do you?"

With a growl, the agent turned on his heel and stomped to the door. Hand on the knob, he looked over his shoulder and spit out, "I think we'd better bring in Eva and have a chat with her. I'm sure we can convince her to tell us," then stormed through the door.

With a hardened look, the guard also left. The door closed behind him and the lock clicked shut.

At the mention of Eva's name, Jack's laughter faded. They wouldn't really bring in his mom, would they? And yet, down inside, he knew they would in an instant.

Jack lay there on the floor for what must have been hours. Wracked in pain as he was and his hands still fastened behind him, he could not find the strength to sit up or even roll over.

Finally, the lock snapped open and the door swung inward. Still behind the table, Jack lifted his head to see who it was, but all he could see through the chair legs were the shoes of a guard, followed by an expensive pair of black shoes topped with black pants. The tabletop hid the rest of the two men from view. With a grunt, Jack let his head fall back, eyes closed. Within moments, the guard grabbed his arms and wrenched him up from the floor. With a moan of pain, Jack found himself in the chair once again.

On the other side of the table stood his half-brother Robert, shaking his head.

"Jack, Jack," he sighed. "What have you done now?"

Jack stared back. "Nothing you wouldn't have."

Robert took a deep breath and let it out all at once. "You had everything you wanted and threw it away. Now who will take care of your mother?"

"I would think her son would want to, wouldn't you?" Robert returned his gaze without expression and Jack continued. "I'm not her only son, you know."

Robert sat down at the table and spread his hands flat against its surface. "But you're the one she looks to for support."

Jack snorted. "Only because you left. Because you disowned her." A moment of heavy silence fell in the room and the truth settled like a suffocating blanket. "She never stopped caring about you."

Robert waved his hand in dismissal. "What I've done is in the past. What's done is done."

Even after all this time, Robert's supreme arrogance still amazed Jack.

He continued. "It doesn't matter anyway. Not many know I have a half-breed in the family. Eva—"

"You mean Mother."

"Yes, whatever. She's been out of the social circles long enough that only a few remember her—or you. Regardless, I'm here to talk about you." Robert tipped his head in what Jack could only imagine was a look of sheer annoyance. "I'm your last chance, you know." He leaned back and crossed his arms. "Your last chance to confess. If you don't tell me what they want to know, I'm afraid you'll go to prison." He spread his hands in a gesture of helplessness. "My hands are tied."

Jack raised one elbow as far as he could and looked toward his hands. "Really? Because it looks to me like I'm the one wearing the cuffs."

Robert shook his head and sighed. "I'm just trying to help. Can you not appreciate the gravity of your situation?"

"Oh, I understand." Jack nodded. "I understand that you love your fine house, your car, all the luxuries that life can afford. I also understand that you have gained these things out of your own ambition. You rejected Mother because she didn't fit in with your plan to succeed at all costs. She was going to hold you back, wasn't she? So you kicked her out."

Robert raised his eyebrows. "Are you quite finished?"

"No, I'm not." Jack shifted in his chair, trying unsuccessfully to bring relief to his throbbing shoulders. "I also understand that the gens are nothing more to you than tools. Tools to do the things you don't want to do."

"Of course." Robert raised his eyebrows. "That's why you were made. That's the way it's supposed to be."

Jack snorted. "If that's what you want, you should have thought farther ahead. You shouldn't have given your creations the ability to think because that will be your downfall."

"Is that what this is all about?" Robert looked at Jack incredulously. "You think that you and your friends deserve rights?" His voice was laced with skepticism. "I'm sorry to disappoint you, Jack. That will never happen."

"We'll see about that." For a panicked second, Jack hoped he hadn't said too much.

Robert sat regarding Jack for a moment, then pushed away from the table and left without another word.

After several minutes, the guard reached up to his ear and touched his communicator.

"Yes." After a few moments, he continued. "Yes, sir. Right away."

"Come on." He pulled Jack to his feet by the arm. "I think they're done with you." He hauled Jack down the hallway, pushed him back into the bare cell, and uncuffed his hands. Jack stumbled in fatigue and tried to catch himself, but his numb arms gave way and he fell heavily to the floor. Barely able to hold his trembling hands in the air, Jack examined them, first on one side and then the other. From the wrist down, they were swollen and red, nearly purple, and he wondered if they would ever be the same again. As his arms eventually started to tingle back to life, he hugged them to his chest. Before long, the tingling became sharp jolts of pain and he rocked side to side, moaning in agony.

Across the street from Jack's house, Amber leaned up against a wall and shifted from one foot to the other. She glanced up the street one direction, then the other, and a seed of worry sprouted in her mind. He should have been home by now.

She looked up at the dusky rose-colored sky. It would be dark soon. Time to go. Not safe to be in Gen Town after dark. She pushed off from the wall, hitched her bag up on her shoulder, shoved her hands into her pockets, and turned up the street toward home. As she went, her mind jumped from one terrible scenario to another.

What if Jack was waylaid and beaten again? Or worse yet, what if he was called in for questioning? No, she shook her head, he probably just had to work late.

Roughly 15 minutes after leaving the gen quarter, Amber reached her destination. Her apartment was modest-sized but located in a very safe area of town and well furnished by her parents. They paid the rent as long as she was in school.

She unlocked the door and stepped inside. The shades had been drawn since morning against the heat of the day, leaving the interior cool and shadowed, just the way Amber liked it. And quiet. Here she could be alone, away from anyone else and the noise outside. Inwardly, she thanked her parents for renting the place for her—at least until she graduated.

Here, away from the prying eyes and ears of society, she could truly rest. She tapped her earbud and activated the voice control.

"Call Kennan."

After a click and a short delay, her friend accepted the call.

"Amber!" Kennan's voice came through bright and cheerful. "To what do I owe the pleasure of your call?"

"Hey, Kennan." Amber wished there was someone else to call, but as the son of the president of the Moran-Burke Technologies conglomerate, he could best leverage his connections in the computer industry to hopefully find Jack. "Can you talk?"

"Um, just a sec."

She waited a few moments, then heard a *click*. Probably a door.

"Okay. I had to find a quiet place. What's up?"

"I lost a package." To anyone else, including government eavesdroppers, it would sound like a benign conversation. Such was their code.

After a few moments of silence, Kennan responded, his voice now quieter, serious. "Which one?"

"The one from Summit." They had established a code word for each member of the insurgency leadership group, and as Jack was the top leader of the group, "Summit" was the name they had given him. "I was wondering if you could trace the package for me."

"Yeah. I'll see if I can find it."

"Okay. Thanks. Let me know."

"Will do," Kennan replied, and Amber terminated the call. Another of their rules was to keep calls as brief as possible. But with Kennan, she was happy to cut it short. She liked Kennan well enough, but she didn't want to spend the rest of her life with him. To Amber, it was painfully obvious Kennan would rather be more than friends, but Amber was content to keep things the way they were.

Well, that's it then, she thought, and flopped down onto the overstuffed sofa. There was nothing else she could do for now.

Just then, her stomach grumbled and Amber realized she hadn't eaten since breakfast. She hauled herself off the couch and went to rummage through the kitchen, coming up with a nutrition bar from the cupboard. That would do for now. She peeled off the wrapper and dropped it in the trash bin, then headed back to the front room to study for a bit.

She sank her teeth into the chewy bar and picked up her handheld from a side table and dropped herself back onto the couch. She navigated to the portion of text assigned by her professor. *The History of Art*. Amber knew she had some talent as an artist and wanted to pursue a career that would allow her to indulge in her love for drawing, but to earn said degree, she had to take art history. She tried to push her worry for Jack out of her mind and settled in to study for the big test next week.

The guard propelled Jack down the hallway and into the back of a police truck. The vehicle lurched into motion and eventually they arrived at the justice building. They pulled around back to the prisoners' entrance and Jack stepped off the vehicle into the glare of a mid-morning sun. Jack was hustled into a long, narrow room and left seated on a bench with about twenty other prisoners, a mix of both gens and humans.

Jack settled on the bench and glanced up at his neighbor, a compact, muscular man, a little shorter than Jack but twice as wide. Just one prisoner in a row of others clothed in bright orange jumpsuits, hands cuffed. Jack offered an uneasy smile and the man grunted.

"Been here before?" His voice rasped like two pieces of sandpaper rubbing together.

Jack shook his head.

"Didn't think so." He eyed Jack's street clothes. "You don't have the look. What'd ya do?"

Jack searched his mind for what to say. *I'm a political prisoner bent on gaining rights for gens* just didn't seem like a smart thing to say.

"I...I hacked into government computers."

With raised brows, the prisoner eyed the wounds on Jack's face. "Looks like the machines fought back. Did ya get anything good?"

Jack shook his head and crossed his arms. "No. I was really close but...no."

He grunted. "Too bad. Maybe next time. Someone needs to take 'em down a notch or two. Full of themselves, they are."

Jack shot the man a glance. "What makes you think I'll get another chance?"

The prisoner snorted and looked straight ahead. "You look like a smart kid to me. If anyone can figure out how to get out of this place, I figure it'd be someone like you. If not," he shrugged his orange-clad shoulders, "you're not as smart as I thought."

The conversation fell silent and Jack sank into deep thought. Maybe the man was right. Maybe he'd get another try. With new purpose, he ran his eyes around the room to see if he could find anything that might allow a chance of escape. All he found was the eyes of a guard coming his way, his expression fixed in a look of sheer boredom.

"All right, let's go. Everyone up."

As one, the prisoners shuffled to their feet and turned toward the door at the end of the wide hallway.

As they stood, Jack's neighbor looked over his shoulder. "Remember what I said."

"Quiet!" A nearby guard scowled and shoved the prisoners along, but Jack just grinned. No matter how unreasonable the concept, it was encouraging to think he might have another chance.

Jack followed the other prisoners into the first courtroom he had ever entered in his life. They filed in and stood in a line, each awaiting their turn.

A quick inspection of the austere room revealed rich, brown wood paneling covered the bottom half of the walls, trimmed with expensive wide moldings. A massive desk stood in the front of the room and behind that, a blonde woman sat, attired in a black judge's robe, scribbling on a screen with a stylus. Without looking up, she called out, "Next."

One prisoner after another was called up, justice meted, and the man ushered out. Before long, it was Jack's turn. He rose and, looking over his shoulder to the gallery, was surprised to see his half-brother Robert sitting in the back row of the room. He returned Jack's look with no expression or recognition of any kind.

Jack walked to stand in front of the judge's bench, as directed. A prosecutor stood behind a table, scrolling through screens on a trim electronic tablet.

The judge folded her hands and glared down from her perch. "What do we have here?"

"Jack Metcalfe," the prosecutor replied, his voice weary and monotone. "Unauthorized access of protected files."

"How did he gain access?"

"He was a network administrator at the Ministry of Religion, assigned only to keep data logs. He's also involved somehow with a group of gen rebels."

The judge barely glanced at Jack. "For crimes against the government, I sentence you to life at River Island."

"Next."

Jack knew he'd have a steep penalty to pay, but life at River Island? A rock formed in the pit of his stomach and his mind went numb at the swift sentencing. River Island was a self-contained island off the coast of the mainland reserved for hardened criminals. Even though there were no walls, once there, a person rarely left. He had heard that with no airports, the only accessible transport was hovercraft or boat and it generally took several hours to get there. According to rumor, a few had tried to flee, but with so great a distance and the ports locked down, the only way to embark was via a raft or small homemade boat. Most perished before reaching land. It's almost as bad as being shipped off-world, he thought.

Jack's next thoughts flashed to his mom and then to his friends and compatriots. Now that he knew that the intelligence agency was at least somewhat aware of their activities, he worried about his friends' and family's safety—and the future of their cause. He hung his head, thoughts dragging him down into a fog of despair.

As soon as they left the courtroom, Jack was told to bare his arm and a clerk injected a tracking chip halfway between his wrist and elbow. Then a bright orange jumpsuit was thrust into his hands and he was told to strip down and don the garish garment. Afterward, he was barely aware of cuffs being fastened around his wrists and ankles, connected one to the other with a chain that didn't allow him to touch his face without bending over. Then he was shoved into a temporary holding cell with a dozen other prisoners.

The door clanged shut behind him and he looked for the first time at his fellow prisoners. Long faces all around, they spread out around the cell, each seeking an empty spot where they could sit on the floor and lean against the wall. When the spots along the walls filled up, the remainder sat in the middle of the room, most with legs folded crisscross.

No furniture, benches, or beds of any kind, and an open-air toilet in the corner of the room pretty much guaranteed that there would be no privacy for any of the prisoners for the foreseeable future.

After several hours had passed, Jack knew he was hungry but had no appetite, which was fine because there was no food. Nonetheless, the effects on all were obvious. Tempers flared as the prisoners fought for room to stretch out in the cramped space. Jack had been lucky to be one of those who initially found a place against the wall and he was determined to not give it up to anyone. So he sat elbows on knees, then cross-legged, shifting from one position to another but not leaving his space lest he lose it to another.

With no window in sight and constant artificial lighting, Jack lost track of the time they were there. But one thing was for certain, they had been there for several hours before a guard arrived and opened the cell door.

"Let's go." He motioned with a baton to the prisoners, one hand on the open door. One by one, the morose pack rose to their feet and filed out into the hallway, heading for an open door. A bus waited outside. They were herded into the vehicle and found their seats as it lurched into motion.

Once again, Jack examined the cuffs on his wrists and the chain that attached them to his ankles. Now sitting, he leaned forward and buried his face in his hands, dreading the days ahead.

Chapter 7

J ack stood on the dock in the midst of a long line of prisoners destined for River Island. Snugged to the dock, a large hovercraft rested in the water, awaiting its cargo. One by one, forty prisoners crossed the gangway and stepped onto the gun-metal gray boat, then into a cabin, where they were seated on long rows of benches that ran from fore to aft. All except Jack bore the gens' characteristic red skin darkened to a deep rusty red from exposure to the sun.

Jack found himself seated between a scrawny wisp of a gen and another about his size, the smaller tight-lipped, eyes shifting constantly from one spot to another, his straight black hair chopped raggedly above the shoulders. The other glared at Jack with hardened eyes, hands balled into fists in his lap.

Their stony looks extended to most of the men in the close-packed cabin. Jack hated to think what kind of society he would be arriving at once he reached the prison island. His mind traveled to where these gens had come from, the things they had done. But at least there were some, Jack noted with relief, who did not appear to be hardened criminals. Jack had never realized how harsh the legal system could be on gens who crossed the line, whether it be a simple offense or a genuine crime.

From time to time, the prisoners were allowed to stand and stretch their legs or shuffle to the back of the cabin to relieve themselves in the open facilities and guzzle a cup of stale, tepid water. After several hours, true to rumor, he gathered from the guards' conversation that they had almost reached their destination. Soon the tune of the motor changed and the craft settled down into the water as it continued to glide forward. After motoring slowly for some time, the boat bumped into the dock and drifted to a stop. The prisoners were goaded to their feet and they shuffled off the boat to stand in ranks on a large, square wooden landing, which formed the end of a pier leading up to a sprawling, boxy compound. Jack squinted in the glare bouncing off the austere, tan-colored buildings, the harsh sunlight piercing his eyes. Rivertown.

Standing in the last row, the hot sun beat down onto Jack's throbbing head and he squinted in the glaring sunlight. Guards lined the dock, spaced apart every six meters or so, guns in hand. The weapons didn't look like much, but Jack had heard what great damage they could cause. One bullet, only as long as half a finger, would explode upon impact, potentially blowing away half a man's body. The prisoners stood quietly, eyeing the guards, afraid to step out of line.

Out in the harbor, heavily armed small craft patrolled, motoring slowly across the water, running both offshore and across the mouth of the U-shaped harbor, protecting the fortress onshore—both from outsiders getting in and prisoners trying to get out.

As Jack stood in the hot sun, he swayed from the hunger that consumed him and his head swam drunkenly. Just then, the guard in front of the prisoners received a call on his communicator and, upon its completion, yelled, "Move 'em out."

A couple of guards stood behind Jack, one at each corner of the square formation. When it came time for Jack to step forward, his head swam dizzily and he hesitated. The guard behind Jack shoved him forward with his weapon, and as Jack fought to maintain his balance, he reflexively threw his hands out in front of him. With a jerk, he reached the end of the chain and stumbled. For one horrifying moment, he knew he was going down. He tumbled forward and crashed into the back of the prisoner in front of him, which pushed that man into the back of the one in front of him. As Jack crumpled to the ground, the guard drew back a boot and viciously kicked him in the lower back. Jack grunted in pain. The jostled prisoners ahead of Jack looked over their shoulders and glared.

"Sorry about that," he mumbled, attempting a wry grin. "Got tired of standing."

The guard tugged at the orange fabric of Jack's jumpsuit. "Get up, dog!" he snarled. Apparently he'd missed Jack's attempted humor.

Jack half lurched and was half dragged to his feet and roughly pushed forward, although he noticed the guard did not push him quite so hard this time.

The prisoners were herded down the dock and into a metal-sided building, its outer surface dulled by the coastal weather. Inside the building, oppressively hot air lay heavy and stifling. The prisoners were formed into a single-file line and paraded past a desk in an excruciatingly slow progression. When each reached the desk, a guard held a small device up to the prisoner's arm, scanned the identification chip, and then referenced the corresponding record that popped up on an electronic handheld resting in the crook of his arm. Identification confirmed, the prisoner progressed to the next guard, who shoved a small lightweight bag into his hands.

Soon it was Jack's turn. The guard scanned Jack's arm, reviewed the ID record that popped up on his handheld, and then shot him a glance.

"Jack Metcalfe? You wouldn't happen to be Stan Metcalfe's son, would you?"

Jack's heart seemed to stop for a moment. "Excuse me?"

"Your father. Is he Stan Metcalfe?"

Jack slowly nodded, wondering how in the world this guard would know that. "Y-yes, sir," was all he could manage.

"Hmph," the guard grunted, and with one last look of scrutiny, waved Jack on.

The next guard shoved the small sack into Jack's hands and he moved on, following the prisoner in front of him. When they reached the doorway leading outside, Jack looked back over his shoulder, the guard's words ringing in his ears. The guard stared back.

Once outside, Jack followed the other prisoners onto a bus. They were driven to the edge of the compound, up to a pair of wide gates. Loops of razor-edged wire stretched across the tops of the gates as well as along the length of the wall. A square tower perched on the wall next to the gate, tall enough for the guards to see both inside and outside the compound. Armed guards took position outside the doors of the bus and the doors swung open with a swoosh. One by one, the prisoners stepped off the bus. Their cuffs and chains were unlocked and removed and the prisoners herded toward the gate.

A guard peered down from the tower and then turned to a console in front of him. Shortly, the gates swung open, and the guards motioned with their guns for the prisoners to exit the compound. Once all prisoners had left, the gates swung shut, leaving a pack of orange-suited strangers standing with their backs to the fortified prison facilities. After one last look behind him, Jack turned his face toward the sad excuse of a town that lay in front of him.

Hot, scorching sunlight beat down upon ramshackle buildings of mud brick or rough-hewn lumber. A few gens and humans alike squatted or stood, leaning against a wall here or there, some with arms crossed. For the most part, their clothes were shabby and shoes mostly worn out. They warily eyed the newcomers with guarded looks. A few smirked with skeptical amusement, but all examined them from a distance.

These seasoned prisoners reminded Jack of the gangs that roamed the gen quarter at home and he knew that these were not likely men to be trifled with. Jack unzipped the front of his jumpsuit and shoved the bag inside, then zipped it back up again. There'd be plenty of time later to discover the contents.

With a last glance at his fellow newbies, Jack moved cautiously into the town. A few buildings down, two children peeked around a corner at him, with faces smudged the same color as the dirt road. Trash lay along the side of the road and collected in the corners and against the sides of the rudimentary buildings. No electricity, no cars, no electronics to be seen anywhere. Jack felt as if he had stepped back in time a few hundred years.

After walking for about a half hour, by Jack's estimate, he reached the other side of the settlement. After even just that short of a walk, the bruises and contusions on his torso, head and shins throbbed. To make matters worse, his head swam with dizziness from hunger and he licked dry lips with a tongue that felt like cotton.

He found a quiet corner and stepped aside, then pulled the bag out of his jumpsuit and looked inside to find a lightweight pair of pants, a shirt, and twenty credits. He sighed and shook his head. Hopefully food wouldn't cost much here. At home, that would buy only enough food to last two days—three, if rationed.

Nonetheless, credits were credits and he needed to eat. Turning his back to the flat desolate land beyond the edge of town, he started back up the street, walking until he reached a brew house he had passed earlier. A simple, hand-lettered sign outside read, "Brew, Eats."

Rough mud brick formed the exterior, the same dismal color as the gray-brown dirt road. A rough-hewn wooden door hung loosely on its hinges and complained with a loud squawk when Jack tugged it open. Inside, crude wooden tables stood drunkenly here and there in a hodgepodge of seats for a handful of customers. A man behind the bar recognized Jack's presence with a nod.

"Have a seat. I'll be with you in a minute," the man growled.

Jack stumbled to one of the tables on the far side of the room and lowered himself into a chair with his back to the wall. The chair wobbled on uneven legs as Jack leaned forward, elbows on the table.

The proprietor swiped a rag stained with grime across the bar and called out to Jack, "What'll ya have?"

Jack wiped a hand across his face. "What'cha got?"

"You must be new here," the man replied. "I have *chicha*—a local brew made out of corn mash—or there's water. I don't recommend the water."

Jack snorted. That figures. "Then I guess I'll have the brew."

The man nodded his approval. "If you're hungry and can afford it, I've got vegetables, potatoes, and chicken." He eyed Jack's bright orange jumpsuit. "But it looks like you're fresh off the boat, which means you probably don't have enough credits. I'll cut you a break," he said. "For ten credits, I'll give you a plate of vegetables and a mug of brew."

So much? Jack thought. He tried not to gape, instead closing his eyes in a prolonged blink.

The man grinned crookedly, revealing yellowed teeth in the early stages of decay. "Down the street it'll cost you double...or more. You'll not find a better deal in town."

With a deep sigh, Jack relented. "Fine. Bring the vegetables and brew."

The man turned back toward the wall, grabbed a spoon and plunged it into a pot resting on a warming tray. He scooped out of the pot a spoonful of the contents, then filled a mug from a nearby keg. He stepped around the end of the bar and placed the plate in front of Jack with a clatter, followed by the mug. Jack leaned forward and examined his expensive dinner. Boiled, limp, wrinkled carrots and one of Jack's least favorite foods, turnips. Water pooled in the center of the plate under the vegetables. He decided to try the brew first.

He lifted the mug to his nose and took a sniff, trying not to wrinkle his nose at the heavily fermented smell. He took a cautious sip and the room-temperature liquid filled his mouth with a bitter flavor and burned his throat as it went down. A shiver of revulsion shook his shoulders and traveled down his back.

A smirk crossed the man's face. "You'll get used to it. It only takes one bout of dysentery from the local water before you change your mind and decide it's not so bad."

Jack turned back to the unappetizing vegetables in a new light. "D'ya have a fork?"

"Oh, yeah." The man turned back to the counter and fished under the bar, surfacing with a bent fork, which he examined, then proceeded to wipe on his shirttail. He handed it to Jack, pulled out a chair, and sat across from him.

Jack looked the fork over and proceeded to pick some kind of unrecognizable dried substance from between the tongs. He hoped it was food.

The man watched, unconcerned. "Name's Oscar. What brought you here to River Island?"

Jack gnawed on the end of a rubbery carrot. He eyed the man, unsure of how much to say.

Oscar shrugged. "Just curious. Everyone here has a story. Some deserve to be here, some don't. Keep it to yourself if you want. Doesn't matter. We're all in the same boat. Well, at least we all came over on the same boat." He chuckled at his own joke.

Jack forced the unappetizing bite down his throat.

Oscar leaned forward, arms crossed on the table. "There's one thing you need to know, kid." He paused and rubbed his jaw, regarding Jack in all seriousness. "You have two choices. You can stay in town and scrape by or you can leave town. But you should know that it's God-forsaken, barren land out there. If you can grow things, you might be able to sell some scraggly crops in town." His gaze shifted down to Jack's uncalloused hands. "But if not, you're probably better off staying in town."

Jack tried one of the turnips—the spongy root squeaked against his teeth and brought a new shudder. The carrots were better.

"You any good at fixin' stuff?"

Jack shrugged. "Sometimes."

"Hmpf." Oscar leaned back in his chair. "If you're handy with electronics, there might be a place for you here in town. If you pick your friends carefully, you might survive."

Jack's stomach rumbled and he stuffed another disgusting carrot into his mouth. At least it was food. "You got any suggestions?" he asked the brusque man.

"Yeah. Maybe. There's an old guy I know you'll probably want to talk to. Any of the electronic stuff we get comes from him. Name's Diego. Maybe you can work out a deal with him."

After getting directions from the bartender, Jack finished his dinner, thanked the man, and set off to find the old technician. Following the directions he'd been given, he walked two blocks, then turned off the main street and followed one street after another. The farther he got from the center of town, the more dilapidated the neighborhoods became until finally, he turned down a narrow alley and found the dwelling Oscar had described—a rundown, ramshackle wooden building. Little more than a shed, really. Jack knocked on the door, careful not to prick his knuckles on the splintered wood. A menacing snarl inside the shack raised the hair on the back of Jack's neck.

"Door's open," growled a muffled voice.

Jack flat-palmed the door and pushed. It didn't budge. Pushing more firmly, the door broke away from the tight jamb and swung free. Jack grabbed for the door's metal handle, catching it just before it crashed open. The snarling only increased with the opening of the door and Jack could see a dog's eyes glinting in the gloom. Hackles raised, the animal rose slowly to its feet. Jack froze.

Beyond the dog, a long workbench stood, behind which perched a wrinkled old man, head bowed over a jumble of what appeared to be odds and ends, wires and tools. A small lamp on an articulating arm extended over his workspace, its glow illuminating the man's project more brightly than the feeble light peeking through a small, smudged window guarded by two crisscrossed bars. Focused on his work, the man didn't look up.

"Perro! Down!" he snapped. The dog's snarling decreased to a low growl and the animal lowered itself down onto the floor.

As Jack's eyes adjusted to the dim light, a cluttered room came into view. Shelves stood floor to ceiling on all sides, filled with a litter of parts for lamps, electronic boards and other parts, components bristling with wires, and cables of all sizes. Larger items like empty computer cases sat on the floor in front of the shelves, most covered with a layer of dust.

From where he stood, Jack eyed the man at work. Soldering iron in hand, the old man held a tin wire to a small electronic board, his head tipped away from a thin trail of smoke that rose from the melting solder. Laying the tools down, he gently tested the connection, and once satisfied it was secure, he glanced up with eyes that appeared small through the narrow scratched glasses perched on his nose. His gaze met Jack's, brows drawn together in a frown.

"Diego?"

"Yeah." His glance flicked down to Jack's orange suit and back up again. "What d'ya want?" he asked in a voice laced with a Latino accent.

"I'm Jack." He held out his hand, which Diego ignored. Perro's growls grew in volume. Not the response Jack hoped for. Hesitantly, he withdrew his hand. Might as well get to the point. "Oscar sent me. He said you might have work."

After a moment's hesitation, Diego replied with a grunt. "Don't hardly have enough work for myself. Why'd he say that?"

"He said we might be able to work out a deal. I'm willing to work for food and a roof over my head."

"'S that right?" He turned back to his project, picking up the component, turning it over and examining the other side. "What can ya do?"

"Oscar said you piece things together and sell them. I can at least do that."

Diego searched Jack's face doubtfully. "Okay," he finally said. "If you're so good, what is this?" He held the part out toward Jack.

As Jack took a step forward, the dog rumbled another growl but stayed put. Jack gently shoved some wires aside and perched his parcel on the edge of the worktable, then took the piece from Diego. Perro kept his canine eyes riveted on his prey and Jack couldn't stop himself from swallowing nervously, but stood his ground, determined not to show the animal any fear.

Jack turned the part over from one side to the other, examining front then back. He hadn't seen one of these in quite a while. "Looks like a logic board from a 927 desktop." He handed it back and glanced around the table. "I don't see any other parts though. You planning to build a working computer from it?"

Diego snorted. "That's the general idea." He gestured with one hand to the shelves around the edges of the room. "I think I have enough parts here somewhere, but there's no sense draggin' 'em out if the connections aren't solid." Diego paused and then seemed to pull back inside his shell as if he'd said too much already. "At least you know what it is."

Gotta get this guy to relax, Jack thought. He looked around once more. "Looks like you have plenty of things here to fix. I can help."

Diego chewed on his lip, then said slowly, "You don't want nothin' but room and board?"

Jack nodded.

Diego picked his way through a small pile of equipment and pulled a lamp off a shelf, the bulb dangling by loose wires. He thrust it into Jack's hands. "Fix it," he commanded.

Jack took the LED lamp and pursed his lips. This shouldn't be too hard. But it'd be nice to have a table.

Diego crossed his arms and watched.

Jack placed his parcel under the table and pushed aside a few items to clear a slightly larger area to work. With a screwdriver borrowed from Diego, he disassembled the light fixture, checked the connections, and reassembled it. Repair finished, he offered the small lamp back to Diego. "All it should need now is a battery."

Diego took the lamp back. "Good job," he said grudgingly. "But now you've found my biggest problem." He placed it back on the shelf. "Batteries are hard to come by—other parts too, for that matter."

Jack waited for an explanation.

"All we get comes from the compound." He jutted his chin in the general direction of the harbor. "Either from the guards' trash or sometimes we can bribe something out of one of 'em. Batteries can be the hardest to get." Diego sighed and thought for a moment, then continued. "Tell you what." He turned back to Jack. "I'll put a roof over your head. I don't always have food to spare, but I'll give you some workspace if you want to scavenge for parts, bring 'em here, and fix 'em. Anything you sell, I get half."

Jack sighed. It was probably the best offer he'd get. He nodded.

Diego jerked a nod toward one corner of the room. "You can put your stuff there." When Jack hesitated, Diego continued. "It'll be safe. Perro'll make sure no one takes anything." He gave Jack directions to the dump with instructions to come back before the end of the day if he wanted a place to sleep.

Jack turned toward the door and Perro snapped his head up off the ground and watched him leave, eyes glinting.

Pulling the door shut behind him, Jack turned down the shadowed street, following the directions Diego had given him. His thoughts wandered to home. His mother, Amber, and the others, and he wondered how they were doing.

Jack made his way to the dump and began sorting through piles of junk discarded by the soldiers. And that's really what it was—junk. And scraps of rotting food, broken pottery and, yes, broken electronics. He began making a pile of parts that might be usable, batteries (probably dead), broken lamps, and other odd pieces of junk. Maybe the wires could be salvaged at least. Once in a while, he came across other electronic parts, but those were few and far between. On the plus side, it looked as if some of the batteries might actually be in decent shape as they were contained within other devices that were broken.

When Jack's pile grew large enough, he began to hunt for a crate in which to put the stuff. There was just enough stuff that he'd never be able to cart it to the shop otherwise. All the while, as he worked, his mind pried on the mystery of the guard's words about his father. What did it mean? How and why would the guard know the name of Stan Metcalfe? His father was nothing but a good-for-nothing drifter...wasn't he?

Jack loaded the stuff into his crate and carted it back to Diego's shop. Neither the man nor his dog were there. Picking up a broken lamp, he separated the broken illumination mechanism from the base and inspected the latter. It looked to be functional. Sorting through the clutter on Diego's shelves, he found parts sufficient to cobble together a lamp of sorts—the ugliest he had ever seen, but when he flipped the switch, surprisingly, it worked. The light was dim, but it worked.

As he finished tightening the parts together, Diego returned, Perro close behind. Diego crossed the room and inspected Jack's work.

"Hmph," he grunted. "Not bad. Should be able to at least get a few credits for it."

"Really?" Jack was surprised that anyone would be willing to pay even one credit for the ugly thing.

Diego raised one eyebrow. "It's better than what many have here in Rivertown." He scratched Perro behind one ear. Diego was short enough and the dog tall enough that he only had to lean over slightly to reach the dog's massive head. Perro returned the gesture with a sloppy lick. Without looking up, Diego turned back toward the door. "Just came to tell you it's time to lock up. Follow me if you're hungry."

Leaving the contraption of a lamp on the workbench, Jack followed Diego out and waited while the man pulled a padlock out of his pocket and locked the door. After a tug to make sure the lock held, Diego turned and shuffled to the building next door. Perro followed with glittering eyes fixed on Jack in an unwavering glare.

The outside of Diego's house was in no better shape than his shack of a workshop. The man pulled a key from his pocket and inserted it into a padlock nearly identical to the one on the shop's door, with the exception that this one was corroded with rust. With a couple of tugs, Diego wrenched the lock open and unfastened the door.

Jack followed Diego inside the one-room hovel. Shelves mounted haphazardly in one corner held a couple of pottery bowls, under which a rough wooden cupboard stood, the top of which formed a countertop. Diego lugged a cloth sack out of the cupboard, scooped a cupful of flour out of the bag, and poured it on the countertop. Forming a depression in the center, he then poured a small amount of water into the shallow well and began to mix the two together with a spatula. He mixed in a pinch of salt from a small tin and another pinch of baking soda and formed the dough into four biscuits, which he plopped onto a battery-powered hot plate and covered them with a domed lid.

While he worked, Jack eased down onto a wooden chair that accepted his weight with a series of creaks and pops. He shifted and the rickety chair wobbled until Jack wondered how much longer it would stand. He leaned forward, elbows on a rugged, rectangular table, the top of which measured roughly one meter by one-and-a-half meters.

In another corner of the room, a pallet rested on the floor, covered crudely with a blanket or two, with another wad of blankets strewn across the top. Perro flopped down onto the floor, placed his head on his paws and watched Jack with an occasional glance up to his master preparing the food.

Once the biscuits were baking on the cookplate, Diego drug a crate from one edge of the room up to the table and sat down, leaning forward onto the table. His eyes searched Jack's.

"So what'd ya do?"

Jack was trying to figure out how to answer the man when he clarified his question.

"What'd ya do to earn a trip to River Island? Ya didn't kill anyone, did ya?"

Realization dawned on Jack and he shook his head, then took a deep breath. "Got caught looking through top-secret files."

"That's it?" Diego raised an eyebrow. "Ya didn't even draw blood?"

Jack grinned and shook his head again. "I assure you, you'll be safe. I won't murder you in your sleep or anything like that."

Diego nodded and seemed to relax a bit. A quiet veil dropped over the conversation as he waited for Jack to continue.

Jack leaned back and the chair complained with a groan. "I worked for the Ministry of Religion and they took exception to me poking through files outside of my area."

Diego stood to peek under the lid at the biscuits, then clamped the lid down once again. He retrieved a lamp from one end of the counter—a lamp that looked even worse than the one Jack had cobbled together. He flipped the switch on. Nothing happened. Jiggling the illumination bar that extended upward vertically from the battery base, the lamp flickered awake. Placing it on one end of the table, he took his seat once again.

After a bit of polite conversation, Jack's curiosity turned toward his new hometown and his host.

"So how long have you been here?" he asked Diego.

Diego grunted and replied, "Too long."

Jack waited as the man sorted through his memories.

"I quit counting a while back, but it's probably been 25 years."

"What happened?"

"I was a thief." He ran a hand through cropped black hair. "Those politicians have some pretty nice stuff." He smiled a crooked grin. "Had a nice little business going. I'd break into their houses, take their pretties, and sell 'em on the black market to gens and humans alike. Didn't matter to me who bought 'em," he paused, "but I could always get more, sell the better stuff in town. That was my downfall," he sighed. "Had a couple of real nice handhelds I'd just lifted. Turns out the guy I sold 'em to was *la policía*."

Diego grabbed a couple of bowls from the shelf, scooped a couple of spoonfuls of room-temperature brown beans from a pot on the counter, and stabbed a metal spoon into each.

The smell of baking biscuits filled the room and Jack's stomach rumbled. Diego uncovered the biscuits, flipped off the hotplate, and plopped one into each bowl atop the beans. The other two biscuits he slid onto the counter. Sitting on the crate, he placed both bowls on the table and dug into his with a bent spoon.

Jack chewed a mouthful of beans. Even though they were cold, Jack was so hungry, he hardly noticed how bland they were. As they ate in silence, Jack remembered the guard's words again and he began to wonder for the first time who his dad really was. What had he done to warrant the attention of the authorities?

Before long, however, the food was gone and the bowls scraped clean. Diego took them to the sideboard and wiped them clean with a dirty rag. He tossed the two remaining biscuits to Perro, who gobbled them up in two bites.

That night, Diego tossed Jack a blanket and then settled himself down on the pallet. Perro snugged up against the pallet, head on his paws.

I guess anyplace on the floor will do, Jack thought. He spread half the blanket across the floor up against one wall, lay down, and folded the other half across himself.

The next few days held more of the same. The days passed without anything remarkable happening—that is, until one morning when a young boy came to the shop.

"Mr. Jack?" he asked.

"Yeah?"

"The warden wants to see you up at the compound."

Jack's heart pounded with dread. "Me? Why me?"

The lad shrugged. "Dunno," he said and scooted back out the door.

Jack stared absently into the bright sunlight outside, wondering what the man would want him for.

"If I were you," Diego growled from one side of the workbench, "I wouldn't wait. You don't want 'em to come looking for ya."

Jack grunted. He was probably right. Reluctantly, he laid down the tools, and with a nod at the old man, headed out the door, hoping he'd be back.

With heavy footsteps, he headed up to the compound. He reported in at the gates, where the guards checked his name against a list and let him in with directions on how to find the warden's office. He crossed the open space of the compound, his shoes raising puffs of dust with each step. He found a flight of stairs as directed, and at the top, checked in with another guard. With eyes of steel, the guard gestured with a jerk of his head. "Inside, down the hall, and to the left," he growled.

Jack wrenched the heavy door open, headed down the hall, and stopped in front of a door, the top half of which declared "Philip Goldman, Warden" in gold paint on a transparent window. Jack rapped his knuckles on the door and a man seated at a desk inside looked up.

"Come in," came the muffled command.

Jack turned the knob and pushed the door open. "You wanted to see me?"

"Jack Metcalfe?"

"Yessir," Jack nodded.

"Sit down." The warden nodded to a chair off to one side. All four walls of his office were framed by windows on the top half, three of which looked out over the hallway and the offices on both sides. The back window showed a view of the courtyard below, crisscrossed with paths and two stunted trees.

The man finished what he was doing, then turned to Jack, hands folded on the desk in front of him.

"Jack Metcalfe." The words were not a question but a statement.

Jack sat motionless, waiting, wondering what the man was thinking.

"Your father's Stan Metcalfe, right?"

Jack nodded cautiously.

"So how is your father?"

"I wouldn't know, sir," Jack said slowly. "I haven't seen him since I was a small boy."

"Hm. Is that right?" The man leaned back and jacked his jaw to one side. "He hasn't tried to contact you or your mother in all that time?"

Jack shook his head, his thoughts racing as he tried to piece together the reason for the man's questions.

The warden scrutinized Jack's face, his expression unreadable. "You know, I find that hard to believe. I had heard he was quite the family man."

Jack sat motionless, figuring that anything he said could do more harm than good at this point. After several moments of silence, the man finally spoke.

"I see you need some persuading. I'll tell you what. If you change your mind and *happen*," the last word laced with sarcasm, "to remember something, you let me know. If you remember enough details, I might even be able to get you off this God-forsaken rock." After a moment of silence, he added, "You're dismissed, but think about it. If you *can't* remember, things might not go so well for you."

"Yessir." Jack stood and left the man's office, his thoughts spinning. How could he tell him something he didn't know? And why did the man care?

Chapter 8

J ack returned to the Rivertown settlement deep in thought. What should he do? If he just made something up, they were sure to find out. But if he didn't tell them anything, he could be beaten—or worse. He wondered if maybe he should leave the settlement. Maybe if they couldn't find him...

Wiping the sweat from his brow, he headed for the far edge of town. But when he got to Oscar's bar, he changed his mind. Stepping up to the door, he pushed it open and strolled into the cool interior. Oscar looked up with a smile.

"Hey there, Jack! How's it going?"

In reply, Jack slid onto a stool at the bar. Oscar drew a mug of *chicha* corn brew from the keg and placed it in front of him.

"What brings you out here?"

"Oh, just thought I'd drop in and say hi."

Oscar inquired as to whether Jack had found Diego, to which Jack replied he had and related the deal they had made—a roof and maybe some food in exchange for a share of profits. Oscar listened, chin in hand, and nodded encouragingly.

"So you're settling in then?"

Jack nodded and Oscar continued.

"They haven't given you too much trouble up at the compound, have they?"

Jack chewed the inside of his cheek as the warden came to mind. "No, not really," he replied. He searched Oscar's eyes to see if any guile lodged there, but found none. Oscar had proven to be a friend so far. "But an odd thing did happen."

Oscar raised his eyebrows at the comment and gave Jack his full attention.

"I just came from the compound. The warden called me up there. Asked about my father." He paused. "Why would he do that?" Jack asked the question more out of frustration than a desire to see if Oscar had any answers.

Oscar's eyebrows drew together in a frown and he scooped up a rag and began to wipe an already clean counter. Not the response Jack had anticipated.

"Oscar?" Jack tipped his head to one side to try to catch the bartender's gaze. "Do you know why he'd ask me that? Is there something I should know?"

Oscar paused in his useless polishing and sighed. "Your father," he said. "I've heard rumors of your father."

Jack sat back in surprise. "*My* father? How do you even know who my father is?"

Oscar's eyes finally met Jack's and realization dawned on the older man's face. "You don't know, do you?"

"Know? Know what?"

"That your dad is a hero of sorts."

"My father. A hero. Yeah, right." Jack couldn't keep the skepticism out of his voice. "I have trouble believing that. My father was good for absolutely nothing. Probably still is, for that matter—if he's still alive."

Oscar scratched his head. "Well, that's not what I've heard."

This time it was Jack's turn to be surprised. "What exactly *have* you heard?"

"Well, um," Oscar laid down the rag. "Word is that Stan stood up for the gens."

Jack stared at the man for a few moments and finally found the words to ask, "Well, why haven't I heard this if it's true?"

Oscar shrugged. "Maybe those who worked with him are here. But I really don't know. But here on River Island most have at least heard of Stan Metcalfe."

Jack pushed his drink aside. "Why? What else do you know?"

Oscar leaned forward onto the counter, arms crossed in front of him. "That's where it gets fuzzy. Some say he led the Underground, some say he worked for Religion. Either way, his name is held in high respect."

"Religion? As in the Ministry of Religion?"

"So I hear, but he's not there anymore."

Jack caught his breath. Could it be he had been right under Jack's nose the whole time? "So he's here? On River Island?"

Oscar shook his head. "No, I don't think so. Sorry to get your hopes up. I know pretty much everyone in Rivertown and I'm pretty sure he's not here. In truth, no one knows where he is—or even if he is still alive. He just disappeared."

Jack hung his head and rubbed his forehead with one hand. Discovering more about his father had been too much to hope for.

Oscar's voice cut into Jack's thoughts, his tone consoling. "Hey there," he said softly. "Don't take it too hard. I thought you knew. Maybe I shouldn't have said anything, but you would have heard sooner or later. In fact, I was wondering if that's why you were here. Maybe the warden thinks the same thing."

Jack sighed, suddenly wanting to be alone. He dug a coin out of his pocket and laid it on the counter and rose to leave.

A frown crossed Oscar's face. "You okay?"

Jack's troubled thoughts ran into the empty spaces of his mind like poisoned water, filling areas he had starved for years, raising thoughts he had refused to think about for so long. But these were things he didn't want to talk about. Instead, he simply nodded. "I need to go." He shoved his hands in his pockets and turned away from his untouched drink, crossed the threshold and stepped out into the harsh, hot sunlight.

As he continued his previous path toward Rivertown's outskirts, Jack tried to sort out his whirling thoughts. He had always known his father might still be alive, but it had been easier to think of him as dead, believing he'd never see him again. And to be honest, that still was fine with Jack. He didn't need his father.

And yet, he couldn't shake the doubts that Oscar had inadvertently planted in his mind. What if his father truly was a hero? What if he really did fight for the gens? Jack shook his head. It couldn't be true. Either way, he thought, Stan had abandoned the gens as much as he had abandoned his family. And that spoke ill of him and his character. It was easier to continue thinking of him as good for nothing rather than to consider for the first time that maybe that wasn't the case.

When he reached the outskirts, Jack stood and gazed out onto a wasteland, a mirage of heat waves shimmering in the distance. So, with nowhere else to go, he drew a deep breath, turned back toward the ragged town, and returned to Diego's shop.

When Jack arrived, Diego watched him enter, his gaze intent. Perro too watched him fixedly, but at least he didn't growl this time.

For some reason Jack couldn't fathom, Diego said nothing, for which Jack was grateful. The man just turned back to his work.

The next morning, Jack was called again to stand before the warden. Yet this time, when he checked in at the gate, one of the guards regarded him with a cruel gaze and turned to follow Jack with a sneer. Jack headed for the administration building as he had been directed the day before, but before climbing the stairs, the guard grabbed Jack by the arm and spun him away from the stairs, pointing instead to another door.

"That way," he growled.

Jack gestured back toward the stairs. "But I got a message the warden wanted to see me."

"Yeah, he does," the guard sneered. "But not up there." He gestured with his gun. "Open the door."

With a feeling of dread, Jack heaved the door open and stepped inside, the guard following close behind. "Keep moving," the man said, jabbing the barrel of his weapon into Jack's back.

A ball of anger began to form in Jack's gut. "Where are we going?"

"Just move." The guard shoved Jack again and he stumbled forward. Looking back over his shoulder, he saw his captor's face twisted in a look of malicious glee.

Before long, they reached a side room off the main hallway and the guard nudged Jack through the doorway, the barrel of his weapon hard against Jack's ribs. A table stood in the middle of the room, a chair on each side.

"Sit," the guard commanded.

With a glare at his captor, Jack lowered himself into one of the chairs.

The guard stepped back outside and locked the door. Jack watched him go, determined not to show any fear, but inside, his heart pounded with adrenalin.

Before long, the warden appeared and the guard unlocked the door, let him in, and then took a position just outside.

"Jack," the warden began. "You've had all night to think about our conversation, so today I'd like to talk about whatever you've remembered since yesterday."

Jack took a deep breath. Yep, just as he feared. Might as well start with the truth. "Like I told you yesterday, I don't know anything."

The warden struck Jack across the face so quickly he hardly knew it was coming. "Liar!" the man shouted. "I want you to tell me where your father is. Right now!"

His jaw aching, Jack shook his head in puzzlement. "What makes you think I know where he is? I haven't seen him for years. In fact, I barely remember him. That's how long it's been since he abandoned us."

The warden leaned forward, fists braced on the table. "You can't tell me you don't know," he growled. "Your father was a rebel and now here you are, following in his footsteps. You must have had contact with him. Like father, like son."

Jack leaned back and folded his arms. The man circled behind Jack like a shark circling its prey. Hearing the rasp of wood on leather, Jack looked over his shoulder, just in time to see a billy club swinging his direction. It landed with searing pain across Jack's shoulder, then again, and again a third time, but this time across the back of his head. Jack swayed in his chair and clutched at his head. The room spun crazily and specks of light flashed through his eyes.

The man paced away, tapping the club on the palm of his hand. "You will tell me."

Anger rose up inside Jack and he snarled through clenched teeth, "I...don't...know."

The warden wheeled around and clubbed Jack across the other shoulder. He couldn't help but cry out in pain.

"You know, you can't save your dear old dad. One way or the other, we'll find him. But it will certainly go better for you if you cooperate." With that, he spun on his heel and stalked out, leaving Jack moaning in pain. Within seconds, the guard reentered, hauled Jack to his feet, and propelled him out into the hallway. He pushed him down a series of corridors until he stopped at a door, unlocked it, and tossed Jack inside like yesterday's garbage. Jack made his way to a cot in the corner and crumpled there into a ball, carefully laying his pounding head on the scratchy blanket folded into a square on one end of the bed.

Later that night, the warden visited him once again, and again Jack was beaten, this time worse than before. Several days followed in like manner. The warden came, asked where his father was and what he knew, Jack denied it, and the warden beat him.

After a week or so—Jack couldn't exactly remember how long it had been—he lay aching in his cell one night, head pounding, ribs throbbing, welts covering his body. The beatings had also revived his previous injuries that never had the chance to heal up. Jack drew his legs up onto the cot and lay with both eyes closed—one voluntarily, one swollen shut—and his thoughts travelled to his mother. And her God. Then he thought of the gens and their gods. Apparently the old beggar's prayers to the nature gods back in New Santiago hadn't done any good. But then again, he thought, surely his mother was praying to her God too. If that were the case, neither camp seemed to be paying much attention.

Snap.

A key turned in the lock and Jack turned toward the door as quickly as his pounding head would allow. He cracked open the one eye that could still see and peered to see what torment this new visitor brought. To his surprise, Diego poked his head around the edge of the door, and seeing Jack, he quickly slipped inside and eased the door shut. His eyes grew large and round as he took in Jack's disheveled state.

"Thank God I found you," the old man said. "And look at you," he tsked. "I figured you must be here somewhere."

"How'd y'find me?" Jack's voice came out more slurred than he had hoped.

"Well, you didn't come back and I got a bad feeling. I figured you ran into some kind of trouble. When I asked Oscar if he'd seen you, he mentioned you'd been called up to the compound again."

Jack struggled to organize his scattered, broken thoughts, to make sense of what Diego was doing here and why. "But how'd you get in?"

Diego smiled a crooked grin. "It's amazing what a little coin will buy. Sometimes that's the only way to open a door."

The door opened once again and a cleaning man entered, carrying a set of blue-striped coveralls that matched the ones he wore. Diego motioned him in, then sat on the bed and put his arm under Jack's shoulder blades and helped him sit up. Jack moaned as the pounding in his head increased.

"Oh, you're in a bad way, aren't ya?" Diego's voice came soothing and calm. He pressed a bottle up to Jack's lips. The *chicha* corn beer that met his lips was as vile as always, but it was wet and Jack willingly swallowed several mouthfuls. Diego continued. "Good thing I found you. We have to get you outta here before it gets worse. It wouldn't be the first time a prisoner died here." He picked up Jack's feet one at a time and slid them into the legs of the coveralls.

He nodded his thanks to the cleaning man, who then slipped out. Before long, Diego had Jack dressed, slipped a cap on his head, and helped him up to stand wobbling on his feet.

"Can you walk? You're gonna have to if we're to get you out."

Jack's thoughts whirled and he tried to figure out what was happening. "Out where? Where are we going?"

"Why, out of this building and off this island." Diego nodded resolutely.

Jack's head began to clear just a bit and he started to understand what was happening. "Why are you doing this?"

Diego looked at the floor for a moment, a thoughtful expression on his face. "Oscar let word out that you're Stan Metcalfe's son. That means a lot to some people out there. For your dad's sake, if nothing else, a plan was hatched to break you out. If you're really his son, it's certain the warden won't let you go until he finds out where your dad is. He probably wants the reward. *Si*, I'm sure that's what it is."

"Reward?" Jack shook his head to clear it as much as he did so out of denial and confusion. What in the world had his father done to be on the government's "Most Wanted" list?

Diego turned his head and regarded Jack quizzically. "Yeah, you didn't know? Hmph." He wrapped an arm around Jack's waist. "Well, we can talk about that later. For now, we've got to get you out of here."

Diego cracked the door open and peeked out, looking down the hallway first one direction and then the other. Satisfied, he urged Jack forward. "Let's go."

They stepped out of the room and Diego guided, half-carried Jack down the hallway. After a few twists and turns, they descended a staircase and entered a large room. Inside, the air lay hot and heavy and blasted Jack in the face as they entered.

"*Ai*, it's hot in here," Diego complained, steering Jack around large baskets of laundry on wheels. "But this here's a shortcut," he said. He gingerly let go of Jack and looked him over carefully. "Can you walk on your own?"

Jack nodded and kept walking, hoping he looked more steady than he felt.

"Just keep your head down and don't look anyone in the eye," Diego instructed. "Your golden eyes shine like the Madonna!"

Scattered here and there throughout the room, a handful of gen workers loaded or unloaded laundry into and out of machines, their faces red, sweat trickling.

"Head for the door over there." Diego gestured with his chin, his voice low. Just before they reached the door, Diego snatched a duffle bag up from the floor and, passing through the door, shoved it into Jack's hands. "I brought the stuff you left at my place, mostly because if you don't have anything to carry it will raise suspicion." Jack must have looked confused because after a glance at his face, Diego said, "I forgot to tell you where we're going. We're putting you on a boat with a group of contracted workers heading back to the mainland. The contractors usually sign up for only a limited period of time, then return home when their contract is up. Not many stay here once they find out what it's like. Hopefully you can pass off as one of them."

Jack just nodded, the effort to speak too great. Before long, they stepped outside and Diego pointed toward a group of roughly thirty-five or forty workers standing near the dock about fifty meters away. Diego tugged on Jack's arm and they stopped. He looked down at the ground and said softly, "That group over there's the one you want. Join them, keep to yourself, and maybe you'll make it on board undetected." He clasped Jack's hand in his own. "Good luck, my friend. May *Dios* go with you."

Jack nodded once and voiced his thanks in a low voice. He tucked his cloth bag under his arm and eased over to the group, eyes on the ground. He positioned himself off to one side, hoping he was close enough to be accepted, but far enough away to not draw attention. So far, it was working. The others, busy talking amongst themselves, barely looked up when he moved to the fringe of the group. Soon a guard motioned them forward and they moved closer to the dock. Jack nervously eyed the guards positioned off to one side, spaced evenly along the walkway, watching each worker pass by.

Ahead, a soldier, gun hanging from his shoulder, stood with a handheld, checking the workers' IDs one by one as they passed by. A feeling of terror rose in Jack's mind and he wracked his brain for a plan. He opened his bag and rifled through the items inside, searching desperately for something he could use that would satisfy the guard.

Soon it was his turn. Still digging through his bag, he stepped up to the guard. His heart beat a staccato rhythm as if it would leap out of his chest and flee if his feet didn't move soon.

"ID?" the guard growled.

"I...I'm looking." Jack tried to still the tremor in his voice. "I know it's here somewhere."

The guard sighed impatiently. "Come on, hurry up." Jack could hear the frown on his face without even looking up.

After a few more moments, the guard tugged on his sleeve. "Step aside and let the others through while you're looking," he said in a tired voice.

At the touch on his arm, Jack shot a glance to the guard, and just before meeting the man's eyes, he remembered Diego's instructions. But by then, it was too late.

"Hey!" The guard grabbed Jack by the chin, wrenched upward, and scrutinized Jack's battered face. "I don't recognize you. What's your name?"

Panic took over and Jack's feet seemed to move of their own volition. He turned away and began to limp-jog toward the boats. Frantically, his eyes ran the length of the dock, searching for somewhere to go. Meanwhile, the guard called out behind him, "Stop! Get back here!"

With every step, Jack's body cried out in pain. He tried to go faster, but he simply didn't have the strength. He knew it was probably hopeless, exposed out in the open as he was, but running was better than going back to the cell. Behind him, the guard yelled, "Stop him!"

Crack!

Jack heard the gunshot only a millisecond before he felt the bullet enter his right leg. With a grunt, he tumbled to the ground. He rolled onto his side, clutched at his thigh, and moaned. The clomp of approaching boots sounded behind him. They stopped next to him and a foot pushed against his side, rolling him over onto his back. His hat fell off into the dirt and, blood dripping hot through his fingers, he looked up with his one good eye and met the guard's gaze.

"Gen!" the guard sneered with disgust and spat on Jack's clothes.

Unable to hold his eye open any longer, Jack let his head fall to one side and all went dark.

Chapter 9

G^{*roan.*}

Someone needs help, Jack thought. With effort, he stirred, trying to wake up. He took a deep breath but the effort drew stabs of pain to his side and he moaned, only to realize that he was the one making that noise. He tried to open his eyes but only one responded, the other still too swollen to open.

And he hurt everywhere. It was hard to tell where one pain ended and the next began. He tried to bring his hand to his face, but couldn't. A gentle tug and a glance revealed his hand was cuffed to the rail at the side of the bed he lay on. The other wrist matched, cuffed as it was to the opposite railing.

He lifted his head as far as the throbbing pain would allow and peered around the room. He found himself lying on a slab of some sort covered with an almost spongy pad maybe four centimeters thick. Stark white walls enclosed a room that held several such beds—maybe eight. He didn't make the effort to count them. Of those, only one other was occupied and its tenant out cold.

Jack looked toward the open door. "Hello?"

No answer.

He lay still and reflected on his situation. Slowly it all came back. The warden, the beatings, Diego thanking God that he had found Jack and the attempted rescue, and then the shooting.

The *squeak* of rubber soles on linoleum sounded out in the hallway until they reached the doorway. When they stopped, a young man in his early twenties, dressed in the uniform of an orderly, looked inside. He glanced at Jack, then turned and left.

Jack parted parched lips and called out in a croaking voice, "Wait," but he was gone and Jack was alone once again with several empty beds and a comatose patient across the room.

However, he didn't have long to wait. Soon another young man appeared, this one a bit older and wearing a loose-fitting smock and pants much like the orderly's but this one had a name tag. *Joshua Ward, Nurse Practitioner*, it read.

"So you're awake." Joshua walked up to the head of Jack's bed and pulled a small instrument down from a rack that Jack hadn't seen before in his painful review of the room. The NP held one of Jack's eyelids open and looked into his retina, then gently moved to the other and slowly pushed it open. The pressure brought stars to Jack's vision and he winced. The young man took a quick peek at the eye then let it close. "Sorry about that. I know that hurts but I have to do my job."

Jack ran his tongue over dry lips, hardly any saliva left to moisten them. "Water?" he croaked.

"Oh, sure. Just a minute." Joshua ducked out of the room and returned shortly with a small cup of water. He held Jack's head up and put the cup to his lips. The liquid was cool and sweet, nothing like the brackish water in the outskirts.

"Easy there," Joshua cautioned. "Not too fast."

Jack sucked in a swallow of the most wonderful thing he'd tasted since leaving the mainland. Joshua gently lay Jack's head back down onto the mat.

Jack regarded his blurry benefactor. "Where am I?"

"You're at the infirmary, pal." Joshua returned the instruments to their rack on the wall. "You caused quite a stir out there, you know."

Jack grunted. *That can happen when a man fears for his life*, he thought. He shifted his legs and a spike of pain shot through the right one.

"Easy there." Joshua put a hand on Jack's leg and parted torn fabric to inspect the wound. "That was a fool thing you did, running from the guards." He lifted the edge of a dressing and peeked underneath. "What were you thinking?"

Yes, what indeed was I thinking? was what Jack thought, but what he said was, "Now what's going to happen?"

Joshua snorted and shook his head. "Well, you won't be going anywhere in the near future, I can tell you that much. But as for what's happening today, I couldn't tell you for sure. I suppose the warden'll send for you sooner or later. But for now, you're not leaving this room until I say so." Joshua turned to leave.

"Wait." Jack tugged at his wrist restraints. "Can you help me out?"

Joshua looked back and smiled a crooked grin. "You seem like a nice guy but the fact that you're here on River Island tells me otherwise. And you're a flight risk. Sorry, pal. The cuffs stay on."

As Joshua left, Jack lay his head back and sighed. Now what? Nothing to do but wait. His troubled mind turned to thoughts of home. His mother, Eva. The senselessness of Ryan's death. And with that last thought, Jack's ire rose. He thought of the humans. Of the injustice. Of the plight of the gens and the abuse of his friends. And in the light of all the injustices, everything else faded. Even his wounds didn't seem to hurt quite so much.

He looked around the room, tugged on his wrist restraints, and growled in frustration. There had to be something he could do. He tried to open his swollen eye and did, in fact, manage to crack it open, but not enough to see. *Well, it's a start*, he thought.

And so he lay fuming on the slab of a bed, wishing he could will things to be right. But some things require more than just willpower. Some things require action. And as soon as he got off this bed, free of these restraints...

Warden Goldman walked through the doorway, stopped next to Jack, and clasped his hands behind him.

"What have we here? The prodigal returns."

Jack glared at the man. A tyrant ruling his own little kingdom.

"And I thought you were happy here with us." The warden wore an expression of forced innocence, blinking with feigned sadness. "But Jack, we couldn't let you go without saying goodbye."

The thought crossed Jack's mind that he'd love nothing more than to spit on the man, returning the favor Goldman's guard had paid him on the dock, as it were. But for one thing, he didn't have enough moisture in his mouth to even attempt it, and if he did, he was laying on his back and would probably only succeed in spitting on himself. Besides, the man wasn't worth it and there were some lows to which Jack refused to sink. Instead, Jack stared the man in the eye and said, "Changed my mind. Decided to stay," he slurred.

The warden smiled. "Ah! That's the spirit. I'm glad you feel that way because I'd like to make sure you're well taken care of. All you have to do is tell me where your father is."

Jack rolled his eye and would have rubbed his face, but when he moved his arm, he reached the end of the restraint and his hand drew up way short. "Can't tell you what I don't know." He shifted his gaze back to the man. "Like I said before. Or don't you understand English?"

Goldman's face grew hard. "Now that's the kind of attitude that won't get you anywhere." He motioned toward the doorway and Joshua reentered, brow wrinkled in a frown. "Joshua here understands what needs to be done, don't you, Joshua?" He looked at the nurse practitioner with raised eyebrows.

"I told you before," Joshua muttered, "I don't answer to you and I will not inject this man with a lethal dose without a judge's order. The medical board would have my license once they found out."

No, he might not do it, Jack thought, *but I'll bet the warden could make Joshua's life difficult.* Then Jack realized the import of what Goldman had said. A lethal dose? His heart beat harder and he nervously licked his lips.

"If you want it done," Joshua continued, "you'll have to do it yourself."

The warden clenched his jaw and glared at Joshua. "You'll wish you hadn't said that," he spat, then turned on his heel and strode out.

Joshua regarded Jack intently for a few moments. He opened his mouth to say something, then closed it and gathered his thoughts. "Stay right there. I'll be right back," he finally said.

Like I have a choice, Jack thought.

Chapter 10

*S*queak, squeak.

The squeal of worn wheels in the hallway intruded on Jack's despondent thoughts. The sound grew increasingly louder until Joshua appeared, pushing a lightweight gurney. He rolled it up next to Jack's bed and fished a key from his pocket.

"Come on," he said. "We have to get you out of here."

Jack's mind reeled in confusion.

Joshua met his eyes and offered an explanation. "I checked your file," he said. "Something the warden said made me question what you were doing here. Why you are here. I looked into your file, put it together with what he said, and came to my own conclusion. I'm not convinced you deserve to be here. You certainly don't deserve to die. And if I don't help you, you're a dead man."

He slipped the key into the lock on one wrist restraint, unfastened it, and pulled Jack's hand free, then unlocked the other as well. He put an arm under Jack's shoulders and pulled him into a sitting position. "Do you think you can move over to the gurney?"

Jack nodded. At this point, he'd manage to dance a jig if it meant he'd get out of this place. With Joshua's assistance, Jack scooted over to the gurney, then Joshua slid his legs over as well. Jack lay back and closed his eyes. That was more work than he'd thought it would be.

"I want you to just lay there." Joshua maneuvered the gurney toward the doorway, stepped ahead and peered both ways down the hallway. The way clear, he maneuvered the contraption into and then down the hallway, the soft rubber soles of his shoes barely squeaking as he walked. "I want you to pretend you are comatose," Joshua said, "an unconscious patient whom I need to rush to the mainland to seek medical attention. Understand?"

Jack grunted an affirmation and closed his eyes. Joshua wheeled Jack down the hallway and out the door.

"Halt! What's going on here?" A guard stepped in their path and barred the way with his weapon. "Where do you think you're going?"

Joshua's cool, calm response surprised Jack.

"I need to get this patient to the mainland." Joshua's words came out with the clinical rush of a seasoned professional. "He's a key witness and some idiot shot him," he said dryly. "Now he's likely dying and I have orders from the medical director to bring him to the hospital on the mainland for medical attention. I don't have the facilities here at the clinic to address his injuries properly."

A moment of silence ensued and it was all Jack could do to not open his eyes. He heard the guard shuffle his feet.

Joshua pressed on. "I'm sure you don't want to be the one responsible for this man's death."

After another moment the guard cleared his throat and Jack heard him step to one side.

"All right then," the guard said. "Go on through."

Hope sprang within Jack, and for the first time he thought that maybe this would work. The gurney squeaked on. Another door opened, then shut and Jack let his head loll to one side. They passed outside and the harsh sunlight shone hot upon his face. They continued a short distance until Jack heard the soft lapping of water and smelled the rank brine of the harbor. The cry of a gull in the air came to his ears like the free song of a bird in the Garden of Paradise. Yet he dare not let his hopes get too high. They still had a long way to go.

Joshua's voice came again. "I need to get this man to the mainland."

"Where are your papers from the warden?" The voice grew nearer.

Jack felt someone bump the gurney and he could feel the presence of a person leaning over him.

"Isn't this the guy that got shot this morning trying to escape?"

"Yeah, and now he's dying. I have verbal orders from the medical director to get this man to the mainland," Joshua said. "If I let him die, there'll be hell to pay."

"Hmph." After a silent moment, the guard spoke again. "All right then. Come aboard."

The gurney moved forward, bouncing as it crossed the gangway. Before long, the sun no longer shone on Jack's face and he could tell they had entered a cabin of some kind. The gurney's wheels squeaked to a stop and he heard Joshua lock them in place.

A voice called into the room. "Where are we going?"

"Get us to the main harbor," Joshua snapped, "and pray we're not too late."

Jack felt the practitioner check the wound on his leg. As Joshua leaned over, he whispered, "You're doing fine."

Jack heard the boat's engines start up and the craft move away from the dock. He had never realized how difficult it was to lay still when you had to. An itch formed on his cheek, and the longer he thought about it, the more he wanted to scratch it. But Joshua had said to remain still and he dared not risk blowing their cover. Instead, he tried to think about something else.

He needed to come up with a plan—something that he could do to facilitate their escape once they reached the harbor, but this was uncharted territory and he didn't even know where they were going. He heard Joshua settle down nearby, presumably in a chair, and time stretched on interminably. Before long, the lull of the engine drew him into a restless sleep. The next thing he knew, the rumble of the engine changed and he felt their momentum slow.

"Here we go." Joshua's voice came low, barely audible. "You're doing great." He unlocked the wheels and pushed the gurney back the way they had come. More bumps told Jack they had disembarked and he heard a new voice bar their path.

"Where are you headed?"

Joshua repeated their story, and to Jack's surprise, the guard allowed them passage.

Despite the excitement of their escape, or perhaps partially because of it, Jack tired. His body ached, his leg throbbed, and every bump brought a new wave of pain. However, in spite of that, his thoughts drifted to Amber and he thought for the first time that maybe his concern for her was more than that of a friend. Suddenly he realized that he missed the sight of her brown eyes, the soft touch of her hand on his arm, and the sound of her voice. And he hoped she felt the same. Just then, he felt the gurney stop and heard Joshua speak once again.

"I need a vehicle for transport to the hospital."

Jack heard someone to one side relay the request on their communicator, and before long, a vehicle drove up, doors were opened and the gurney pushed inside. Joshua climbed inside and the doors shut behind them.

"We're almost there, Jack. You can open your eyes now. Are you okay?" Joshua fussed over the bandage covering Jack's bullet wound.

Jack snorted and moistened his lips with the tip of his tongue. "I suppose so," he said. "As well as can be expected."

Joshua chuckled. "I suppose you have a point. Hang on. We're almost there."

"And where is 'there'?"

"Well, the ambulance is taking us to the hospital, and from there, well, we'll probably have to sneak out of the hospital."

With that pronouncement, a troubling thought crossed Jack's mind. "And what will you do now that you've helped me escape?"

Joshua raised his eyebrows with a grimace. "Well, I suppose my career is basically over. I can't go back now or I'll be the one in prison. But I just couldn't stand by and watch Warden Goldman kill someone who is probably innocent. Not again." He leaned back and put his hands in his pockets. "I thought about it quite a bit on the trip over and it occurred to me that maybe the underground needs someone with medical skills."

Jack bit his lip and thought for a moment. "Yeah," he said. "I might know someone I can hook you up with."

"I thought you might."

The ambulance sped through the city, sirens blaring. Within fifteen minutes, they reached the hospital. Joshua moved toward the back doors and put his hand on the latch, but before he opened it, he turned to Jack. "I don't think you have to feign unconsciousness, but try not to look too alert, okay?"

Jack offered a wry grin and nodded. Joshua opened the doors, hopped out, and before long, an orderly rushed up to help. They wheeled Jack through the sliding doors and into an emergency room teeming with activity. Joshua wheeled the gurney to one side and a nurse rushed up, an ED in her hand.

"What do we have here?" Her voice was all business.

Joshua rested one hand on the gurney. "This man needs to see Dr. Hollingsworth."

The nurse raised an eyebrow. "I take it this isn't an extreme emergency?"

Joshua took a deep breath. "No, not completely. This man is a shooting victim and I think the bullet may have shattered his tibia. I called ahead and spoke with Dr. Hollingsworth for consultation. He's supposed to meet us here shortly."

The nurse nodded. "Very well. Take him to Bay 4. You can wait there."

Joshua nodded curtly and pushed the gurney forward. When they reached Bay 4, Joshua paused, scanned the room, and then continued on, pushing him through a swinging set of double doors into a hallway beyond. There he stopped and put a hand on Jack's shoulder. "How are you doing?"

Jack reached to gently touch the wound on his leg. "Did the bullet really shatter the bone?"

Joshua gave a crooked grin. "No, not even close. It's really not too bad, considering. It didn't hit the bone and I've removed the bullet. Let's get you somewhere safe and after a few days at least, you should be able to walk a bit. It'll hurt like anything, but you should be able to get around at least." Joshua looked down the hallway and around the corner. "Stay here. I'll find a wheelchair and be back in a couple of minutes."

Before Jack could respond, Joshua was gone. Jack struggled up to a sitting position and gingerly swung his legs over the side of the gurney. He leaned forward a bit and braced himself on the edge, and looked nervously up one side of the hallway and down the other, hoping no one would question what he was doing there.

Within a few minutes, however, Joshua reappeared as promised, pushing a wheelchair. He helped Jack into the chair and wheeled him toward the front lobby. He stopped at the front desk and asked the woman on duty to call a cab. He then wheeled Jack out the front doors, moved to one side, and stopped.

"Now it's your game, Jack. Where do we go from here? Who do you know?"

Jack took a deep breath. Mentally, he ran through the databanks of his mind, trying to think of someplace to go, maybe a friend of a friend who might take them in. Then a thought came to mind. Pedro—The Fixer. He had heard rumors of this man through the underground's network. He was supposedly a compatriot rebel who also happened to be a master of disguise. It just might work.

When the driverless cab arrived, Joshua helped Jack inside the taxi, returned the wheelchair to rest near the hospital doors, ran back to the car and climbed in, shutting the door behind him. He pulled out a crypto card and inserted it into a reader on the console, waited a millisecond for it to register, and drew it back out.

Jack looked to Joshua in concern. "Won't they be able to trace us from your card?"

"Probably, if they look—which I'm sure they will, unfortunately. Can we program the car to take us to a location fairly near where we need to go so they don't trace us to your contact?"

"I think so," Jack agreed. "It's probably our best option."

He gave Joshua an address, which Joshua programmed into the console and the vehicle moved into motion.

"First thing we have to do is get rid of your tracking chip," Joshua said as he pulled a pen knife out of his pocket.

While the car was moving, he deftly sliced the skin and pried the tiny capsule out of Jack's arm, then pressed a clean piece of gauze to the fresh wound and taped it in place.

That done, Jack leaned back and scanned the interior of the cab. He ran his hand along the smooth leather covering the inside of the door.

"First time in a network cab?" Joshua grinned.

Jack nodded. "They usually don't let gens ride in these."

Joshua raised his eyebrows. "You were raised gen?"

"Yeah. My mom married one and her family disowned her so she went to live with him." After a few moments of silence, Jack continued. "Would you still have helped me had you known that?"

Joshua looked straight ahead and jacked his jaw to one side. Then he nodded slowly. "I assumed you were raised in the human quarter. Your height and hair color, you know. But would I have helped? Yeah." He nodded slowly. "Yeah, I would have. No matter what your race, Goldman was wrong to put an innocent man through hell."

"Well...in that case, you should fit right in with the underground."

Joshua took a deep breath. "I guess I'll have to at this point."

Chapter 11

The cab cruised the streets of New Santiago, the neighborhood growing seedier the farther they went. Finally, they pulled onto an old street, where townhouses stood silent in a row like disapproving, elderly spinsters peering down on the street. The car slowed to a stop at the curb in the middle of the block, its motor barely purring as normal. Jack and Joshua leaned toward the windows, peering up and down the street.

"Is this the right street?" Joshua's eyebrows creased inquisitively.

"I'm not sure but it's what I remember," Jack replied. "I guess there's nothing to do but check it out." Unsure how the process worked, Jack asked, "Will the car stay here?"

Joshua nodded. "It will stay where I leave it until I release it. I'll just be charged until then. Let's get you out and I'll pull the car around the corner."

Jack nodded. That would have to do. Joshua climbed out, went around to Jack's side and helped him out, then over to the steps of an old building, where Jack took a seat. Then Joshua jumped back into the car and it pulled away.

Jack flicked at the rusted handrail next to him with a fingernail. He prayed to whatever god might be listening that they'd find help soon and tried to formulate what he would say when they knocked on Pedro's door. What if they knocked on the wrong door? He didn't want to reveal their situation to someone who would betray them in exchange for a possible reward.

After maybe fifteen minutes, Joshua returned. He lifted Jack's arm across his shoulders and helped him up. Slowly, they made their way up the stairs and knocked on the door. After about thirty seconds, the door opened. Before them stood a grizzled man probably in his fifties. He looked them up and down and frowned. The smell of fried food wafted out the door and Jack's stomach rumbled. He hadn't realized how hungry he was.

"Yes?"

Jack licked his lips and began his prepared speech. "I'm looking for Pedro."

The man studied Jack's face, then flicked his gaze to Joshua and back again. "That's me."

Jack swallowed the lump in his throat. *Here goes.* "My name's Jack and this is Joshua. I believe we have mutual friends. May we come in?"

Pedro opened the door further and stood aside, motioning them in. Jack noticed he didn't invite them to sit down. "What's this about?"

"Um, I heard your name from a friend in the underground." Jack waited for a reply but received none so he continued. Too late to back out now. "I'm wondering if you can get a message through to someone for me." Jack had no intention of contacting any of his friends or family and thus jeopardizing their safety any further but somehow he needed to find out if this man could help them or not.

"And who are you?" Pedro crossed his arms in front of him. "You've told me your names, but who are you?" His gaze shifted down to Jack's leg. "And how did you hurt your leg?"

Jack shifted his weight onto his good leg and placed his hand on Joshua's shoulder for support. He took a deep breath. "I was shot by guards on River Island, and Joshua here," he tipped his head toward his friend, "helped me out."

Pedro's eyebrows shot up. "You were on River Island?" He thought for a moment. "I need more information but you might as well have a seat before you fall down."

Joshua helped Jack to the couch, where Jack gratefully took a seat. Pedro sat across from them in a wooden rocking chair.

"You escaped?"

Jack nodded.

"Huh. Let me guess. Now you need shelter."

"Yes sir." Jack searched Pedro's eyes to see if any guile lodged there. So far, no warning flags. "I heard sometime back that you might be sympathetic to the underground's cause."

Pedro snorted. "If you heard that, you probably heard a lot more about me than that." Jack waited for him to continue and Pedro sighed. "All right, then. I do have connections to the underground. Maybe we can find a way to help you. What did you say your name was?"

"Jack Metcalfe."

Pedro leaned forward, elbows on his knees, hands clasped in front of him and regarded Jack for another moment. Then he stood and paced to one side, swiping his hand across his mouth and came back. "I might've heard of you. Are the authorities hunting for you?"

Jack nodded and Joshua looked from one to the other, silently taking it all in.

"Hm. Then you'll need a disguise. We can find a place for you to hole up a bit until that leg of yours heals."

"That would be ideal." Jack's hopes sprang anew. There was hope after all.

"All right. You can stay here for now and I'll get you fixed up. I've got a spare room in the back, but you'll have to sleep on the floor. There's no bed."

"That's fine, sir," Jack said gratefully, then tentatively added, "You wouldn't have any food, would you? We haven't eaten for a while."

Pedro grinned. "It so happens I just fried up some Indian bread. Would you like some?"

Jack's mouth watered. Even Joshua's eyes lit up.

"Let's get you settled in the back. You need to get off that leg. Then I'll bring you some."

With Joshua's help, Jack reached the back room, where Pedro took some blankets, folded them in half, and spread them out on the floor. Joshua grabbed Jack's elbow and lowered him to the floor, where Jack stretched out full length. The hard floor felt like a featherbed to his tired, wounded body. Joshua went out to release the car and within just a couple of minutes, Jack was sound asleep.

Sometime later, a nudge on his shoulder roused him.

"Jack." The voice coaxed him from the darkness his exhausted mind had fled to. "Jack, wake up." Jack opened his eyes a crack and found Joshua leaning over him. "Come on. You need to eat something."

Joshua helped him sit up, his back resting against the wall, throbbing leg stretched out in front of him. He handed Jack a piece of fried bread, the slightly crispy golden crust still warm.

This must be what manna tastes like, he thought. He remembered the stories his mother used to tell him from her worn, no, ragged Bible. She spoke of manna, the food the Israelites' God had sent them straight from heaven when they needed it. They were stories from a book so old the stitched binding barely held together. Myths from another age.

His stomach comforted, Jack fell into a dreamless sleep. Hours later, he awoke and found a piece of the bread still in his hand. As he rolled a bite of the chewy bread around in his mouth, he took in his surroundings. The dim room had a wide, short window about half a meter tall and about one-and-a-half meters wide, mounted up near the top of a dingy wall that hadn't seen paint in years—or even a cleansing scrub, for that matter. Along one wall, rough wooden crates stood in a crooked line on a dusty concrete floor.

Jack struggled to his feet and limped out into the shadowed hallway. "Hello?"

"In here," Joshua's voice answered. Within a couple of halting steps, he reached the flat's front room. His friend sat at a tiny table in one corner, hunched over a piece of paper, pencil in hand. After jotting down a few more words, Joshua looked up. "How're ya feeling?"

"I've been better." Jack gingerly lowered himself onto the nearby lumpy couch, hoping that merely sitting down wouldn't rip the tattered upholstery. He jerked his chin toward the paper laying in front of Joshua. "What are you working on?"

"Well," Joshua ran a hand over his close-cropped, black curly hair and leaned back. "I figure we're going to need some supplies if we're going to get out of here. I was just making a list of things we could use." He ran his eyes over the paper. "We definitely need to get you into some kind of disguise."

Jack snorted. "Yeah. It's kind of hard to hide my eyes."

"Exactly. But your friend here seems to have all kinds of things at his disposal. I think we can get you a pair of contact lenses to change the color of your eyes. Of course you'll have to dye your hair."

Jack nodded.

Joshua chewed on the inside of his cheek. "But then what?" An inquisitive look creased his brow with worry. "What do we do next?"

Jack leaned back and folded his hands in his lap. After a few moments of thought, he replied, "I think we need to split up. We'll be harder to find that way." He took a deep breath. "And I have some unfinished business I need to take care of."

Joshua raised one eyebrow and Jack hurried on. "Believe me when I say it's safer for you if you don't know. Besides, the insurgents here need you. Pedro can point you in the right direction."

Joshua nodded. "I figured that might be the case."

Jack bit his lip and regarded his new friend. "I'm sorry to have dragged you into this."

Joshua gave a dry chuckle and turned away. "Don't take the blame for something I did of my own accord. I suppose it was only a matter of time until that place got to me. It's not right—what they do there."

After several moments that spoke volumes in their silence, Joshua picked up his pencil and resumed writing. Shortly, the front door creaked open. Joshua shot a glance toward the door, eyes round, while Jack tensed and looked over his shoulder. After a second, however, he breathed a sigh of relief. It was only Pedro.

The wiry man scooted inside and latched the door behind him. Moving into the kitchen, he lowered a satchel onto the table and unzipped it, removing an assortment of vials, small boxes, and the like.

Jack limped over to join him. "What is this?" he asked.

"It's your ticket to freedom." Pedro smiled up at him. "At least I hope it is." He raised two of the vials to eye level and gave them a shake. "Your new eyes."

Jack leaned forward and took a closer look. There in the bottom of each vial rested a small contact lens the color of the angry ocean on a stormy day. "The blue is so dark."

"Has to be," Pedro replied. "Gotta cover those pockets of gold in your head." He chortled at his own joke.

Jack shook his head, then stilled, frozen with a sobering realization. "Pedro," he began slowly. "How much will all of this cost me?"

Pedro sobered and scrutinized Jack's face. "Well, I figure you don't have any money so I'll make you a deal. I'll fix you up with new hair and eyes, and all I ask of you is your corneas."

Jack stared at the man in disbelief. He had known the price would be high, but this? He took a deep breath and sighed, backing away. "No," he shook his head, "I can't do that."

After a moment of silence, Pedro burst out into laughter. Jack looked at the man in confusion. He shot a look to Joshua and found mirrored there the expression of confusion he felt on his own face.

Pedro wiped tears from the corners of his eyes. "You should see your faces." Perhaps the old coot had lost his sanity. "I'm not going to take your eyes," he gasped. "If I did, you couldn't see, no matter what lenses I got for you." He gestured to Joshua. "You of all people should know that." Pedro's laughter subsided into a chuckle. "Where was I?"

"We were discussing payment," Jack prodded the odd little man.

"Hm?" He shot Jack a glance. "Oh, right. Payment. As I was saying, I know you don't have any money." His expression turned serious. "I'll help you under one condition." He paused. "I asked around. You're Stan's boy, aren't you?"

Jack ran a hand across his face. Again? What was up with this Stan?

Pedro nodded. "I thought so. I also heard you've been following in his footsteps." At a sharp look from Jack, Pedro motioned for him to calm himself. "Don't worry. I didn't tell anyone you're here." He motioned to the couch and waited for Jack to settle himself. "Now, as I was saying, I heard you're trying to help the gens." He crossed his arms over his chest. "If you are, that's enough payment for me."

Jack sat frozen, unable to find any words other than the beginnings of a feeble protest. "But..."

"Eh," Pedro waved his hand in the air. "Don't worry about it. Maybe someday I'll need a favor from you."

Jack clamped his mouth shut and the rudimentary makings of a plan snuck into his mind, but they involved an idea he'd rather not think about. Surely he had plenty of other options left without resorting to that.

Chapter 12

J ack stood in front of a mirror, looking over his new disguise. Pedro had worked his magic and now he understood why the man was so revered in the underground as The Fixer. One with a skill like his who could visibly turn a person from one race to another, particularly when it came to gens and humans, was rarely seen. Jack ran his fingers through his now-black hair and examined his eyes, turning his head one direction and then the other, unable to detect any fault in his new eye color—a fashionable dark navy blue that some humans had been adopting of late. The man was a genius, Jack thought. Just the color itself set Jack apart as one of the upper class. Not just anyone could afford to have their eyes genetically altered to a new color. To do so permanently was a costly medical procedure and, as a result, some had begun to purchase lenses like Jack's new ones, but they weren't cheap. He shook his head at the man's skill and generosity. These lenses alone probably cost what it would have taken him six months to earn if he still had the network administration job at the Ministry of Religion.

With a deep sigh, Jack reflected on the life he had lost. He mourned the loss of the job, not only because it provided the perfect chance to spy on the Ministry office activities, but also because he truly liked the work. He shook his head and turned away from the mirror, wondering if he'd ever have such an incredible opportunity again. And then there were his friends and, most of all, his mom. Jack would do anything to keep the authorities away from Eva and her gentle soul.

As Jack stared at himself in the mirror, he pondered his next move. Somehow, he still had to find a way to get the Ministry's secrets, but where could he go? The offices were closed to him now. He limped back into Pedro's front room and flopped down onto the couch, rubbing his sore leg. It still ached horribly, but at least he could walk. One thing was for certain—if he didn't get out of this house, he'd go stir crazy.

He glanced over at Pedro sitting at his little desk, focused intently on creating some kind of identification papers for another client.

Jack rubbed a hand over his smooth chin, wishing he had the genes to grow a beard. That would definitely complete his disguise. Then a thought came to mind that had been roiling around in the back of his head, one that he'd been trying to ignore. But Jack was getting desperate and he couldn't think of a better plan.

"Pedro," he said, then paused. "You said you'd heard about my father. Do you know where he is?"

The older man continued working for a few moments, then sighed and slowly looked up at Jack. "Are you sure you want to know that? That's dangerous ground to head into."

So he does know something, Jack thought. He nodded. "I have to go somewhere and I can't think of a better place to start. If he truly is involved with the underground like you say, I need to know what he's doing." He snorted, then looked up at the ceiling, eyes closed. "And what are they going to do if I'm caught? Throw me in prison?"

Pedro chuckled. "I guess you have a point. Okay. I'll tell you what I know. I haven't heard anything in a long while, but last I heard, he'd built a secret research facility somewhere out in the desert."

Jack shot his gaze toward the old man. "What?! Why?"

Pedro tipped his head and shrugged. "I suppose you'll have to ask him to find out."

"If I can find him, that is."

Pedro nodded. "I'm told that it's hidden somewhere east of here in the Mojave Desert."

"Hmph," Jack grunted. "So how can I get there?"

"That's the tricky part. You have to have a guide, I hear." He went back to work. "I'll see if anyone knows."

Later that evening, after the sun had set, Pedro slipped out. He never said where he was going, but when he came back a couple of hours later, he sank into the couch across from where Jack sat in a tattered chair. He peered into the kitchen to make sure Joshua was still seated there. Then he stared deeply into Jack's eyes and spoke in a voice so low that Jack had to lean forward, elbows on his knees, just to hear the man. "Are you sure you want to know about your father?"

Jack swallowed and returned the man's steady gaze. *This is a truth I have to face, no matter the outcome*, he thought. He nodded mutely, afraid to trust his voice lest the tremor he felt inside would be evident when he spoke.

After a few silent moments, Pedro moistened his lips and continued. "I found out he's still in the desert. Still at the lab. I don't know its exact location—apparently that's a closely guarded secret—but I know the general area. I can tell you how to get close, but from there, you're on your own."

Jack nodded again and waited for him to go on.

"The lab is hidden somewhere on the eastern edge of the Mojave Preserve," he whispered. "That's all I can say. That's all I know."

"Okay." Jack leaned back in the chair and the knowledge lay heavy in his mind. Jack thought he hadn't ever wanted to see his dad again, but given what he knew now, Stan was a mystery that he couldn't ignore any longer. Part of Jack remained angry that the man had abandoned them, but even still, a new flicker of hope sparked inside. Maybe Stan had a good reason for leaving after all. In a way, Jack hoped that wasn't true, that his dad truly was a scoundrel so he could continue to justify the anger and hate he had felt for so long, emotions that he wasn't sure how to let go of if things were to change. So far, he had been able to redirect his anger into pushing back against the authorities and thus help the gens. Or so he had thought.

"There's a little old town called Goffs. I can help you get there. You need to find a woman named Maria Castillo. That's all I know." Pedro stared intently into Jack's eyes, as if to gauge his intent. "If you still want to go, you should leave tonight."

Jack returned his look with a slow nod and then said, "I'll go."

Pedro slapped his knees. "Very well. I think you chose well." He then stood quickly and turned toward the kitchen. "Meanwhile, I'll find something for us to eat."

Joshua stepped into the front room, passing Pedro on the way, and took a seat on the couch, his forehead creased into a frown. "What's up?" he asked Jack. "What's going on?"

Jack brushed a piece of lint off his pants leg. "Looks like I'm leaving tonight."

Joshua grunted. "Your dad?"

"Yeah."

Joshua nodded. "I thought you might go if given the chance. Anything I can do?"

Jack shook his head. "I appreciate everything you've done for me," he said. "Thank you for this opportunity for a second chance."

"I like to think someone would have done the same for me," he said and turned back to his notebook.

Before long, Pedro returned with a satchel, which he shoved into Jack's hands. "You ready?"

Jack nodded.

"Then let's go," Pedro said and headed for the door.

Jack slung the sack over his shoulder and clasped Joshua's hand in a firm grip. "Thank you again, my friend."

"Be careful—and go with God. Maybe I'll see you around someday."

Jack smiled. "Yeah, I hope so," he replied and turned to follow Pedro out the door and into the night, keeping to the shadows as much as possible. It amazed Jack how quietly the wiry man could walk. Although Jack's leg was starting to heal, he still had a pronounced limp. But at least he could keep up. That wouldn't have been possible a few days earlier.

The two men walked for about an hour, eventually reaching a warehouse with docks stretched across the back of the building. Inside the fence, a cargo truck was parked in front of nearly every open shipping door while others lined up in the lot waiting their turn. For once, Jack was grateful the transport trucks were on the ANN grid. There were no drivers to hide from. Or warehouse workers for that matter. Those had been phased out many years before in favor of an automated system that robotically loaded the trucks.

Pedro stopped in front of a locked gate and waved a card over the lock's sensor. With a click, the latch came free and the gate swung slightly open. Pedro cracked the gate open just far enough to slip inside, then waited for Jack to come through, and closed the gate once again with a click.

Pedro led Jack from the shadow of one truck to another, stopping to check the ID number on the front bumpers of several trucks as he passed by. After a half dozen or so, he stopped with a grunt and motioned Jack toward the back with a tip of his head. Jack stepped around to the back while Pedro grasped the handle, unlocked it and tugged the truck's cargo door up.

"Aren't they usually locked?" Jack whispered.

Pedro nodded with a grin and mouthed, "Bribery." In the dark, Jack could hardly read the man's lips.

Pedro motioned Jack closer and pointed to a lever just inside the door. "See this?" he whispered. "Keep this lever flipped up and it won't lock. Flip it down and you're stuck." He pressed a watch into the palm of Jack's hand. "Trucks are on a timed schedule. In ten hours, at eleven, open the door, flip the switch toward the locked position, and step out onto the bumper." He patted the bumper that extended out just far enough for a man to stand on. "The truck won't stop. Pull the door shut, make sure it locks, and jump off."

Jump? Jack thought. *This should be fun.*

"You'll be in the desert near an overpass," Pedro continued. "There's water and food in the bag. Follow the side road north about 16 kilometers and you'll come to Goffs. You'll find Maria there."

Jack grabbed a handle on the back of the truck to pull himself up, but Pedro gave a little tug on his sleeve.

"Jack, be careful. I hear they don't like strangers out there. They shoot first and ask later."

Jack jerked a nod and clasped Pedro's hand with a firm shake. "Thank you, my friend."

With a smile, Pedro nudged him toward the truck and Jack climbed in. Pedro double-checked the lever to make sure it was up, then with a "Godspeed," he pulled the door down, shutting Jack into the dark. Jack lowered himself to the floor, stretched his bum leg out in front of him, and pulled the satchel into his lap. He leaned his head back, eyes closed, and took a deep breath. Didn't matter if his eyes were open or not. He couldn't see an inch into the darkness that surrounded him. And he began his vigil.

Jack jerked his head up with a start and searched the blackness in confusion, then remembered where he was. He rubbed his hands on his face and then ran his fingers through his hair. Must have fallen asleep. Then he realized what had woken him. The truck eased forward, silently powered by energy streaming from a central power source.

After a series of twists and turns, Jack figured they must be on the open road because the truck had settled into a steady pace, following the directions transmitted by the central Shipping Transportation Center. He checked the lighted digital watch Pedro had given him. Still several hours to go so he settled back and dozed off again, the hum of tires on pavement lulling him to sleep.

When he woke, the air had grown warmer and stuffy in the enclosed space. He checked the watch again and found, to his surprise, it was almost time to hop off. He waited until the designated time, then eased the cargo door up. Just like Pedro had said, the desert stretched out behind the truck, heat shimmering off the wasteland in glimmering waves. Scrub brush dotted the landscape in a valiant effort to survive the harsh conditions. He looked at the road speeding by at maybe 120 kilometers per hour. This was going to hurt.

He held onto an outside handle, closed the sliding door and made sure it latched. With a deep breath, Jack clutched the satchel to his side and jumped, aiming for the edge of the pavement and trying to land on his left side away from his injured leg. Trying to emulate the stories he had heard about the importance of rolling when one lands to avoid injury, he partially curled into a ball but still hit the ground hard. Nonetheless, he rolled onto his back, then over and then over again, coming to rest on his stomach, face in the dirt. He raised up onto his hands and knees, blowing dust from his nose and wiping loose dust from his eyes, watching the truck speed off into the distance.

Jack gingerly ran his hands over his aching arms and legs, making sure he was all in one piece. A scrape running down the side of his left arm had already begun to bead up with blood. He dug in the satchel and found a couple of apples—probably quite bruised by now—and a few pieces of smashed flat bread laying loose in the sack. He also found vials for the contacts—thank goodness they were still intact—and an extra pair of clothes, socks, and a plastic bottle of water that somehow survived the impact. His fingers grazed across something hard. He fished out a small crypto card, then smiled. Pedro had thought of everything. With some effort, he tore a hole in the toe of one sock and slipped it up over his arm, gingerly easing it over the oozing scrape. He stood, brushed the dirt off as best he could, and looked around.

He stood in the middle of a flat wasteland, which stretched out in every direction. The truck, already growing smaller in the distance, sped toward a barren range of dark mountains, the remnant of a volcanic eruption untold thousands of years ago. A small town shimmered in the heat at the foot of those mountains. Jack took a sip of water and headed toward the town with a *step, limp, step, limp.*

It didn't look like the town was that far away, but after a while, it seemed to Jack he'd been walking forever. He'd heard that things looked closer in the desert than they really were and now he had proof that was true. A couple of hours later he finally reached the town.

As Jack walked into the outskirts of town, a gust of wind blew at his back, swirling the dirt into a dust devil that spun crazily across the pavement in front of him. The hot sunshine baked into his skin, its rays beginning to sting a bit as his skin started to burn. Only a few people dotted the sidewalks ahead. Jack assumed the rest had gone indoors to escape the early afternoon heat.

He looked about for a place to get out of the sun if nothing else. Time to see how many credits were on the card. Down the street, a small store beckoned like an oasis and Jack limped that direction. When he reached the building, he pushed open the clear door and a wave of cool air washed over him. He filled his lungs with the refreshing draft. Inside, half a dozen cold cases held a variety of bottled drinks. The clerk behind the counter barely glanced up. Jack perused the selections and chose one of the least expensive, a large bottle of water to replace his now-empty bottle.

Jack placed the bottle on the counter and fished out his card. The clerk glanced up as he reached out to scan the bottle. To Jack's surprise, the man didn't scowl when their eyes met, but then Jack remembered his new contacts and realized the man had no idea he was half gen. Jack flashed him a wide grin and even though the clerk simply grunted in response, Jack couldn't swallow the sense of glee he felt with the results his new persona had already granted.

Emboldened, he asked, "I'm looking for Maria Castillo. Do you know where I can find her?"

But with that question, the man shot Jack a prolonged look. Even though Jack could've sworn there was a certain look of knowing there, the clerk replied, "Nope. Don't know her."

Has to be lying, Jack thought. But with no other recourse at hand, he nodded and picked up his purchase. "Thanks anyways."

Pushing the door open, Jack stepped back out into the broiling heat and it hit him like a blast furnace. He slid into a slim shadow cast by the building and leaned up against the wall, still warm from where the sun's rays had baked into the plaster earlier. He twisted open the bottle cap and downed a swallow, the coolness washing down his throat and easing the dryness of his cotton mouth. What to do next? He still didn't know how to find the woman named Maria.

Before long, two men came around the corner two buildings down and sauntered his direction. He assumed they were heading for the store. But they passed the doors and stopped in front of Jack, eying him with hostile looks. Jack's heart skipped a beat and he tried to paint his face in an expression of neutrality. He took another swig of the water.

"Can I help you?" He squinted at them in the glare.

The taller of the two jutted his chin Jack's direction. "You lookin' for Maria?"

Jack studied his face and then glanced at the smaller of the two, who stood with hands in the pockets of brown work pants. After a few moments, Jack responded. "Yeah, I am. D'you know where I can find her?"

The man grunted and clipped out with a heavy Spanish accent, "Come with me."

Jack hesitated, uncertain whether he should follow the stranger, but so far this was his only lead so he decided to take the chance. He pushed off the wall and headed in the direction the man had indicated. The two men fell in next to him, one on each side, the corners of the larger man's mouth drawn down into a scowl. The other wore a more neutral expression but kept glancing Jack's direction as if to ensure he wouldn't step out of line.

At the corner, the men prodded Jack down a side street. Here the small stores were replaced with run-down houses, some with fences, many with dried-out lawns of brown grass that had fried in the hot summer sun. At one such house, Mr. Macho gestured up the sidewalk.

"This way."

Jack wondered if the man ever smiled.

The house, its color faded to a light green, had a low, gradual sloping roof that showed repair in several places. Across one front window, a strip of wide tape overlay a long crack in the glass. The large man nudged Jack toward the door, then reached in front of him, turned the knob and pushed it open. With a feeling of trepidation, Jack stepped through. Inside, the curtains were drawn, casting the interior into dim shadows.

"Stop there," Mr. Macho said, then dismissed the smaller man with a nod. Without a word, the latter stepped out of the room toward the back of the house. Mr. Macho crossed his arms and stood, feet spread apart, his vigilant gaze boring into Jack.

Jack cast his gaze around the room. A tattered couch, mismatched armchair, and a cheap end table stood in the dim light. No pictures adorned the walls. It occurred to Jack that the lives of these humans were likely no better than many of the gens in the city. He shifted his gaze back to Mr. Macho.

"So, you been here long?" Jack shoved his hands in his pockets and waited for a reply that didn't come. "Hm." He looked the man over. "Talkative sort, aren't you?" And still the man didn't answer. "So, are you planning to feed me to your dogs, or what?" Jack wished the man would say anything instead of just standing there, glaring at him as if he were to be executed for some horrible crime.

"He just might do that," an old woman's voice came from the doorway behind him. Jack spun about to find an elderly woman scowling back at him, the other man standing behind her. She shuffled into the room, shoulders slightly bent, cane grasped in a gnarled fist and stopped in front of the tattered armchair. With the man's hand supporting her elbow, she lowered herself into the chair. She arranged the cane up against the cushion next to her leg, then clasped her gnarled hands together in her lap.

When Mr. Macho saw the woman, a faint look of fondness crossed his face. The other man hovered to one side of the chair, regarding Jack with a guarded look. The way the two men deferred to the old woman reminded Jack of two loyal subjects bowing before a regal queen on her throne.

"Who are you and why are you here?" Her voice scratched with age and yet she spoke with power and confidence. In spite of her advanced years, something about her unsettled Jack, and somehow he knew that if she but said the word, these men would slit his throat without another thought. "Give me one good reason why I shouldn't have my boys take you out in the desert and feed you to the coyotes," she snapped.

With a shiver, Jack knew she could easily make good on her threat. From the look on her face, he wondered if he'd ever walk out of this room alive.

Chapter 13

F ear rumbled through Jack's gut but there was something more at stake than his own safety, he reminded himself. He had to find his father, or at least try his hardest to. He still had a medical mystery to solve and his friends' eternity might depend on what he found here. Jack took a deep breath and looked the old woman in the eye.

"My name's Jack. I'm here to find Stan Metcalfe."

The old woman searched his face for several moments. Jack wondered what she saw there. Hopefully she could not see the hopelessness, discouragement, and fear that threatened to overtake him. Instead, he tried to project a sense of confidence, of immovability.

"Are you Maria?"

She nodded slowly. "I am." The woman paused. "Many people are looking for Stan Metcalfe. What makes you think you will find him here?"

Jack chewed the inside of his cheek, but then, thinking that probably wasn't the best way to show confidence, he forced himself to stop and clenched his jaw instead. He chose his next words carefully, taking a gamble that he hoped would pay off. "I know he's here. Well," he gestured broadly toward the hills outside, "I know he's around here somewhere. Somewhere out there, at least. I need to talk to him."

"Let's pretend I do know this man. What did you say his name was? Stan?" Jack returned her question with silence. Her dark brown eyes glittered as her gaze bore into him. "Say I do know him. What makes you think I would tell you where he is?"

Jack tried to think of a way he could refer to the old woman's rumored underground activities without revealing the ones he had left behind in New Santiago. "I heard he was here. Out in the desert somewhere and that you could show me the way."

"Who told you this thing?" she demanded, her eyes sparkling dangerously.

"Friends," he answered simply.

"You have odd friends to tell you such lies." She gestured to her poor surroundings. "I am just an old woman trying to survive in a worn-out desert town."

Jack couldn't help but smile a crooked grin at her apparent falsehood. "I think you are the one not telling the truth. I think there's more to you than meets the eye. If you are simply an old woman, then I'm..." His voice trailed off as he remembered his disguise, suddenly unsure what to call himself.

She pounced on his uncertain silence as a cat would on its prey. "A what? What are you? All I see is a man, and a scrawny one at that, who shows up at my home with delusions of conspiracy." She looked him up and down. "You speak nonsense. Get out of my house." She locked eyes with Mr. Macho and jutted her chin toward the door. The burly man grabbed Jack roughly by the elbow and shoved him toward the door.

Desperation rose up inside Jack. "Wait!" He sought frantically for the words that would convince her. "I...I'm just trying to help the gens and I need to talk to Stan."

"Stop," Maria snapped. "Why would you, a human presumably from the city—by the look of your clothes—be helping the gens?"

"Because," he swallowed hard, deciding on the spur of the moment to take a new, more dangerous tack. "Because I'm half gen."

"Again with the lies. Get out." She waved toward the door as if Jack were an annoying fly.

"I can prove it!" Jack struggled against the grip Mr. Macho held on his arm. Hope sprang in his chest when the man hesitated and looked at Maria questioningly.

"How would you do this thing?" she asked.

"My hair..." Jack stammered. "I dyed my hair black. And my eyes are not really blue."

This time, the old woman's forehead creased in a scowl. "If this is true," she said slowly, "show me your eyes. Jose," she said to the man at Jack's side, "give him some room."

Jack sucked in a breath, grateful for the temporary reprieve. He pulled away from the man and, reaching up with trembling hands, eased the contact off the surface of his eye. Holding it in one hand, he looked straight into Maria's eyes. With just one glance, her eyes grew wide and she sat up straighter. "Your eyes speak of your heritage and yet your skin is pale."

"My mother is human," he said more softly, "and my father...Stan is my father."

The old woman raised her eyebrows, surprise written on her face. "Your father?"

Jack nodded.

"I must think on this." She motioned the shorter man to come closer. He bent down and she whispered in his ear. Jack wished he knew what she said, but whatever it was, the man headed out the door with a purposeful stride. "Sit," she said and motioned Jack toward the couch with her eyes. "We will wait for Enrique to return."

Gratefully, Jack dropped his bag onto the floor and sank onto the couch. Leaning forward, he replaced the contact into his eye and blinked it into place. *Confidence,* he thought. *I must show confidence.* Despite his thudding heart, he leaned back and rested one arm on the back of the couch. Maria sat motionless, watching his every move. Jack picked at loose threads sticking up from a tear in the couch and waited, trying not to shift under her steady but unnerving gaze. Not for the first time, he wished he was home. His thoughts drifted to Amber and his mother and he wondered where they were at this very moment. After what must have been at least a half hour, Enrique returned. He nodded at Maria and whispered something in her ear.

"You're in luck," she said. "Señor Metcalfe has agreed to see you."

Jack closed his eyes in a long blink. Part of him remained angry with his father. The other part desperately wanted to solve this curious mystery.

"Jose and Enrique will take you there. You may go," she said with a note of finality.

Jack stood and shouldered his bag. "Thank you," he said softly. Maria responded with a nod and he followed Jose outside, Enrique trailing behind. After being in the darkened room, Jack blinked in the bright sunlight. Moving around to the back of the house, Jose stopped beside an ancient vehicle. With no roof and large, knobby tires, it sat high off the ground, probably able to travel over nearly any type of rough terrain. Before this, Jack had only seen images of such vehicles in historical texts.

"Get in."

Jack marveled at the truck, realizing it was probably petrol-powered. He hadn't known that any such vehicles still existed on the planet. The thing had to be a hundred years old. But then as he thought about it, it made perfect sense. This is the only type of vehicle that could operate outside the neural grid. It would be difficult for the government to track the alternatively powered, all-terrain vehicle.

Settling back in the seat, Enrique held out a handkerchief and said, "I must cover your eyes." He then reached forward and wrapped it around Jack's eyes, tying it in the back.

At least it keeps out the scorching sun, Jack thought wryly.

He felt the truck sway a bit as the two men climbed inside. The engine roared to life and the vehicle moved forward. The tires hummed against the pavement until before long, the sound changed. From the bouncing and crunch of the tires, Jack assumed they were now traveling on a rough, dirt road.

With the blindfold on, Jack had trouble sensing the passage of time but eventually the vehicle slowed and angled downward. Jack braced himself against the dash and noted that the surface of the road had changed—they no longer drove over rocks or gravel—and the air had cooled considerably; the sun no longer beat down mercilessly on Jack's skin. He heard the whirr of a motor, signifying a door closing behind them, and the vehicle came to a stop. Enrique and Jose climbed out and Jose removed Jack's blindfold. Jack gratefully rubbed his eyes and then looked around. He stepped out of the vehicle onto the smooth concrete floor of a warehouse-type of room roughly 45 meters long and nearly 30 wide. Realizing he would likely be meeting his father within minutes, Jack felt his heart begin to pound and he chewed his lip nervously.

"This way." Jose gestured toward a closed door roughly two car lengths ahead. He wrested the door open, its hinges squealing in protest. They walked down a windowless hallway, the walls paneled with hard composite panels typically found in city buildings. After passing a couple of closed doors, Jose knocked on the third and a voice inside responded.

"Come in."

Jose pushed the door open, but Jack hesitated, the old doubts rising up in his mind. What would Jack find inside? What would Stan be like?

Jose stood to one side and waited, raising his eyebrows expectantly. With trepidation, Jack stepped through the doorway and his eyes settled on the man inside. What he saw wasn't quite what he expected. Instead of the rough scoundrel he had assumed for years was his father, the one standing before him was slightly taller than a typical gen, his hair characteristically black but his skin a shade or two lighter than normal. His casual tan shirt and navy blue pants were the typical uniform of an off-duty professional office worker. With a shock, Jack realized there must have been a human a couple of generations back in his dad's lineage. Jack snorted lightly. That would explain his lighter skin and blond hair. It wasn't just his mother he took after. He had more of his dad's looks than he realized. Years of bitter anger sprang up inside Jack. In his mind, his father's partly human tendencies made it even more odious that Stan had left his wife and son. From his demeanor and dress, he must have had a good enough job to support his family and yet he had left them in poverty.

Stan stepped out from behind the unadorned, industrial, gray metal desk he had been standing behind. A narrow bookshelf stood to one side, next to an extra chair and an old-fashioned file cabinet. "Jack?" he said softly. "Is it really you?" He stood, arms at his sides. "I never thought I'd see you again."

After a moment, Jack spit out, "You could have whenever you wanted." He didn't care that his words were harsh, his voice hard.

Stan rubbed the back of his neck and took a deep breath. "It's not that I didn't want to."

"Really?" Jack found that hard to believe. "Could have fooled me."

"I was trying to keep you safe by staying away." Stan leaned back against his desk, propping himself up on the heels of his hands. "Would you like to sit down?"

In response, Jack leaned back against the file cabinet and folded his arms across his chest. His mind was a torrent of mixed emotions, but for now, anger was rising to the top.

Stan looked at the ground for the span of several breaths and then took a deep breath, exhaling loudly. "Jack—"

When Stan said his name, something like a dam burst inside Jack and he couldn't contain his anger any longer. "Where were you all those years? Why did you leave us?"

Stan opened his mouth to reply but Jack plunged on ahead.

"Do you realize what you did to Mom? Do you know what you left her to? She has nothing! Nothing!" He was shouting now. "Here you stand in your air-conditioned office, wearing nice clothes," Jack gestured down the length of his father, "while Mother lives in a hovel, wearing threadbare clothes, and barely enough to eat." He stepped forward and roughly shoved against Stan's chest with both hands, knocking the man backward until his back nearly touched the desk's surface. "Why? Did you hate us that much?" Having run out of words, Jack clenched his jaw and breathed hard, fists clenched at his side. "Why?" he spat out once more.

Stan bit his lip and sat back up. "I did it to protect you," he said softly.

"To protect us." Jack paced to one side and back again. "That's funny. To me it looks like you took anything of value and left your family behind to fend for themselves."

"I know how it must look," Stan tried to reason. "But you have to believe me. I wanted to take you both with me. It broke my heart to leave you behind, but..."

he paused, "if they caught me, they would have sent not just me to prison but her too. You would have ended up in a community home. Or worse yet, out on the streets. I couldn't take that chance."

For an instant, doubt crossed Jack's mind but he tried to shove it aside, unwilling to let go of his anger. It had been building for far too long to let it go so easily. "I don't believe you."

Stan ran his hand across his face and he looked to one side. "I suppose I should have expected this. I had hoped it wouldn't be this way but I can't really blame you. I know how you must feel."

"Do you?" Jack said incredulously. "How can you know how I feel? How can you know what it feels like to be left behind, thinking all those years that it was my fault, that you hated me and how Mom suffered because of it?"

Stan looked at Jack, his eyes mournful. "Maybe I don't know what it feels like to be left behind, to feel abandoned. But I do know how it felt to slip out of the house at night, afraid I might wake one of you up, unable to bear the grief you both would face at my leaving. To look back at that house one more time...." His voice caught, the next words came out in a raspy voice. "To think that I probably would never see that house again." The tears began to flow down his father's cheeks. His voice was so quiet Jack could barely hear. "To think that I'd never again see the ones I love the most."

When Jack saw his father's tears, doubt flooded even more strongly through his mind and he turned away lest his father see the weakness. Despite Stan's pleas, Jack still found his father's version of the story hard to swallow. He stomped out of the room and down the hallway to the warehouse and barged through the door. It was then he realized he didn't know where to go. The garage door was shut and he didn't even know which doors led outside. Besides, remembering the barren hills outside, he knew he wouldn't last long out there in the heat. Dropping his bag on the ground, he leaned against the wall and sank to the ground, forearms resting on his bent knees. He closed his eyes and tried to bring his emotions under control. *No matter what he says, he shouldn't have left us,* Jack told himself.

Before long, Jack heard the door leading into the warehouse open and footsteps approach. Jack clenched his jaw, ready to lash out at his father once more. He lifted his head but found not his father, but Enrique standing before him.

"Hey." The man jutted his chin out by way of greeting. "Señor Metcalfe says to tell you that you may leave tomorrow if you wish when we go back to town, but he hopes you will give him the chance to speak with you before you go."

Jack glared at the man. He'd love nothing more than to climb back in that truck and leave, but apparently that wasn't going to happen today.

"He says he will give you his room tonight."

But Jack didn't want to accept anything from Stan, much less stay in his room. "I'll sleep here. Thanks."

Enrique shrugged. "Your choice. But I can show you the food. You hungry?"

At the mention of food Jack realized he hadn't eaten for hours. He grudgingly agreed and stood, following Enrique back inside. He stalked down the hallway, glad to see the door to Stan's office closed. Several paces beyond that, Enrique turned left and Jack followed him into a larger room roughly thirty meters square with a smaller room off to one side that looked to be the kitchen. Jack followed Enrique to the kitchen's doorway and waited as the man banged around in the cupboard. He emerged with a spoon and a container of beans small enough to be an individual serving.

"Sorry. Is all we have for now," Enrique told him. "Dinner will be later."

Jack thanked the man and returned to his place in the warehouse. He settled on the ground and popped the top off the container, plunging his spoon into the saucy beans. They tasted sweeter than those Eva made. Probably had sugar, he thought. Something they could rarely afford at home. In spite of his bitterness, he had to admit they tasted pretty good.

When he finished, he set the container to one side and leaned back against the brick wall. Its cool surface eased the tension in his muscles and he closed his eyes. His thoughts traveled back through the years, reliving nearly every hardship they had gone through. The lack of food, not having enough money to always pay the utilities, the contempt of those around him, of not being accepted by either gens or humans. It angered him to think that Stan must have felt the same antagonism and could have helped Jack through it—if only he'd been there. Slowly he began to realize that he had been so angry he hadn't even bothered to find out what his dad was doing out here in the desert. Why the man had earned the title of *Señor* from those around him. Reluctantly, Jack realized he still had to find that out on the chance it might help their efforts in the underground. He would have to talk with Stan again.

After a couple of hours, the door opened again. Stan stepped into the warehouse and headed Jack's direction, hands in his pockets. Jack crossed his arms and hung his head, not willing to look into his father's eyes, dreading the fact that he had to speak with the man. Stan walked slowly up next to Jack and sat on the floor beside him. For a long time, they just sat next to each other without talking. Finally, Stan broke the silence.

"I'm sorry, Jack. I'm sorry for the pain I caused you and your mother."

After a lengthy pause, Jack stared straight ahead and replied, "What was so important that you had to leave?"

"All of this." Stan gestured around him. "It's a research facility. Before I left New Santiago, I was a lab assistant, working in the facilities that made medicines, mostly antivirus treatments and things like that. There was a portion of that facility that was off-limits to all but a few top researchers. I began to wonder what was behind those locked doors. After a time, I figured that must be where the DNA research was conducted—the same research that limited the gens to the life the humans had decided was best for them."

He paused and took a deep breath. "I started to poke around and found enough evidence that mostly confirmed my suspicions. I wanted to learn how to do what they did. I wanted to learn the secrets, to give the gens a chance to live with God Almighty after they died." A hardness entered his voice. "It's not right that they refuse them this hope. The priests preach forgiveness, how to live with each other and how to live a good life that will usher one into the arms of a loving father for all eternity. Then they abuse the beings they have created. I couldn't deal with the hypocrisy any longer."

Engrossed, Jack's curiosity piqued. "So what did you do?"

Stan's answer came back soft and low. "I broke into the lab, copied all the files I could, and ran. I knew there was no way I could escape detection and hide my actions. Surveillance was too tight for that. If they caught me, I would be executed and all my efforts to help the gens would have gone to waste. I had to leave. If I had taken you both with me, it would have been easier to be caught, and had we been caught, your mother would have been executed along with me. Then you would have been left alone."

Jack shook his head. There was still something he didn't understand. "But if you believe in the providence of the God you profess to serve, don't you think he could have protected all of us? Who were you to make that decision?"

Stan paused before he answered. "You might be right. Over the years, I have relived that day again and again, wondering if I did the right thing. Going over the same doubts you have raised. Wondering if my actions had even saved you or if the authorities had punished you both anyway because of my betrayal. The truth is, Jack, I don't know the answer to your question."

To that, Jack had no reply. It was hard to despise the man when he expressed regret, when he confessed his own doubts, when he obviously had tried to do the right thing. Jack still wasn't ready to embrace his father, but a crack had formed in his hard-hearted resolve. As much as he tried to deny it, the hate in his heart had begun to melt. *Time to steer the conversation toward something less personal,* he thought.

"So what exactly do you do here? You said this is your lab?"

Stan nodded. "The data I obtained—"

"Stole, you mean," Jack interjected.

Stan gave a wry smile and looked sideways at his son. "The data I *stole*...was incomplete. Unfortunately, I'm missing key components in the finished formula so I'm trying to fill in the holes and recreate the therapy that will complete the gens' DNA."

Realization hit Jack like a speeding ANN truck. He had been so clouded by anger that he hadn't wanted to admit the possibility of the truth that now glared in his face. "So...you really are trying to save the gens?"

"Yeah," Stan said dejectedly and hung his head. "Putting together the beginnings of the formula was easy, but over the last couple years my efforts haven't yielded any positive results. There's a key component missing that I just can't figure out."

The two sat in silence for a minute or two, each lost in his own thoughts. Then Stan spoke, his voice lighter, less serious, but with a bit of forced cheerfulness.

"So what about you? I've missed so much. What have you been doing the last few years?"

Jack chose his next words carefully. "I'm in IT. I worked at the government public administration office until recently, then became a network administrator at the Ministry of Religion."

A frown settled on Stan's face. "If you have a position at the Ministry of Religion, what are you doing here? I'm sure they wouldn't give you enough time off to come all the way out here, would they?"

Jack took a deep breath and Stan's eyes widened.

"You lost the job?"

Jack nodded.

"What happened?"

"I, um..." Jack's voice trailed off. It pained him to admit his end goal mirrored that of the man he had hated for so long. "I was caught trying to access secret files in the Ministry's databanks."

"But if you were caught..."

"Yeah," Jack finished the thought that surely rested in his dad's mind. "They sent me to prison." His admission did nothing to lessen the confusion on Stan's face so Jack filled him in on the rest of the story. How he had gone to River Island, how his leg was wounded, and how he had escaped.

"But how did you find me?" Stan's voice was thick with worry.

"The Underground," Jack replied. "I have ties to the Underground. They helped me find you."

Stan chuckled softly and shook his head. "So all this time we've both been working on the same team, toward the same goal. And neither of us knew it."

Jack met his statement with silence, still finding that fact hard to believe. He tried once again to steer the conversation in a different direction, to focus on another aspect of the situation. "You have quite the reputation, you know."

"Me?" Stan's expression changed to one of incredulity.

It was Jack's turn to shake his head. The man didn't even know. "It seems you're a hero in the Underground. And there's quite a price on your head."

Stan snorted. "That last part doesn't surprise me. I'm sure Dr. Fujimoto was livid when he discovered what I'd done."

"Initially, my friends and I weren't connected to the Underground so I didn't know anybody there. It wasn't until I got to River Island that I began to realize something was up. Your name is spoken with reverence there and the warden tried to force me to tell him where you are. But I didn't know."

"But my lab is common knowledge in the Underground?"

Jack shook his head. "No. The man who helped me with my disguise had to ask around, and even then, he could only find someone who had heard of Maria."

Relief washed over Stan's face. "Ah, Maria. She's a gem." He paused. "I'm glad our location is still a relative secret. If we are found, I don't know if I could move everything quickly enough to save the lab." Stan turned his head and took in Jack's hair and then looked into his eyes. "Nice disguise, by the way. I wondered about that. Even as a baby, your eyes were never blue."

"Thanks." Jack smiled. "But all the credit goes to a guy named Pedro. They call him 'The Fixer.'"

"I'll have to remember that. But hopefully I won't need his services in the near future."

For the first time, Jack felt a spark of compassion for his dad and he realized he wanted the man to succeed. He shifted. The hard floor was becoming, well, a bit too hard to be comfortable.

Stan seemed to note his discomfort. "There are certainly more comfortable places to sit, but before we go back in—if you want to, that is—I want to ask you something else."

Jack waited expectantly.

"Did you have any luck in your efforts to access the top secret files?"

"No." Jack shook his head. "I think I know where they are kept but I hadn't yet been able to breach the security walls." Then an idea sprang to mind. "Maybe I could try again somehow. Perhaps the data would be helpful in your work here!"

Stan exhaled loudly, doubt written on his face. "No. It's too dangerous." The forcefulness in his voice surprised Jack.

"But if it helps us reach the goal, it'd be worth the risk."

But Stan shook his head determinedly. "I can't ask you to do that. You already tried. If they catch you again, you'll be executed."

"But surely you know people in the Underground who could help me, don't you? You've been involved longer than I."

"No," Stan repeated. "I can't help you risk your life. I lost you once. I don't want to lose you again."

Resentment reared in Jack's mind and the few minutes of camaraderie they had experienced disappeared.

"You don't want to lose me? You haven't been my father for years and you still aren't now. You gave up that right when you left. I have my own life to live, with or without your support. And I don't need your help. In fact, I was already planning to leave in the morning."

Stan took a deep breath. "I'm sorry you feel that way, Jack. But if you want to leave, I won't stop you." He looked at his watch and stood. "But for now, why don't you come in? Dinner should be almost ready. Murray's really quite a good cook."

The pain and anger in Jack's heart overcame any sense of hunger he might have felt. "I'm not hungry," he grumped.

"Okay." Stan looked at the ground and nudged a piece of gravel with his foot. "If you change your mind, come on in. I'm sure there will be plenty," he said, and walked back into the main facility.

Jack stood and walked across the warehouse and tried a door next to the main garage door. Thankfully it opened and Jack slipped out into a black night. He'd never been in the desert at night and the multitude of stars in the heavens surprised him. So many pricks of light spread from horizon to horizon. At home, he'd only been able to see the brightest ones. As he reflected on that, he thought of his mom, then Amber, and he wondered if they were looking up at the same stars. Sudden longing filled his heart, and at that point, Jack determined to go back. Stan had already broken Eva's heart once and Jack didn't want to be the one to cause her more pain. And Amber. He missed their conversations, their friendship. He smiled to think of the times they had spent together. Surely she would help him. After all, they already had been partners in this venture, and now that he had some contacts with the Underground, it shouldn't be too hard to gain more support in the city. He nodded his head. Yes. That's what he would do. If Stan wanted to stay with his test tubes and chemical analyzers—or whatever he had in there—that was fine with Jack. He didn't need him.

Jack's thoughts continued to run along those lines as he worked out a plan for what he would do next. When his stomach growled, he stepped back inside the warehouse. Rummaging around in his satchel, he pulled out one of the apples and made a dinner of that, then crawled into the back seat of Jose's truck and lay down. He stretched out and rested his long legs on the top edge of the door—there was no window to fill the opening—and eventually fell asleep.

He woke at dawn, a kink in his back from the cramped seat and his legs numb from lack of circulation. He sat up and wiggled his feet, grimacing as the spikes shooting through his legs announced the feeling was coming back. Once they recovered, he stepped inside, found the facilities to relieve himself and returned to the truck to wait for Jose and Enrique. He didn't have to wait long. When they arrived, both men seemed surprised to find Jack already there. Enrique muttered a good morning, then went to open the garage bay door. Jose climbed into the driver's seat without a word and pulled the truck outside, after which Enrique closed the door and hopped in.

"What? No blindfold?" Jack asked.

"Señor Metcalfe," Jose replied, "he say there's no need."

Jack grunted, surprised in a way that after last night, Stan trusted him not to reveal their secret. *Whatever*, Jack thought. At least he didn't have to face any awkward goodbyes. Jack couldn't care less whether he ever saw the man again.

Chapter 14

The truck bounced across the desert, lurching from sand to rock, up one hill and down another. All the terrain looked the same to Jack. Now that he was free of the blindfold, he could see that the "road" to the facility was actually only a culvert that ran between the mountains of rugged basalt. The loud noise of the engine kept conversation to a minimum, for which Jack was grateful.

By mid-morning they reached the little town of Goffs and pulled up to Maria's house. With Maria now assured of Jack's trustworthiness, she quickly made arrangements for him to ride back to New Santiago with two Underground associates. Names were withheld for everyone's protection. Though the two men seemed friendly enough, Jack had little desire to talk. After several attempts at conversation, they gave up and left Jack to his thoughts.

After several hours, they reached New Santiago, where Jack connected with another vehicle traveling to the city center. Anxious to reconnect with Amber and his family, Jack didn't take the time to look up Pedro and Joshua. Instead, he asked to be dropped off in the human quarter near the university, thinking to find Amber first. It would probably be easier to avoid recognition near the university than in Gen Town, where he knew more people.

Once again, Jack chose to ride in silence, his mind filled with a combination of happy thoughts about reunion, but also darker thoughts of impending danger and risk.

To his surprise, the people around him did not regard him with looks of disdain—then Jack again remembered his disguise. Of course. He looked human now, no longer a gen. He grinned to himself at his newfound freedom.

Reaching his destination, he thanked the driver and made his way toward Amber's apartment, somewhere he had rarely dared to go before. With his distinctive golden eyes, he had been too readily recognizable and he had wanted to keep her from harm. As it was, he realized that he was taking a chance now, but it was worth it to see her again.

Knowing the route she usually took home, Jack found a place to wait near the edge of the university grounds. He mingled in with the students, who gave him barely a glance. After all, he was the right age and race to be one of the upperclassmen. He leaned back against the edge of a half wall and waited. Just as he was about to give up hope, he saw her heading his direction. With barely a glance, she passed him by. When she was three or four steps past him, Jack called out, "Amber."

She turned and searched the crowd. Not seeing anyone she recognized, she turned back and kept walking. Jack called again. She turned around, this time with her forehead creased in puzzlement. Jack pushed off the wall and took a couple of steps in her direction.

"Hello, Amber."

At the sound of his voice, her eyes grew wide and her jaw dropped in surprise. Then, brow furrowed, she shot a glance first to one side and then the other, grabbed his arm and tugged him down the sidewalk away from the school.

Jack didn't care how he looked; he couldn't wipe the grin from his face. It was so good to see her. After everything he'd been through in the past couple of months, it felt as if he hadn't seen her for years.

"Have to get you out of here," Amber muttered under her breath. "We'll talk at my place." She set a good pace and walked quickly, continually shooting quick glances sideways at Jack as if to assure herself he really was there.

Jack's leg had been healing well, but after about five minutes of walking, he began to tire and his limp became more pronounced. Thankfully they were almost there.

Soon they reached the complex where Amber lived. Leafy palm fronds hung over the sidewalk, which meandered through lush tropical gardens with various types of palms, ferns, and flowers. A narrow stream burbled happily through the gardens, passing under a wooden footbridge only a few paces long. The sweet smell of star jasmine drifted past Jack's nose and their footsteps thudded hollowly as they crossed the bridge. Amber turned off the main sidewalk, practically sprinted up to her door, and with a furtive glance over her shoulder, waved her keycard over the lock plate. The lock clicked and Amber shoved the door open, pulled Jack in behind her, and quickly shut the door. She leaned back against the door, out of breath, and just stared at Jack. Then she dropped her things on the floor, reached for him and wrapped her arms around him in a tight embrace. Jack gladly returned the hug. She laid her head on his chest, her hair tickling Jack's chin.

"I can't believe it's you." Then holding him at arm's length, she took in the sight of his eyes and hair. "Look at you." One corner of her mouth turned up in the barest hint of a grin, then it was gone and her eyes grew serious once again. "Jack, what's going on? How did you get here?" She opened her mouth to say more but the words didn't come.

As for Jack, he still couldn't wipe the grin off his face. He pulled her into an embrace once more and inhaled the faint spicy scent of her perfume. "It's just so good to see you," he murmured.

After a few seconds, Amber scooped her bag up off the floor. Taking Jack by the hand, she pulled him into the front room. He limped after her, leg throbbing from their hurried walk. Catching sight of his gait out of the corner of her eye, she looked at his leg then up at his face.

"Jack! You're hurt! How did I not see this earlier?"

Jack tried to not grit his teeth as he lowered himself onto the couch. "Eh, it's not that bad," he said, even though the pain pulsed through his thigh with every beat of his heart. *But she doesn't need to know that,* he thought. No need to make her worry. "I just need to sit down."

Amber regarded Jack with furrowed brow. "Not likely. I know you—it probably hurts like crazy. Here. Put your foot up." She moved a throw pillow to the far end of the couch. "What happened?"

Jack dropped his pack on the floor and shook his head. "I'm not sure where to start."

"How about you start at the part where you disappeared? You talk and I'll get us something to eat. You must be famished." Amber headed into her tiny kitchen and washed her hands at the sink while watching Jack through the opening in front of her, a pass-through to a bar with two stools.

Jack's stomach rumbled. "That'd be great, Amber. Thanks. I haven't eaten since breakfast."

She rummaged around in the refrigerator, pulling a few items out and clanking them down on the counter. "Well?"

Jack took a deep breath. "I'm sure you heard—or figured out by now—that I was arrested at work."

Amber nodded, her lips pressed together in a fine line. "That was the rumor on the street. When you didn't show up at your house, I figured that's probably what happened. Then your mom went to Robert and asked him and he confirmed the rumor was true."

Worry raised in Jack's mind when Amber mentioned Eva. "You've seen my mom? Is she okay?"

"You haven't seen her?"

Jack shook his head.

"Your mom's, well, she's not doing that great, to be honest. If it weren't for Ethan, I think she'd probably curl up in a corner and never come out."

Jack's heart broke at the news. The thought that he had been the source of her pain was hard to swallow.

Amber busied herself at the counter. "I've been trying to keep an eye on her too, making sure she eats and all that."

"Thank you," he said quietly. "I really appreciate that."

Without acknowledging Jack's comment, she steered the conversation back to the topic at hand. "So what happened next?"

"At the trial, I was sentenced to River Island—"

Amber's jaw dropped. "River Island?! No one leaves there. How'd you get out?"

"I'm getting there," Jack said good-naturedly.

Amber carried in two plates, a sandwich on each, two canned iced teas tucked in the crook of her arm.

"Ah, that looks good!" Jack took the plate she held out to him. Frankly, he didn't care if it was only peanut butter between two slices of bread, as long as it was edible. He took a big bite, and after he'd swallowed, launched back into his story.

He filled her in on his adventures on the island, told her about the warden and how he had threatened Jack with a lethal injection. Then he told of how he got shot, then about Joshua and how the man had helped him escape.

"So he just wheeled you out of the hospital?"

Jack nodded.

"So where is he now?"

"I'm not sure." Jack licked a smudge of dressing off his thumb. "We found a guy in the Underground who took us in and fixed me up with this disguise. When I left, Joshua stayed there. I'm not sure where he went from there but he'll have to stay under the radar now. He threw everything away just to help me. I'm still not sure why he did it."

Amber nibbled on a corner of her sandwich. "So after you left there, you came back to the city?"

Jack shook his head. "No, there's more."

Amber raised her eyebrows at that and waited while Jack took several swallows of his drink. The cold liquid trickled soothingly down his throat.

"I kept hearing about my dad, and how there's this bounty on his head. So I decided to see if I could find him."

Amber tucked her feet up under her on the couch. "And did you?"

Jack grunted. "Yeah. I found him." He couldn't keep the bitterness out of his voice. Amber waited, her eyes riveted on Jack's face as he pulled his thoughts together. He sighed deeply and adjusted his leg a bit. "Turns out he's some kind of researcher or scientist or something. He's got this hidden lab where he's trying to make an antidote for the gens."

Amber's eyes grew as round as saucers. "You're kidding me, right?"

Jack rubbed the back of his neck. "No, that's the truth. He's about got it done too, but there's one missing ingredient he can't figure out. We got to talking and I told him how we've been trying to find the formula in the computer banks. I thought if we worked together maybe I could try again and maybe find the answer this time. I figure he probably knows people here in the city, in the Underground, who might be able to help us."

Amber's eyes lit up. "That'd be great! If we could hook up with the rest of the Underground, we might have a chance!"

"That's what I thought too."

Amber's smile faded. "But…"

"He refused. Said he lost me once and doesn't want to lose me again." Jack wished he could get up and pace without his leg throbbing. "What gives him the right to play Father now? Like I told him, he gave up that right when he left us."

After a few moments of silence, Amber spoke, her voice quiet. "So why did he leave? Did he tell you?"

"Yeah." He picked a piece of lint off the back of the couch. "Said he didn't want to hurt Mom and me. It was supposed to protect us." He looked deep into Amber's eyes. "Didn't work, did it? That's okay. I don't need his help. We can do this without him."

Amber collected the dirty dishes and carried them back to the kitchen, the expression on her face unreadable. Jack stood and flexed his sore leg a bit, then walked the few paces over to perch on one of the bar stools. He leaned forward, elbows on the bar, and watched her rinse the dishes.

Jack continued. "I was thinking that maybe we could poke around ourselves and see if we can find the Underground contacts we need. It sounds and looks like the network is more organized than we had thought before. It shouldn't be too hard to find them."

"Jack, listen to yourself." Amber ran a brush around the dishes. "Don't you think there's a reason why we didn't know they existed before? And we're on the same team they are." She dropped the brush, turned off the water, and rested the heels of her hands on the edge of the sink. "They're well hidden and plan to stay that way. Besides, you can't go poking around. True, you have a great disguise, but it's still too dangerous. You're a wanted man now. There's a price on your head, for goodness' sake." She snatched a towel off the counter and vigorously wiped her hands. "Do you think that if you go up to the Ministry offices that no one will recognize you? In passing, it's fine. But your face is still Jack's face."

"But Amber..."

"No, listen to me." Amber folded the towel in quarters and laid it on the counter. "Jack, your dad is basically right. It's very dangerous." She came around to the other side of the bar. Jack opened his mouth to speak, but Amber placed her fingertips on his lips and continued. "I know that you are fully aware of how dangerous it is. No matter what you say, we can't do this by ourselves. But with your father's contacts, we might stand a chance. We need an edge." She paused. "Think about it, Jack. You know I'm right. We need him. Somehow you have to convince him to let us help."

Jack looked down at the ground. As much as he didn't want to admit it, Amber's words had a ring of truth.

She placed her hand on his arm. "Jack, I thought you were as good as dead," she whispered. "I still can't believe you're here. I didn't think I'd ever see you again. Please don't do something so foolish as trying to do this by yourself."

Jack placed his hand on hers and looked her in the eye. "I missed you so much, Amber. I certainly didn't think I'd be back here. I almost died."

"But you didn't," she replied. "Can we keep it that way?"

Jack pulled her into a hug and she laid her head against his chest and seemed to snuggle in. Jack had to admit that the feelings he had for his friend just might be turning into more than a friendship. They had been close for so long, but it almost seemed as if they had just entered a new type of friendship they'd never had before.

"Please," she whispered.

At that point, Jack realized he would do practically anything for her. He couldn't tell her no. "All right, Amber." He stroked her hair gently. "For you, I'll go talk with Stan again."

Comfortable. So comfortable.

Wrapped in a cocoon of warmth and eyes still closed, Jack's only thought was that this had been the most comfortable night's sleep he had had in months. Then Jack remembered where he was. The couch in Amber's apartment. He stretched and smiled. All of the recent events seemed worthwhile if that's what it took to bring Amber and him together.

He smiled and glanced over to the other side of the room where the display softly glowed with a soothing picture of a pond with lily pads and lotus flowers. Her parents had given the display to Amber one year for her birthday. When resting, it looked like a beautiful painting created in the tradition of the old masters. In fact, it was possible to create your own work of art on the touch-sensitive screen, but Amber preferred to display a copy of a priceless work of art painted more than 300 years before by a now-obscure artist—someone named Monet, he thought she had said. But the multi-function device could also be used to stream movies, and last night, Amber had chosen a movie that was probably 50 years old—and one of her favorites. Not many knew her well enough to crack through the shell she had built around her heart, but Jack knew she loved old things. She said they brought her peace, comfort from a happier day gone by, back when things must have been less complicated. Sometimes, she said, she wondered if she had been born in the wrong era.

Reluctantly, Jack left the warmth of his blanket and padded into the kitchen. He rummaged around in the cupboards until he found the coffee and measured enough directly into the carafe to make a full pot, then filled it with water. It was surprising, really. After so many years, there was still only one way to make a satisfying cup of coffee—coffee grounds and hot water. He added the water, flipped the switch, and within minutes, the brew was ready—the coffee fragrant and hot, the grounds collected and confined into a filtered pouch that could be lifted out and tossed in the trash.

Within ten minutes, Amber emerged from her bedroom, wrapped in a fuzzy robe and rubbing her eyes.

"Mm." It was a cross between sleepy contentment and a moan. "I thought I smelled coffee. Smells great."

Jack grinned, happy to see her pleased. He poured a cup for each of them, and while Amber sat at the small dining table, he prepared a quick meal of oatmeal and raisins. He didn't know his way around her kitchen very well, but those ingredients were easy to find.

Placing the meal on the table, he pulled up a chair across from her and dug in. After just one bite, Amber glanced up. "How are you going to get to your dad's?"

"I'll find the people who brought me. They said to contact them if I needed anything."

She nodded. "That's good. Do you need anything to take with you? Water? Food?"

"Water would be good." He blew lightly on the steaming oatmeal. "Nutrition bars would be good. The really filling ones."

"Okay. I can pick those up for you easily enough today."

Jack grimaced. "I have a few credits on a card but I'm not sure if it's enough."

She shook her head. "Don't worry about it. It's not much. Are you sure that's all you need?"

Jack chewed, the fresh raisins sweet and chewy. A rare treat. "Mm-hm. It's not terribly far. It'll only take a few hours to get there."

Amber looked up, one corner of her mouth turned up in a wry smile. "You're not going to tell me where it is, are you?"

Jack shook his head quickly. "No. If they find out I was here, well, let's just say it's better that way."

"Fine with me." Amber turned back to her oatmeal. "I don't think I want to know."

That was good with Jack. No sense putting her at risk. He looked up at Amber. Even though her hair was mussed from the night's sleep and she had no makeup, she still looked beautiful to him. Self-consciously, she glanced up and caught his gaze.

"Ugh." She ran her fingers through her hair, trying in vain to tidy the white bangs in front. "I must look awful. I didn't even brush my hair."

"You look great," he smiled, scraping the last of the oats from his bowl.

"Riiight." She regarded him skeptically, her voice dry and doubtful. She took their bowls to the sink and rinsed them. "I have a class at ten thirty. After that I can stop by the store. Will that be okay or are you planning to leave sooner than that?"

Jack shook his head and leaned back. "No, that's good. I don't think my ride will be ready until at least then."

"But how are you going to find them without tipping off the police? You know they monitor all communications."

"I thought of that." He tipped his head and looked at her hopefully. "Maybe you could call them for me? You don't need to know any names. Just tell them a package needs to be picked up. They should give you a time and I'll go meet them at a rendezvous point we talked about before."

Amber agreed and shuffled off to get ready for her day. Jack poured himself another cup of coffee and peeked out the window, careful not to open the blinds all the way. The sun was just coming up.

Over the top of the neighboring buildings, striated lines stretched horizontally above the horizon in alternating ribbons of orange and lavender and peppered with puffs of the same color clouds. Below, the sky glowed a golden peach. Above, the sky brightened to cornflower blue, with the exception of the pinkish yellow wisps of vapor overhead. Beautiful. For not the first time, Jack wondered if maybe there really was a God who, his mother had always said, orchestrated such beauty in nature. It seemed too gorgeous to just happen by chance.

With a sigh, he turned away from the window. Letting the blinds fall back into place, he returned to the front room and settled on the couch, alone with his thoughts. He missed his handheld. It had been a faithful device and had served him well. With nothing to fiddle with, his thoughts returned to his father. Stan. The hero. The obstinate, unhelpful hero. Initially, when they had talked at the lab, Jack had felt the first stirrings of hope that maybe he actually did have a father worth talking to. But he had been wrong, he thought bitterly, then wondered why he had let Amber talk him into going back. With a deep sigh, he ran one hand through his hair. Well, it was settled now. He had promised to go and he would not let her down. Somehow, he'd make this work, even if only to please Amber.

After an hour or so, Amber came out looking much more awake. Her spiky white bangs fell down over one eye and the black layers in the back didn't poke out every which way any longer. This morning she had paired her characteristic black pants with a black loose jacket over a gray pullover shirt.

"Guess I should make that call." She picked up her communicator bud off a side table and inserted it in her ear. She touched it and requested the number Jack gave her, then gave the message he had relayed to her that morning. When finished, she turned to Jack.

"They said five o'clock."

He nodded. "That'll work. Thanks."

Amber scooped up her handheld and plopped into a side chair.

"Gotta study?" Jack returned his cup to the kitchen.

"Yeah. I have a test this morning and want to look over my notes first."

"Okay. I'll leave you alone. Have to shower anyways. Mind if I use your launderer?"

"No, go ahead," Amber said absently and focused on the text.

In the bathroom, Jack placed his clothes in the machine and turned it on. By the time he finished his shower, they'd have processed through the cleaning cycle and be ready to wear. When he finished and came back out, Amber was ready to go.

"I'd better get going." She stuffed her slate in her purse and slung it on her shoulder. Jack walked her to the door, wishing she didn't have to leave.

She reached up and smoothed his hair back gently. "You look so different with black hair...and blue eyes." Then she kissed him lightly, her lips soft and warm, and a thrill ran through Jack. With a quick smile, she turned to the door. Hand on the latch, she looked back over her shoulder, her face stern.

"Promise me you won't go out."

"I promise," he agreed. Even though he longed to step out for some fresh air, he didn't dare risk it.

While she was gone, Jack rambled around the apartment restlessly, trying not to think of the days ahead, of facing Stan again. But his thoughts visited the topic again and again, trying to figure out what to say. Eventually, he gave up and scrounged around until he found a few scraps of paper and a pen in a drawer. He sat at the table and jotted down one idea after another, but as soon as he wrote one down, he crossed it out. Nothing seemed right. He didn't want to appear to be crawling back pathetically, nor did he wish to be demanding. That surely wouldn't get him anywhere. How could he appeal to Stan's sensibilities and convince him to let Jack help by doing the only thing he knew how? One thing Jack knew for certain—he'd never be able to contribute anything meaningful in the lab. Probably all he could manage would be to clean the equipment.

Amber returned about four-and-a-half hours later. Jack heard the lock click open and looked up to find her pushing the door open with her hip, shoulder bag swinging and a carryall bag in her arms. Thankful to have something else to do, Jack leapt to his feet and took the bag. Looking inside, he found the water and nutrition bars, along with several other items.

She pushed the door closed firmly. "I thought I might as well get a few other things while I was at the store."

Jack carried the bag into the kitchen. She pulled out the water and nutrition bars and handed them to Jack.

"These are for you."

He thanked her and put them in his bag. While he checked to make sure he hadn't forgotten anything, Amber made two more sandwiches.

"I wish I could make something better for you to eat before you go, but I'm sure you're in a hurry."

Jack nodded and sat at the bar. "This will be fine. Thank you." As he watched her, his heart grew heavy, already dreading the thought of leaving.

Amber plated his sandwich and placed it in front of him. Still standing in the kitchen, she took a bite of her own. All too soon, Jack was finished and it was time to go. He drank a large glass of water, not knowing when he'd get another and wanting to save his bottle for later.

"Guess I'd better get going." Jack wrapped his arms around Amber and held her close. After a minute or so, Jack reluctantly released her and, holding her hand, returned to the front room to collect his satchel. At the front door, they hugged once again. Then Jack looked into Amber's eyes, a hand on each of her shoulders.

"I need you to do me a favor. Please don't tell my mom I was here."

"But Jack, don't you want her to know you're okay?"

"I do want her to know that, but...I don't want her to have knowledge that will cause her harm." Remembrances of Stan leaving home flitted through Jack's mind, and while it still infuriated him, he found himself doing the same thing his father had done. But there was one big difference. "I'll be back. Then I can tell her myself."

Lips pressed into a thin line, Amber nodded her head. "Okay. I'll let you tell her." Then she raised her finger and pointed at him accusingly. "But you'd better come back."

"If I don't, I'll be dead." Now that the words were out of his mouth, they fell on an uncomfortable silence. Jack shuffled his feet and put his hands in his pockets. "I'll miss you." He tried to keep his voice upbeat. "But hopefully I won't be gone long."

"Yeah. Hopefully." Amber stood on tiptoes and kissed him on the cheek. "I'll miss you too." Jack pulled the door open and stepped out. He turned back and tried to offer an encouraging smile. With a final "goodbye" he turned and walked away rapidly, afraid he'd change his mind and stay. The door clicked shut behind him.

With the good rest he had had over the past twenty-four hours, Jack's leg felt much better and he walked quickly away from the complex, head down, hands in the pockets of his jacket. He doubted anyone would recognize him, but he still wanted to put as much distance between Amber's apartment and himself as possible. No sense tempting fate. Besides, he had a long walk ahead.

Roughly an hour later, he reached his rendezvous point, glad he was early. Nearby, a small park beckoned so he went over and found a bench on which to wait. He pulled the scrap of paper from his pocket and reviewed his list of ideas again, still not happy with what he had written in his brainstorming session earlier. He stuffed it back in his pocket and leaned forward, forearms on his knees. He wished he could see his mom. In his mind, he could hear what she would probably say, offering reassurances that she would pray for him and yet, in spite of her prayers, he had endured so much.

And he still didn't have a clue what to do. He certainly didn't have time to visit the shrine of the nature gods, but his mother had always said he could talk to her God wherever he was. And so in desperation, he looked down at his hands folded in front of him and whispered, "God, if you're there, I could really use some help."

Then he sat back, puffed out a breath, and shook his head at his own foolishness. Why was he doing this anyways, he questioned. If there was no god, there was no such thing as a soul. And yet, so many of the gens believed there was and, Jack reminded himself, if he succeeded, it would give them a reason to live, a reason to hope for the future. And maybe, just maybe, his mom was right. There was no harm in giving it a shot, was there?

Not wanting to stay on the bench so long as to be conspicuous, Jack stood and ambled down the sidewalk, walking around the park. By the time he got back he checked his watch to see it was almost five o'clock. He leaned up against a tree where he could keep his eye on the street and waited. Sure enough, before long, the car he was waiting for turned the corner and cruised up the street. As it grew closer, Jack could see it was the same man who had dropped him off the day before. He sauntered out to the street, and when the car drew even with Jack, it stopped and he hopped in. The car immediately resumed its path.

"Thanks." Jack settled into his seat. "I appreciate the ride."

The man grinned. "Sure. No problem. Glad to help out."

The two didn't have much to say on the road. Jack assumed the man was part of the Underground but he didn't know for sure. The unspoken code seemed to be that the less one knew, the better off they were. And that was fine with Jack.

The man told Jack that he had arranged for the same party to pick him up and take him back to Goffs. *Good*, Jack thought. That was one bridge crossed that he had been concerned about.

Once in the city center, the connection was made and soon Jack was headed a second time toward the little town in the desert. Jack looked sideways at his driver as the old man rambled on about the weather, about the plants and animals in the desert. The man's cheerfulness was refreshing and the things Jack was learning about the desert might come in useful some day.

With the man chattering so much, the few hours required to reach his destination seemed to go quickly, and yet it had to be at least midnight when they arrived. His driver knew exactly where to go. He pulled up at Maria's house and as Jack stepped out of the car, the man leaned over. "Young man," he called, "may God be with you, wherever you go."

The same words his mother used to say. Jack smiled at the fond memory and genuinely thanked the man. He watched for a moment as he drove off, then hurried up to Maria's door and knocked.

Before long, the door opened and there stood Jose, his eyebrows raised in surprise. Jack couldn't help but smile. That was the most expression he had ever seen on the man's typically stony face. After a moment, Jose stood aside and motioned for Jack to come in.

"Wait here." The man's accent revealed he usually spoke as much Spanish as English, if not more.

Jack didn't have long to wait. Before long, Maria shuffled in and settled in her tattered chair. She rested both hands on the cane standing in front of her.

"So you've come back."

Jack nodded. "I need to..." He was going to say he needed to see his father, but he wasn't sure how much Maria knew. She likely didn't know of their father-son relationship. "I need a ride out to...the place I went before," he said, unsure what to call the facility.

"Mm-hm." She nodded. "Why else would you be here, *mijo*? Somehow I knew you would be back." She searched Jack's face, seeming to know more than he liked and he shifted uncomfortably. Finally, she spoke again. "Jose will take you. Go with him." She turned to the young man. "You need to leave now," she said kindly. With a single nod, Jose obeyed and moved for the door.

With a thank you to the old woman, Jack followed Jose, relieved to be outside once again. While he appreciated Maria's kindness, her manner still unnerved him. He had the feeling that with her, no one held any secrets.

Jack followed Jose around to the back of the house and waited while he fueled up the truck. Before long, they were crawling inside and once again bouncing across the desert. Now that the height of summer had passed and the days were grower cooler, so too were the nights. Jack zipped his jacket shut and flipped the collar up against the back of his neck. One wheel plunged into a dip and Jack braced a hand against the truck's door. The headlights shone thin streams of light into the dark, barely enough to illuminate the rough path.

After roughly an hour, they pulled up to the bay doors. Jack motioned that he'd open the door and he hopped out, glad to be out of the bouncing truck. Jose drove the vehicle inside and Jack closed the door behind them. Jose cut the engine and the ensuing silence pressed in like a blanket. Being the middle of the night, Jack wasn't sure what to do now. He certainly didn't want to wake everyone in the facility—however many that was. Might as well sleep in the truck, he thought. He started to climb back in but Jose motioned for Jack to come with him.

"*Ven*. Come." He turned and headed for the door.

Jack dug his pack out of the truck and slung it over his shoulder, rushing to catch up. At roughly one a.m., the facility was quiet and dimly lit. Jack followed Jose down the hallway to a door that opened up into a small room with two sets of bunk beds, all four mattresses bare and empty. Jose stretched out on one of the lower beds and closed his eyes. Jack murmured a thank you and lay down on the other bottom bunk. It was then he realized how tired he was. It didn't take long to fall asleep.

When he woke in the morning, Jose was gone. Jack groaned and rubbed his face, his body still lethargic and muscles slightly sore from fatigue. He stretched and sat up on the edge of the bed, trying to collect his thoughts and wondering what time it was. Eventually he stood and ventured to the doorway and looked out into the hallway. The smell of coffee and some kind of food drifted down the hallway from the dining area. He headed that direction. The only person there was at the stove, busily cooking something. A coffee urn stood on a long counter, a couple of mugs nearby. Jack tentatively approached the man.

"Excuse me, may I have some coffee?"

"Hm?" He looked up. "Sure! Help yourself. Cups are on the counter."

"Thank you," Jack murmured, trying to sound more awake than he felt.

The man spooned some eggs into a moderately sized serving tray. "I'm Murray. Weren't you here a couple of days ago?"

"Yeah, that was me." Jack poured the coffee into a cup, its fragrant, tantalizing steam pulling him in. Coffee was something his mom had prepared only on special occasions. These rebels must have good connections, he thought. They certainly eat better than a lot of gens.

Murray placed the tray on the counter next to another covered dish already there. "There aren't that many of us so I usually know where everyone is. I didn't know you were coming back. Does Stan know you're here?"

Jack shook his head. "No. He's not expecting me."

Murray pulled the lid off the other tray, revealing at least a couple dozen strips of fried bacon. "It's not much, but help yourself. When you're done, I can take you around and we'll find Stan."

Jack's mouth watered as he looked at the steaming food and he realized he hadn't eaten anything since he'd had a nutrition bar the previous afternoon. He took the plate Murray held out to him and scooped a spoonful of eggs onto his plate, then a couple strips of bacon. Murray served himself and joined Jack at the table.

"So what brings you out here?" Murray pulled in his chair and shoved his fork into the eggs.

"Um...I'd rather not say." Best keep that to himself for the present.

"That's okay. Don't worry about it."

The two ate in silence for the few minutes it took to consume the food. Though simple, it was the best thing that Jack had tasted in quite some time. Once finished, Murray took their plates and placed them in the sink.

"I generally cook so the others take turns at cleanup." Murray headed for the door. "Come on. Let's go find Stan."

Jack took a deep breath and followed. He still didn't know what he was going to say when he faced the man.

First they checked the office but no one was there.

"Gotta be the lab." Murray did an about-face and headed farther down into the facility than Jack had ever been.

They stopped at a door with a glass window in the top half. Murray motioned toward a man inside. Masked and gloved, he leaned over a counter, working with a variety of vials in trays. But that was the extent of Jack's knowledge, except for the computer that stood off to one side. It was a TH3100, one of the best on the market for its size. Once again, Jack was amazed at the resources they had here.

Murray excused himself and left Jack standing outside the closed door. Stan seemed engrossed in his work so Jack leaned back against the opposite wall to wait in the hallway. Stan fiddled, for lack of a better word, with the equipment, then referred repeatedly to the computer. After probably 15 minutes or so, the scientist lifted his head and rolled his shoulders back, stretching against the bent-over posture he had assumed for who knew how long. As he stretched his neck, tipping his head from side to side, he noticed Jack out of the corner of his eye. He whipped his head round to focus his attention on Jack, his eyes wide. He pulled off the gloves and walked toward the door. Pulling off his mask revealed a wide smile on his face. Laying the gloves and mask on a table nearby, he opened the door.

"Jack!" With one quick motion, he closed the door behind him and began to reach out to shake Jack's hand. "You came back!" Changing his mind, he hugged

Jack briefly. At the unexpected embrace, Jack felt stiff as a board. Embarrassed, he shoved his hands in his pants pockets and looked down at the floor.

"Yeah." He couldn't think of anything else to say.

"Well," Stan interrupted the awkward silence. "Um. Been here long?"

"Got here last night. Jose drove me." Jack wished his sentences didn't sound so clipped. He thought of Amber and his promise to ask the man for help. *Must be friendly*, he thought. "So...looks like you're hard at work." Jack cringed inside at his weak attempt at conversation.

"Yes, well, there's always work to be done." Stan walked slowly down the hallway. "Coffee? I mean, would you like some?"

"Sure," Jack replied. *At least he doesn't seem to be much of a conversationalist either*, Jack thought as he walked with Stan back to the dining area, where his host poured them each a cup.

Stan motioned with his head toward a table along the wall. "Would you like to have a seat?" Without waiting for an answer, Stan headed for the table and placed both cups down, one on each side, and the two sat across from each other. "It's good to see you," Stan said and took a sip of the brew.

Jack ran his thumb along the rim of his mug. "I thought maybe I should find out a little more about what you do out here." Well, that was at least partly true anyway.

Stan's eyes searched his face. "You know I've been praying for you," he said quietly.

Jack looked off to one side at nothing in particular. So that's the way it was, was it? He had no idea his mom and Stan shared their faith. "I don't know that it's doing any good." He sipped from his cup, but not carefully enough. The hot liquid scalded his tongue and he swallowed quickly.

"After you left," his dad continued, "I got to thinking. Maybe you were right."

Jack looked at his dad in surprise. "About what?" He thought he knew, but it wouldn't hurt to ask.

"Seeing you again after all these years stirred up feelings I hadn't felt that intensely for years."

Evading the question, Jack thought, and he tried to keep his eyebrows from raising skeptically.

"Maybe I let my feelings get in the way so I couldn't look at the situation logically. I prayed that God would protect you and bring you back here safely."

Jack leaned back in his chair and folded his arms in front of him. "You sound like Mom."

Stan smiled and looked down at his coffee. "I'm glad to hear Eva's kept her faith. I hoped she could lean on that after, well..."

"After you left, you mean."

His voice dropped almost to a whisper. "Yeah. After I left." Then he took a deep breath and seemed to collect himself a bit. "I was thinking that if you'd give me a second chance, maybe we could work together as you suggested to reach our common goal."

"But how? I don't know anything about lab work." Jack hoped that he could steer the conversation in the direction he needed to go.

"I know that." His dad nodded. "But God protected you and brought you back. He must have designs for your life. Something that you are particularly suited to do."

Maybe there's hope, Jack thought. He leaned forward, elbows on the table.

"Didn't you say you were a network administrator?"

Jack nodded.

"What else do you like to do?"

"Programming. Computer hardware repair. I had a used Orichi handheld slate. It was old, but I had done a lot of work on it. Upgraded it, customized part of the hardware and software."

"So what happened to it?"

"I don't know. They arrested me at work and I had to leave everything there."

Stan grimaced. "Hm. I'm sorry."

"Yeah. I wish I had it now. I had so many things in there. My projects, notes—encrypted, of course." He sighed. "I hope no one was able to break my codes. If I'm lucky, they didn't pay any attention to the old slate."

Stan smiled. "You talk like it was an old friend."

"Yeah. It seemed that way."

"Can I ask what your projects were?"

Jack regarded his dad for several moments. He guessed there wasn't any harm at this point in telling him. He rubbed his hand across his face. "One thing I was working on was a communications network that would be undetectable by the police."

Stan's eyebrows shot up with interest. "Sounds expensive."

"No, not really." Now here was something Jack could talk about. "You see, all the earbud communicators use two frequencies, one weak and one strong. Theoretically, if the frequencies are placed close enough together, the weaker of the two can be masked by the stronger one, but they have to be far enough apart to not interfere with each other." Jack paused to see if he had lost his dad, but he still seemed engaged so Jack continued. "Then if the data signals are sent in encrypted bursts, that is, sending fewer packets with larger amounts of data, then they are less likely to be detected."

"Fascinating!"

Jack was somewhat surprised his dad seemed truly interested.

"I assume this is for use by the gens?"

Jack nodded. "Our group of insurgents has had trouble communicating with each other. It's been pretty risky. So I thought that if I could develop something like this we could even customize commercially available earbuds and not have to build the devices from scratch. But...I didn't realize the Underground network was so big. Do you know if they're already working on something like this?"

Stan shook his head. "Not that I know of." He paused. "So you weren't officially part of the Underground?"

"No. I was kind of leading a small group of insurgents. We banded together because we felt the gens weren't being treated properly."

Stan leaned back. "No wonder you wanted contacts in the Underground. I thought you knew."

Jack just shook his head.

Stan thought for a bit. "So you lost your notes for the project?"

"Yeah." Jack sighed. "They're all gone."

"So...do you think you could remember enough to try again?"

"Possibly." Jack shrugged. "But I don't know where I'd get that kind of equipment."

"Maybe we can help. You've probably noticed we're pretty well funded. In fact, I think one of our benefactors sent us a few earbuds, but we haven't used them for fear of detection. Even out this far."

"Hm. Well, I'd need a testing room—kind of like a giant Faraday cage that could block out all types of transmissions so none get out or in."

"That might be doable. I'll see what I can do. Of course, you'll need to stay here for a bit."

Jack felt a genuine smile cross his face. It felt good that he and his dad could find a way to work on the same team—and he looked forward to possibly being able to have the materials he had needed for so long to develop his technology projects. "I suppose so." He thought briefly of Amber and Eva but he was certain he could either get word to them or return to the city before too long. This was going to be great.

Within ten days, Stan was able to obtain the materials and tools Jack needed to work on his projects. A room was set aside and work was begun to shield the working area from outside communications signals. Jack was hanging shielding panels on the wall when he heard a voice behind him.

"Hey Jack!"

Jack stopped and turned around.

"I brought you something."

Stan handed him a roughly half meter square box.

Curiously, Jack broke the seal. He set the parcel on a stack of boxes and opened the lid. When he looked inside, his jaw dropped in surprise. There on a bed of packing material lay a handheld, a few years old, but incredibly clean. Reverently, he lifted it out of the box and inspected the device. Although he still thought of his old slate fondly, this one was much nicer and he looked forward to inspecting it in great detail.

Jack looked at his dad and shook his head. "I don't know how to thank you."

"Don't worry about it." A wide smile stretched across Stan's face. "Consider it payment for all your hard work."

Stan left and Jack just stood in the middle of the room looking around at the building materials and the small stack of boxes containing the earbuds, tools, and testing devices. *This just might be the best day of my life*, he thought.

Excited by the prospect of finally being able to build his devices, Jack plunged into his work. One week became two, which became three and then four. As he worked, memories of Amber increasingly began to surface. He could hear himself telling her, *I won't be gone long.*

Jack laid his tools down and leaned back, pressing his shoulders together. It was time to test the earbuds. Hopefully for the last time.

"Hey there. I wondered where you were. You missed dinner again." Stan leaned against the doorframe, hands in his pockets.

"I did?" He glanced at his wristwatch. "Huh. I didn't realize the time."

"I know this is important, but you've been working like a madman."

"Yeah, I've been making real progress too. I get a little obsessed sometimes."

"You don't say?" Stan grinned. "So how's it going?"

"Actually, I'm almost finished." Jack stood and stretched. Stan entered the room and looked with interest at the earbud Jack had been working on.

"Is this it?"

Jack nodded. "I just tested the frequencies of this one to make sure both incoming and outgoing are in the proper ranges."

"It looks just like the others."

Jack grinned. "Yeah. That's the idea."

"Have you tested it?"

"Just getting ready to. Wanna help?"

"I'd love to." Stan's eyes sparkled enthusiastically. "What do I do?"

Jack shut the door to his lab, now dubbed The Cave, turned the earbud on and handed it to Stan. "Put that one on." He picked up its twin lying within arm's reach on the long worktable and tapped it on. He inserted it into his ear while walking the end of the table cluttered with electronic parts and tools. At the end, he reached for a square monitor, a cube that measured roughly 30 centimeters on every side. "Ready?"

Stan nodded and Jack flipped the switch.

"Can you hear me?"

"Yeah. It sounds normal."

Jack checked the measurements on the monitor and grinned. "Just like it's supposed to. Signal's nice and strong on the primary frequency and the one we're using doesn't even register."

"Wow! That's amazing!" Stan removed the communicator and rolled it in the palm of his hand. He gestured to it and then Jack's. "Are these the only ones?"

"So far." Jack took his out and returned to his workstation. "Now we need to test it long distance and make sure it works on the global network."

Stan frowned. "Isn't that kind of risky?"

"Could be," Jack shrugged. "But it has to be done." He straightened his tools. "And I need to get back to the city."

"I see. What's the rush?" Stan started to hand the device to Jack.

Jack glanced up. "No, you keep that one." He paused. "I have obligations there. I promised someone I wouldn't be gone long."

"Ah." Stan closed his hand over the earbud.

Jack nodded.

"When are you planning to leave?"

"I'd like to leave today, but I thought I'd shoot for tomorrow. I need to get some sleep first."

Stan nodded in agreement. "Good idea. If you hurry, I think there's still some food left from dinner."

"That sounds good. But first, let me show you how this works." Together they looked at the monitor and Jack showed him how to test the signal, then he showed him how to test the frequencies on another device. "After I leave, keep the earbud handy and I'll test it periodically to make sure it's still working. I need you to keep it with you because the tests will be very brief in case they malfunction and become detectable. I just need you to watch these monitors to make sure the frequencies and signals don't change. I've built a smaller set of testers that I can take with me. You'll need to move these outside The Cave for them to work."

"Right. That shouldn't be too hard." He paused, then looked up at Jack intently before speaking. "Jack, I've been thinking about your request for Underground contacts in the city. I think the work you're doing here is important and I trust you. To tell the truth, my contacts are from a long time ago, but I'll give you what I have."

A sense of relief washed over Jack. "Thanks...I appreciate that. Maybe it will help me get in." He had almost said "Dad" but the word still felt strange in his mouth. But he was grateful nonetheless.

"Okay, then. Let's get you that food."

While he ate, Stan gave Jack the names of two people who might be able to help—if they were still around—and told him how to contact them. "But be careful," Stan said. "I haven't used those contacts in a long while and I'm not sure how secure they are anymore."

After eating, Jack headed for his bunk and crawled in. Pulling up his blanket, he sighed contentedly, comforted by the knowledge that he had finished two prototypes and would be headed back to the city soon. Thinking of Amber fondly, he drifted off to sleep.

The next morning, Jack rinsed a fresh application of black dye through his hair and reinserted his blue contacts. He grabbed a bite to eat in the dining area, then placed the compact equipment, along with a bottle of water and a couple of nutrition bars, in his old pack. He zipped it up and tested the weight. Not too bad and not too bulky. That should work just fine. He hitched a ride back to Goffs, all the while wishing the car could go faster. He had some contacts to make before he could see Amber.

Chapter 15

The car pulled up to the curb a few blocks from where Stan had told Jack to try first. Jack thanked the driver and stepped out of the car. With a nod, the driver pulled away.

Jack stood in the middle of the sidewalk and looked around briefly to gain his bearings. He had committed the directions to memory for the sake of security. Picturing the map his dad had drawn, Jack thought that Mockingbird Street should be the next one over. With butterflies in his stomach, he walked that direction, wondering what he would find.

He reached the next corner. Sure enough, Mockingbird Street. So far, so good. Now to go down five buildings to number 697. Though he hadn't been to this part of town before, the townhomes looked similar to another older section but this neighborhood had been renovated some years back, the old brownstones fixed up or new constructions built to resemble the old ones that couldn't be saved. The streets were clean and the townhomes, many three stories tall, were all in good condition. The scent of flowers drifted through the air from flowerbeds lining the sidewalk in front of the houses.

Let's see, 693, 695, there it was—697. Jack hitched the pack up a little higher on his shoulder, then wiped sweaty palms on his pants legs. *Here goes,* he thought.

Jack walked up the six steps to the stoop and knocked on the door. No answer. *After all this,* he thought, *please let someone be there.* He knocked again and shortly heard footsteps. They stopped just inside the door, then the lock clicked open and the door swung back just far enough to reveal an elderly woman dressed in pressed slacks and a casual but well-tailored blouse. Her hair was arranged neatly and her make-up applied just so.

"Yes?" Her eyebrows drew down in a frown.

"Um," Jack's voice faltered at the stern reception. "I'm...I'm looking for Stein Ingerstrom."

If possible, the woman's frown deepened, the corners of her mouth drawing down, lips pressed into a thin line. "He hasn't lived her for several years. Can't help you," she said and slammed the door.

Jack gulped. That hadn't gone well. With a deep sigh, he descended the stairs back down to the sidewalk. A breeze caught purple flowers on leggy stems hanging over small green shrubs and they bobbed cheerfully. Jack scowled at them and turned away, already searching his mind for the next address Stan had given him. He had also told him it was all the way on the other side of town.

Within a couple of blocks, he found a bus stop. He fished out the fake ID Pedro had given him and ran it through the scanner. Hopefully it still had a few credits left that would be enough for the fare. Thankfully, the machine accepted the card and Jack moved back farther into the bus. His first instinct was to go to the very back where the gens sat, but then he reminded himself not to. It was still so strange to be accepted as a human, even if only temporarily. He compromised and sat about halfway back, neither in the front nor the back. Hopefully here he would not be noticed.

All the way across town, Jack thought about what he was doing. He couldn't get the old woman out of his head. Her frown, her quick refusal. Then he remembered his father's admonition to be careful. Perhaps the old woman was going to be a problem. Or was she? He sighed. Either way, there wasn't anything he could do about it now. His next task was to find Clare Montague, a woman who had worked with Stan in the lab all those years ago. He knew it was partly because of her help that his dad had escaped.

After getting lost only once, Jack finally found the woman's house—or at least the address he had been given. He found himself in a middle class neighborhood, very neat and tidy, everything just so. Lawns manicured, the flower beds full of colorful blooms.

By the time he arrived, the shadows of night had begun to lengthen. Should be dinner time soon. He knocked on the door but no one answered. Stepping back, he looked around, up one side of the street and then the other. *Maybe not home from work yet?* he wondered. That is, if she still lived here. Jack decided to wait until someone came home, but as he looked around, he realized that there was nowhere to wait in this pristine neighborhood. No parks, no benches. If he stood outside the house, he thought wryly, a neighbor might just call the police. So for lack of a better idea, he started walking down the street. He checked his watch. He'd give her an hour and then come back.

Jack walked one way a half hour then turned around and came back. Nearing the block where Clare supposedly lived, the streetlights clicked on, casting puddles of shadow on the darkening streets. Jack walked on. The only sound in his ears was the twitter of birds settling down for the night. He could barely hear the sound of his own footsteps given the soft-soled shoes he had been given. By the time Jack arrived, the sun had set.

He stepped up to the front door again and knocked. This time he was rewarded. The door opened, and an attractive red-haired woman stood just inside, hand on the knob.

"Yes?"

Jack gulped. "I'm looking for Clare Montague." He tried not to fiddle with his hands, instead shoving them in his pockets.

"I'm Clare. What can I do for you?"

Jack breathed a sigh of relief. Then with a start, he forgot for a moment what to say next. "Um...I need to speak with you about Stan Metcalfe."

The woman's face grew serious. She looked out the door, up one side of the street and then the other. Then she stepped back and motioned with her hand. "Come in," she urged. "Quickly."

As soon as he stepped inside, she closed the door quickly, then leaned her back against it. She looked at Jack with a level glare. "Who are you?"

"My name's Jack."

"And?"

Though Jack had had hours to think about it, he still wasn't sure what approach would best put the woman at ease and get her to help him. "Stan told me you used to work together."

Her brow drew down into a frown. "What do you mean 'Stan told you'? He's been missing for a very long time. Who are you really?"

"I really am Jack. Jack...Metcalfe."

Her eyes grew wide and she whispered, "No. That can't be. You don't look like his son." She fumbled for the doorknob.

"No, wait!" Jack motioned, hand outstretched in an effort to calm her. "I really am. I saw my father this morning. I know where he is."

Clare narrowed her eyes and looked at him closely. "I think you're an impostor. Stan's son did not have black hair and blue eyes. Prove it."

Jack pulled his off pack, placed it on the floor and began to undo the zipper.

"Stop! Right there!" Clare's voice, hard and demanding, caused Jack to freeze.

"It's okay," he tried to reassure her. "I have something you need to see." He glanced up and looked her in the eye. "I'll go slow."

Clare gave a terse nod and kept her focus on his hands. Jack slowly unzipped the bag, then a smaller pocket inside. He reached in and pulled out an old ID card Stan had given him. Standing, he held it out to her.

"Stan said to tell you thanks for the pass. He wouldn't have made it without you."

Clare reached forward slowly and took the card. She stared at it and then back up at Jack. "But your hair. Your eyes. I met his little boy and I know that can't be changed. Where did you get this?"

"Hair can be dyed. And look." Reaching up, he removed one of his contacts. When Clare saw his naked eye, she gasped, then extended her hand and touched his face with her fingertips.

"You really are little Jack," she whispered. She stared at him for a moment, then seemed to come to her senses. She gave her head a tiny shake and blinked a couple of times, then took a few steps away from the door, beckoning with her hand. "Come in, come in."

Jack hesitated. "Is anyone else here?"

"No." She shook her head. "I live alone." She stepped through a doorway on the far side of the room. "I was just making some tea. Would you like some?"

Jack followed her into the kitchen. Apparently, Clare didn't want for much. While her house didn't seem to be very big, her kitchen was well-appointed and sparkling with all the latest appliances. At least it looked that way to Jack. It was the nicest kitchen he had ever seen. Clare dispensed hot water from a spigot by the sink, set it next to a second cup, and dunked a tea bag into each.

"Have a seat." She motioned to a table and chairs. "I hope you don't mind. Sometimes it seems more relaxing to sit in the kitchen than the living room."

Jack smiled. In spite of being visibly rattled, he found Clare's attempt to bring some sense of normalcy to the situation comforting. Soon she joined him at the table.

"Now," she wrapped both hands around her steaming cup. "Tell me your story. What's Stan up to?"

Jack collected his thoughts, reluctant to tell her everything. "Well, he's still working on a gen therapy."

Clare raised her eyebrows. "Really? He's still working on that?"

Jack nodded. "He's almost figured it all out. There's just one piece of the formula missing."

Clare grew serious. "That's why you're here, isn't it?"

"We've been working together. I need to help find the answer."

Clare whooshed out a breath and turned her head to one side. "Have you talked to anyone else?"

"The first person my dad said to contact was Stein Ingerstrom. I couldn't find him so I came here."

Clare looked at him in alarm. "You went to Stein's old house?"

Jack nodded.

"What happened?"

Jack related how he had gone to address Stan had given him and found the old woman who basically shut the door in his face.

"That's not good." Clare ran a hand through her hair. "You're going to have to hurry. We worked with Stein. After your father left, the police arrested him. He refused to talk. He wouldn't betray either your father or the Underground."

"What happened to him?"

Clare looked into his eyes and sighed. "He was executed."

A chill ran through Jack when he thought of his interrogation. His fate probably would have been the same as Stein's had he not escaped.

"It wasn't any secret what happened to him. They like to make an example of those who fall on the wrong side of the law."

"But you're okay, aren't you? They didn't arrest you?"

"No, somehow I escaped. I don't know how." She thought for a moment. "They probably had someone move into Stein's place who sympathizes with the police. It's possible that even now, the old woman has reported you. Whatever you're planning to do, you'll have to hurry. Soon they'll come after you with everything they have. What are you planning?"

"I'm not sure." Jack leaned back. "I don't know if it's best to try to get into the computers or the labs."

"I think your best bet is the lab." Clare chewed on her lip before replying. "I can't do it. They'll be watching me—all the staff, in fact—too closely and they'll know how to find me. You're an outsider. I can tell you how to get in but you'll have to get in and out quickly."

Jack sipped his warm tea.

"I can get you a fake pass. You'll need it. The facilities are at the Ministry offices."

I had been so close and never known it, Jack thought.

Clare gave him further instructions, then pulled on a jacket. "I have to go see about getting you a pass. I don't want to risk using my communicator." She pointed at Jack and said sternly, "You stay here. Since you're wearing a disguise, I assume they're looking for you already. Every time you step outside this house, you run the risk of discovery."

Jack reluctantly agreed even though thoughts of seeing Amber ran through his mind. Their reunion would have to wait.

Clare grabbed her purse and jacket. "I'll be right back," she said and rushed out the door, locking it behind her.

Jack stood in the middle of the room, unsure of what to do next. Never had he thought he'd find himself alone in the house of a woman he had barely met. He thought about testing the communicator but didn't want to risk it malfunctioning and bringing the police to Clare's door. His thoughts ran to his mother. Right about now, she was probably cleaning up the kitchen. He longed to be there, to provide for her, but at least she still had Ethan to watch after her.

He thought of their meager belongings and tattered house and couldn't help but compare it to where he was. Plush, pale tan—almost ivory—carpet covered the floor, on which sat an old fashioned, complementary flowered couch. Three walls were painted a light shade of yellow, and on the fourth, a wooden, built-in bookshelf held books of all types, from chemistry to fiction, both new and old.

Jack lowered himself into an armchair near the bookshelf. He propped his sore leg up onto the generous footstool in front of him and rubbed it gently. Though healing well, it ached after being on his feet all day. He closed his eyes and laid his head back. It seemed he had just closed his eyes, but then with a start he realized Clare was standing next to him, gently shaking his shoulder.

"Wake up, Jack."

Jack opened his eyes, glanced at her, then around the room. His heart skipped a beat at the unfamiliar surroundings, then he remembered where he was and he sighed lightly in relief. He rubbed a hand across his face and turned his groggy attention to Clare. "What time is it?" he mumbled.

"It's about five a.m."

He noticed she wore a different outfit than the one he had seen her in last. He must have been asleep for hours.

"I'm sure you must be exhausted, but you need to get going. I let you sleep as long as I dared. But the longer you wait, the greater chance you have of being discovered." She sat on the nearby couch and leaned forward, elbows on knees. "I have the pass you need to get in. It'd be best if you go just before the offices open. There are always guards on duty and they'll be less likely to stop you if they think you're just an employee arriving early for work. But you'll have to get out before the lab employees show up."

Jack chewed his lip trying to think of how he could work it out.

"Don't worry," Clare reassured him. "I can drop you off and it should only take a few minutes to get what you need." She handed him a small stylus. "This is a data stick. You can transfer the files to it wirelessly and hopefully no one will know the difference should they find it."

He rolled the stick between his fingers. Ingenious, he thought. It looked just like one of the styluses he had used countless times before but they hadn't been data sticks.

"You need to enter the building—I'll show you a back door—turn left, go through the door in front of you and head down the stairs on the other side. The lab will be straight ahead. Scan your pass across the sensor at the right side of the door, and when the light turns green, go in. Head straight down the hallway and go to the third door on the left. Inside you'll find a couple of computers. Any one will do. You know how to transfer the files, right?"

Jack nodded.

"Good." She told him which directory to look for and gave him the main administrative password he would need to complete the transfer. "They shouldn't be able to trace this password back to me." She grinned. "It's not mine." She stood, adjusted her jacket, and slung her purse up onto her shoulder. "After you get the files, you need to get out of there as quickly as possible. I recommend you leave through the front doors because most of the lab techs will arrive through the back door. Hopefully no one will be very early today."

Running over the instructions in his mind, Jack stood and stretched the fatigue from his muscles.

"Got it?" Clare's eyes searched his face.

"Yeah, I think so."

"Come on, then. Let's go. The Ministry offices are across town and if we leave now, we'll get you there just in time."

Clare headed for the door and Jack followed her out, after which she locked the door behind them. A shiny black car sat in the drive next to the house. The

Ashton was probably only a year old, one of the newer models of a still-young company named similarly to one of the old money auto makers that had folded a couple of hundred years before. The new cars held much prestige for those who could afford them. Clare obviously was well paid and he hoped she wouldn't lose it all along with her freedom for helping him.

Clare stepped inside the car and Jack entered from the other side. As they settled in the seats, she grinned over at him. "You like the car, I take it."

Jack could feel his face blush and he ducked his head. He didn't think he'd been that obvious.

Clare programmed the car and it pulled out. Jack took a deep breath. "Won't the police be able to track your car to see who was in the area at the time of the theft?"

"It should be okay." Clare folded her hands in her lap. "Sometimes I go to breakfast at a little restaurant nearby. That's where we're headed now. You can walk the rest of the way from there."

Jack pursed his lips and took a deep breath. She seemed to have it all worked out. Hopefully the rest of the morning would go as planned.

They rode the rest of the way in silence. Gradually the suburbs turned into city, then into places Jack began to recognize. The darkness gave way to glimmers of light in the east, and in the soft light of early morning, they passed a lush green park. The last time he had been here was with his mother. His eyes took in every tree and shrub and his heart ached with a longing to see Eva, to tell her he was okay. *Soon,* he hoped. *Soon.*

Within a few minutes, the car pulled up and parked itself on the street in front of a tiny restaurant nestled in a row of quaint buildings dating back at least a hundred years.

"I know," Clare smiled a crooked grin, "it's a hole in the wall, but they have the best breakfast within two kilometers of the office." She gathered her things together. "I'd ask if you want anything, but..."

Jack returned the smile. "That's okay. I couldn't eat right now anyway."

Clare nodded. "I figured as much. Do you know the way from here?"

Jack opened his mouth to reply but Clare cut him off.

"Oh, right. I forgot, you used to work here." She gave a nervous chuckle, the first indication that she too was on edge.

"All right, then. I guess I'll be off."

Clare turned serious, earnest compassion written on her face. "God go with you, Jack."

"Thank you," he said, wishing he knew the words to adequately describe how grateful he was for all of her help. Then with a deep breath, he stepped out and walked quickly away from the car, not looking back lest he lose his nerve. He couldn't help but think he wasn't cut out for this and he shook his head, recalling all the events that had brought him to this place. How could it be that he was the best one for the job? Then he banished the thoughts from his mind. *Confidence,* he told himself. *I have to focus. Can't lose my nerve now.*

Within ten minutes, Jack arrived at the complex of buildings that comprised the capitol buildings and made his way to the labs. Walking down the sidewalk next to the main lab, the only sound he heard was the tread of his shoes on the sidewalk. The soft-soled shoes were quiet but not silent, and to Jack, his footsteps sounded far too loud on this still morning.

Around the back side of the building, Jack found the door Clare had mentioned. He scanned his pass and the lock clicked. Jack tentatively pulled the door open, bracing himself, half expecting an alarm to sound. But he found nothing inside but the eerie silence of an office devoid of life. Recalling the path Clare had outlined, Jack found the stairs, then the locked door, and he was in. He walked down the hallway, counting the doors on the right. Inside the third door stood a rack of cleaning supplies.

His heart beat faster and he stepped back out into the hall, racking his brain to remember what Clare had said. Wait. Did she say left? Looking back the way he had come, he counted to the third door. He opened it and breathed a sigh of relief. There stood the bank of computers she had mentioned. He quickly seated himself in front of the first one. Just before his fingers touched the keys, he paused. Fingerprints. They'd find his fingerprints on the keys and would discover they were his. He'd had to have them taken when he accepted the job at the Ministry offices. Well, he thought, nothing to be done about it now, and he attacked the keyboard with vigor, anxious to get this done and get out of there.

Within a minute, he found the files. He grinned. It was just like Clare said. A couple of seconds later, the files had been copied to the stylus in his pocket. He put the computer back to sleep and quickly made his retreat. Outside the lab doors, he turned the opposite direction and headed down the hall. Now to find his way out. It should be easy, right?

The farther he walked, the more nervous he became. Where were the stairs? There had to be another set heading up. At the end of the hallway, the only way to go was right. He headed that way and eventually found an elevator. He had hoped for a path less traveled, but this would have to do. Within a minute, the doors opened and he poked the button for the first floor, the next one up. The doors shut and Jack shoved his hands in his pockets, then pulled them out again and crossed his arms. The elevator coasted to a stop and he consciously lowered his arms to his sides, rolling his shoulders in an effort to appear nonchalant. The doors opened and Jack sucked in a breath at what he saw.

Amber. Her jaw dropped and she looked as if she would say something, then she closed her mouth and gulped. Jack ran a hand through his hair and confusion clouded his mind. He stepped out of the elevator and, taking her by the elbow, guided her to the side of the lobby, hopefully out of sight of anyone approaching down the hallways that gently curved away from the elevator in a wide circular path.

"What are you doing here?" he whispered urgently.

Amber's face creased with a stricken look. She looked away and then back again. "J-Jack, I thought you were gone. Out of town."

"Well I'm not. Why are you here?"

"Jack, my parents. They took my parents and said that unless I—"

"Well, well. What have we here?"

Jack closed his eyes at the familiar voice behind him. He released Amber's elbow and slowly turned around.

Robert wore a sneer and a wicked gleam shone in his eyes. "Amber, you never told me you had an accomplice."

"No, it-it's not like that!" She shook her head, panic in her eyes.

"Robert," Jack balled his fists at his side, "let her go. She has nothing to do with this."

"With what, Jack? I didn't think you worked here anymore. There must be a good reason you're here." Jack's half-brother raised an eyebrow and waited for a response.

"Just let her go. I'm the one you want."

"Hm." Robert chewed the inside of his cheek. "Perhaps that's for Amber to decide. I was under the impression that she was working with us now. What do you say, my dear?" He shifted his focus to the young woman. All the color drained from her face and she clutched her black bag in front of her.

She looked at Robert, then to Jack. She bit her lip and tears welled up in her eyes. "Jack, I'm sorry. I have to. They didn't give me a choice," she whispered.

Robert chuckled in triumph and called for a guard. "A very good choice, Amber. I knew you were an intelligent young woman."

A dull pain stabbed his heart and Jack looked at the ground, angry and hurt. Within seconds, a guard appeared.

"If you run a search, I think you'll find this man is wanted by the police."

The guard grunted in surprise, then quickly spun Jack around, cuffing his hands behind his back. Robert took Amber by the elbow and, guiding her down the carpeted hallway, called back over his shoulder, "It's not that good of a disguise, Jack. You could have done better."

Turning his face away, Jack allowed the guard to push him in the other direction, his footsteps heavy and his heart broken.

Chapter 16

S *lam!*

The doors to the prisoner transport truck banged shut and Jack's thoughts went back to the day he was first arrested. He had left everything at Clare's except the stylus and the security pass, both of which the officers had taken a few minutes before. At least they didn't have anything else—like the new communicators he had developed, he thought.

Jack felt numb, barely aware of the bouncing and turns, not caring where he was going. Here he was, back where he started on this horrendous journey—and he had nothing to show for it. He tried to push away thoughts of Amber, but with no success. He couldn't get the image of her face out of his mind. How could she betray him after all they had been through?

The van jerked to a stop and the doors creaked open.

"Let's go," a burly guard motioned.

Jack vaguely noted that disguised as a human, he was treated better than the typical gen, even though he was a prisoner. Once inside the facility, the guard pushed him up to the receiving desk. The clerk on duty, a man with a slight build, peered up and examined the two.

"What'cha got?" the man said in a nasally voice.

"Father Robert Bradley said to bring this one in," the guard growled.

Jack laid his hand on the hand scanner as directed, and with a click, it recorded his prints. In a few seconds, the results popped up on the clerk's screen.

"No kidding," the man squeaked. "This one's wanted by Intelligence."

The guard scanned Jack's face with raised brows. "We got ourselves a good one, huh? Do we process him as usual?"

The clerk shook his head. "No, just frisk him. Make sure he's not carrying anything else. They want him isolated as soon as possible." The clerk gave the instructions as to where to lock Jack up, and before long, Jack found himself in the same cell where his incarceration had first begun. With a sense of *déjà vu*, he slid to the floor, back to the wall, and awaited his fate.

After a time, a guard arrived and escorted him to an interrogation room. After maybe another hour, the door opened and Robert walked in, followed by a guard.

"Hold his head," Robert instructed the guard. The guard grabbed Jack's head in a vise grip and tilted it back. Robert leaned over and peered into Jack's eyes. "Mm-hm. I thought so." He held Jack's right eyelid open and plucked the contact from his eye. Jack didn't dare stir, afraid to incur damage to his eye. Holding the other eye open, Robert removed that contact as well. He rolled them between his fingers and dropped them on the table like pieces of lint.

The guard let go and Jack turned his head to glare at the man. When the guard caught a glimpse of Jack's golden eyes, he froze, but only for a second. Then a hard look overcame his face and he snorted. "Figures," he muttered.

Father Robert threw the stylus and security pass on the table and then took a seat across from Jack.

"You know, Jack, I have to say that I was really surprised to see you at the Ministry offices." He fingered the pass, flipping the rigid card around in his hands. "I see how you got in. But to get one of these," he tossed it onto the table, "you would need to have had help." Robert glared deep into Jack's eyes. "Who was it, Jack? Who else did you drag into this little scheme of yours?"

Jack simply returned the glare.

Robert shook his head. "Always so stubborn." He paused. "At least Amber has chosen the right path."

At the mention of his friend, Jack clamped his jaw even tighter in an effort to not say what he was thinking. How could Robert have turned Amber so easily? Then he remembered what she had started to say and he could keep silent no longer.

"What did you do? Did you do something to her parents?"

The corners of the priest's mouth turned up in a slight smile. "Her parents? No, they just encouraged her to be reasonable."

Jack shook his head. Robert always had a way of twisting the truth until it came out in such a way that would benefit him.

"What about this, Jack?" He picked up the stylus. "I find it hard to believe you'd be carrying a stylus and no computer. You always had some old piece of junk tablet, didn't you?"

Jack racked his brain for something to say that wouldn't give away the stylus' true purpose, but came up with nothing. He wished he were better at this kind of thing. No matter how many interrogations he'd been through at this point, they still weren't easy for him. *You'd think I would have learned something by now,* he thought wryly.

"I suppose you have some kind of files on here or something. Hm?"

Jack looked down and tried not to let the dismay show on his face.

Robert chuckled. "I thought so. You've always been so easy to read, Jack. You must have inherited that from your dad. You gens just aren't very complicated, are you?"

Jack took a deep breath. Not this again. Robert had learned early on how to poke through Jack's armor in just the right places until he became angry.

"Dumb as tree posts, actually. We didn't build you for brains, you know."

Try as he might, Jack couldn't contain his anger any longer. Arms still secured behind him, Jack lunged to his feet. Maybe if he could tip the table over with his legs...but the guard grabbed his shoulders and slammed him back down into the chair.

Robert leaned back, hands off the table, mock surprise on his face. "Now, now, Jack. Don't lose your temper. I'm just telling the truth. I wouldn't lie to you. I'm a priest and the Church frowns on that kind of thing." He rose to his feet. "Well, it looks like I'm not going to get anything from you for now." He scooped up Jack's security card and stylus. "I'll just have these checked out and see what we find. I'll be back later and we can talk again." As he passed the guard at the door, he instructed, "Put him back in his cell. No one talks to him but me. Got it?"

"Yes, Father," the guard responded crisply, his voice all business. But no sooner had the priest left than he turned to Jack with a sneer. "Get up. Time to take you back to your guest quarters." He chuckled at his own lame joke.

Jack stood and walked to the door. The guard shoved him forward with a prod from his billy club. "We don't take kindly to those that don't know their place...*gen*." He jabbed Jack in the back again, hard enough this time that he stumbled a stutter step. The guard shoved Jack back into his cell and slammed the door.

"Wait," Jack called out. "Can I get these cuffs off? I have to go." He tipped his head toward the metal toilet in the corner.

With a scowl, the guard unlocked the door. "Bah. Nothing worse than having to clean up after a gen and the warden'd have my head if he found the mess. Otherwise I wouldn't bother." He unlocked the cuffs, then stepped back out and pulled the barred door shut behind him with a clang.

Jack didn't see the guard again until later that night when he delivered a meager sandwich, the contents of which were unidentifiable and tasted like cardboard.

The next day, the guard took him to the interrogation room once again. After what had to be a half hour or so, Robert arrived, sat, and leaned back in the chair across from Jack, one hand on the table. "You may go." He waved off the guard and waited until he was alone with Jack before speaking.

"You know, Jack, you're in a world of trouble." He waited, seemingly for a response, but Jack steeled himself, determined not to give Robert the satisfaction of a reaction once again. "We found the files on your little stick." He rubbed his jaw with his hand. "That's the second strike against you and...this constitutes an act of treason. You know that carries the death penalty, don't you?"

Though his heart beat rapidly, Jack tried his best to look bored. At that point, he had nothing to live for anyways. Amber was gone and he'd never be able to help his mom again. *Unless, just maybe you could find a way out...* Jack shook himself. Where did those thoughts come from? Suddenly, Eva sprang to mind and a spark flared inside. She needed him. True, Ethan was there, but the wages a hard-labor gen made was barely enough to subsist on. They'd always needed his income to survive. He couldn't give up now!

Jack glanced around the room, then focused on his half-brother.

"I want to show you something." Robert reached into a pocket inside his jacket and pulled out a vial of clear liquid. He leaned forward, elbows on the table, and rolled the vial in his hands. "Do you know what this is, Jack?" With a wicked gleam in his eye, the priest continued. "This is what is going to kill you."

Under the table, Jack rubbed sweaty palms on his pants legs.

"You came so close, Jack." Robert inspected the solution, his voice a reverential quiet. "You see, this is what is commonly used for lethal injections. But what most people don't know," he leaned forward in a mock conspiratorial whisper, "is the drug that kills is also the one that heals."

Confused, Jack's mind raced to put the pieces together.

"In massive doses, the drug is fatal. It just scrambles your DNA until the body can't live. It can be fairly painful I hear. But," he paused, forefinger in the air, "if used in the proper proportion—for instance, a vial just like this—it will mend one's DNA, piecing back together the parts that haven't been connected. Say, those parts that open the door for one's soul to reside."

Jack looked at the vial in a new light. This was what they had been seeking for years and it had been right in front of them all along. He moistened his lips with the tip of his tongue.

"Isn't this what your father has been trying to develop out in the desert all these years?"

Jack felt his eyes go wide.

"That's right. We know about Stan. We know he has a lab out there somewhere and we were hoping you could show us where it is. This is your last chance to accomplish some good in your miserable, short life."

"You'll just let me walk away if I agree to show you where the lab is?" Jack asked skeptically.

"Oh, that won't pardon the charges of treason, if that's what you're asking." He adjusted the sleeves of his jacket, tugging them down farther over his wrist, leaving the vial on the table. "It will, however, ensure that we'll leave Eva and Ethan out of this. But if you refuse, we may have to bring them in for, um, let's call it 'questioning.'"

Jack's mind raced. Maybe there was some way he could change this to his advantage.

"In fact," Robert tipped his head and looked toward the door, "I think Amber's coming in to try and talk some sense into you. Of course, I'd hate to think what would happen to her as well if you refuse." Robert stood. "Tell you what. I'm going to leave that vial right there on the table. That way you can stare your destiny in the face. It's your choice, Jack." He walked to the door. "Take it if you want, but there's nowhere for you to hide and you can't take it out of this room without being caught. All you can do is swallow it...and I don't recommend that."

The door clicked shut behind Robert and Jack sat, hands on the table, palms down, and looked at the vial. Robert was right. There was no way he'd ever get it out of this room, much less the station. His mind raced. If only he could get this back to Stan. Get it out of Robert's hands.

Within a few minutes, the door opened, but Jack didn't look up, expecting it to be Robert.

Instead, a soft voice penetrated the silence. "Jack?"

He looked cautiously toward the voice, not wanting to believe his ears. Amber slipped in and closed the door behind her. She wore little make-up, her face pale, hair straight and flat. Dark circles under bloodshot eyes made Jack wonder if she'd been crying. But still stinging from her betrayal, he didn't move or say a word, even though it felt as if a rock fell into his stomach the moment he saw her. He still loved her, no matter how much it hurt—or how angry he was.

Amber tentatively stepped farther into the room and her eyes flitted from Jack to the vial and back again. Looking at Jack, she bit her lip.

"What are you doing here?" he said tersely.

Amber squared her shoulders, chin held up resolutely. "What are *you* doing here? Better yet, what were you doing at the Ministry offices?"

"Trying to help my friends—not betray them."

Amber closed her eyes for a moment, took a deep breath, and then refocused on Jack. "Jack, you don't understand."

"Or do I?" he snapped. "I saw you with my own eyes. You willingly came to meet my brother and then turned me over to him. Who told you I was going to be there?"

Amber's eyebrows shot up at Jack's accusation. "I didn't know you were going to be there."

Jack sat back, arms folded. "So why were you there?"

"I..." she faltered and looked at the ground, "came to talk to Robert. He demanded I come."

"Really." It was more of a statement than a question. "And what could he possibly hold over your head to make you obey so easily?"

Amber looked deep into his eyes. "My parents."

A tiny crack formed in Jack's resolution to be angry with her. "What do you mean 'my parents?'"

Her reply was soft and low. "They took my parents."

To that, Jack had no response. Could it be she was telling the truth? "So...the question remains. Why are you here? In this room, talking to me?"

The gentle smell of floral spray filled the room and tugged at Jack's heartstrings, reminding him of better days, but he steeled himself, reminding himself of her betrayal.

She coughed into her nearly closed fist. "I'm supposed to convince you to help them." After she said that, her shoulders slumped and she looked at the ground as if a weight had rolled off her shoulders, her defiance melted into sadness.

"So it's true. You didn't know I was there." Jack's hard resolve crumbled and he looked at her in a new light. "They still have your parents, don't they?"

Amber jerked a nod.

Jack sat in thought for a moment, a plan beginning to form in his mind. "You know, you don't have to do this."

"But I do. Robert tells me he's bringing in your mom for questioning."

Jack let out a deep sigh and looked away. Was there no end to the man's cruelty? Didn't he care that Eva was his mother too? Surely it was just a threat. "Amber..." She looked away. "Amber. Listen to me," he commanded firmly. "Robert's bark is worse than his bite. I need your help."

Amber shook her head vehemently. "No, I can't."

"Yes, you can," he whispered forcefully. He leaned forward. "Try to convince me, just like they want you to," he whispered, throwing a quick glance up to a camera watching their every move.

Amber paused, chewing the inside of her cheek. Then realization glimmered in her eye. She straightened her back and glared at him. "No, Jack. You don't have a choice. I don't have a choice. You have to do what they say."

Hope sprang up in Jack's heart. Maybe this was going to work. He cast a glance to the table, near the vial, and then back up at Amber, silently begging her to understand. She barely nodded once. "Why?" he spat back, feigning the anger that until a few moments ago had been real.

"Because they have all the power. We don't. If nothing else, think of your mom." Amber leaned both hands on the table. "Think about it, Jack. You don't have long to decide."

Jack clenched his jaw and looked away, trying to appear angry and frustrated.

When Amber stood back up, she ran her hand over the vial, scooped it up into her hand and turned toward the door. Hiking her bag up onto her shoulder, she slid the vial inside. She jerked the door open and took one step outside the room, then stopped dead in her tracks. Robert stood just outside, lips pressed into a thin line.

"Amber, Amber." He peered down at her. "Did you really think you could get away with that little trick? You know, I'm very disappointed in you. Didn't you think we'd be watching?" He held out his hand. "Now give it back."

With a panicked glance, she darted a glance up at the priest, then down the hallway, and she bolted, running for the far doorway.

Robert grabbed for her arm but came up short. "Stop her!" he yelled. Within moments, a shot rang out. Jack rushed to the doorway of the interrogation room. Another guard hurried to block the way. The burly man firmly held him back, but not before Jack got a glimpse of the scene outside. Amber lay crumpled on her side, a puddle of blood forming under her body.

"Idiot!" Robert yelled. "I said stop her. Not kill her!" He rushed to Amber's side and rolled her onto her back. "Get a medic!"

Jack struggled against the guard in an effort to reach her, but without success. With barely a glance in his direction, Robert snapped, "Get him out of here."

The guard grabbed Jack's arm and twisted it behind his back. "Let's go!" he growled through clenched teeth and forced him down the hallway in the opposite direction.

Agony swelled up inside Jack and he wrestled against the guard's painful iron grip. Stumbling forward, he forced a look over his shoulder. "Amber!" he choked in a broken voice.

They reached the end of the hallway and turned the corner to find two medical personnel rushing to the scene, gear in hand. Too late to avoid a collision, the four went down in a tangle of arms and legs. Jack wiggled his way free of the pile-up and ran. Behind him, he heard the deep voice of the guard.

"Get off me!"

Amid the clatter and grunts of disentanglement and with a mouthful of oaths, Jack heard the man begin the pursuit. Jack flew around a corner, looking frantically for somewhere to hide. He wrenched on the handle of the first door he came to. Locked. He tried another. Also locked. He rounded another corner and, with a sinking feeling, tried the next door. But to his surprise, the knob turned. He pushed his way through the doorway into the dark of an abandoned office. He latched the door behind him as quietly as he could, then felt his way through the dark until he found the desk he had seen before the door shut. Slipping around to the back side, he slid under the desk and crouched there waiting. Within seconds, he heard heavy footsteps pounding down the hallway. They paused outside the door to the office and the man threw the door open. After only a few moments, the light from the hallway faded as he pulled the door shut. Before it latched, Jack heard him mutter something about losing his head. He had to grin.

Sitting alone in the dark, Jack took a deep breath. His mind flew back to the sight of Amber laying on the floor, blood draining from her body. He closed his eyes and forced down the grief that threatened to rise. There was nothing he could do now.

Once it grew quiet outside, Jack crept to the door, cracked it open, and peeked out. With no one in sight, Jack sprinted for the exit, leaving a piece of his heart behind with Amber.

Voices ahead echoed down the hallway. Jack slowed just before two people came into view, a uniformed officer and a woman in street clothes. Jack cast his eyes down and to the side in an effort to hide his golden eyes and sighed in relief when they passed by, engrossed in their conversation.

He passed a few others without incident. *I guess that's the advantage to being taken by the secret police,* he thought. *No one knows I'm here.*

Chapter 17

F ootsore and weary, Jack followed the sidewalk, head down, hands in his pockets. Walking for hours until dark, staying off the main roads, opting instead for side streets. So far, it seemed to be working. And yet, the victory—however minuscule—rang hollow.

He scrubbed his hands on his face to wipe away the sight of Amber crumpled on the floor, bleeding and still. Maybe if he had stayed.... He groaned. No. There was nothing he could have done, even if he'd stayed.

He jammed his hands back in his pockets and ducked down the driveway between Clare's house and her neighbor's and rapped softly.

The curtains on one side fluttered, and within seconds, the door opened. Clare tugged him inside, quickly shutting the door behind him.

"What happened?" she hissed. "When I got there, agents were crawling all over the place."

"I got in just fine." Jack released a deep breath of air. "Found the files and downloaded them. But on the way out..." He related the details of finding Amber, of his capture, then escape. He avoided the part about his true feelings for Amber. And his now-broken heart.

"So now you have nothing?" Clare demanded. "I'm sorry but you can't stay here. It's too dangerous." Her voice resounded with resignation.

Jack nodded. "I just came for my things." He followed her out of the little enclosed porch and into the kitchen.

"Wait here." She disappeared down a hallway.

Jack waited awkwardly in the center of the pristine kitchen until she returned. "I hid your things in case the police came." She gently laid his bag on the table. "I'm sorry. I didn't mean to sound insensitive. It's just that when I saw the agents at the lab, I got worried. Wondered what happened to you. I figured it couldn't be good." She rummaged around in the refrigerator. "Do you need anything to eat?"

"Please," Jack said, realizing that he couldn't remember when he'd eaten last. He sat at the kitchen table and soon Clare placed a plate in front of him with cheese, chopped vegetables, and a folded tortilla.

"I don't eat meat," she said, layering the ingredients onto another floury disc, then bagged it and tucked it into his pack. "There's one for later." She sat down across from him. "Where are you gonna go?"

"I'd rather not say. The less you know..."

She nodded. "I know, the safer I'll be. You sound just like your father."

Jack choked a swallow down. ...*just like your father.* The similarity of their situations was too close to ignore. *At least Stan escaped with something in hand. I, on the other hand, have nothing to show for my trouble.* He sipped from a water glass, trying to hide all emotion.

"Hey," Clare squeezed his hand. "I'm sorry about your friend. Maybe she'll be okay."

Jack looked at her with disbelief. "She was bleeding and unresponsive."

"But she wasn't dead, right?" Clare shrugged. "I'm no medical expert, but it's possible, right?"

Jack finished the veggie burrito, then stood and settled a strap of his backpack on his shoulder. "Um, thanks for...everything." She had tried to do so much for him and he didn't know where to start.

"Tell Stan hi for me, okay?"

Jack nodded. "Thanks again."

"It's the least I could do after all your dad did to protect me."

Jack strode away, trying to project the confidence he didn't feel.

———————◀●▶———————

Jack looked from one side to the other, trying to make sure he was alone. The park was basically deserted—as well it should be at this time of night. He stepped into a dark grove of trees, just in case anyone happened by, and fished the communicator out of his pack. He slipped it into his ear and spoke the code that would connect him to his father. Shortly, Stan picked up.

"Jack? Is that you?"

"Yeah, it's me." Upon hearing his dad's voice, fatigue washed over him and he was struck with the hopelessness of his situation.

"Where are you?" Stan's voice came through anxious. "When I didn't hear from you I got worried. You didn't run into any trouble, did you?"

"Actually, yes, I did."

His dad was silent on the other end as he waited for Jack to continue.

He took a deep breath. "I got in," Jack heard Stan suck in a quick breath on the other end of the line, "but I got caught. I ran into Robert, who turned me over to the police, but then I escaped. It's a long story."

"I guess so," his dad said slowly.

"I'd rather not say anything more here. I'm glad this thing works," Jack said, "but I don't want to say anything else in case it's not secure."

"I understand," came the reply. "Now what?"

"I need to find a way back."

"Uh-huh. I don't suppose you have anything to bring with you?"

Jack understood perfectly well the meaning in his father's cryptic question. "No. Not physically. I do know something though. I need to get back. Maybe you can use the info." He paused. "Do you know how I can find my way?"

"Actually, no. We're not expecting anyone for a while. Can't you plan it on your end?"

Jack sighed. "All right. I'll see what I can do. I'd better go. We need to cut this short."

"Got it. Try to get here as soon as you can."

Jack agreed and clicked the communicator off. He ran his fingers through his hair in frustration. He hadn't known if Stan could help him but it was worth a try. Jack could only think of one more option. Time to give it a shot.

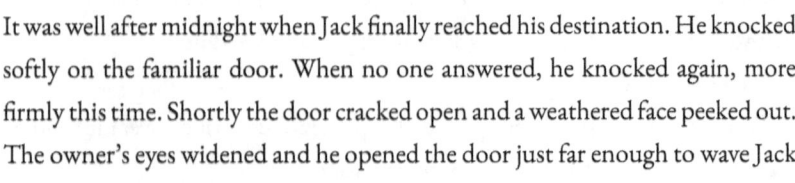

It was well after midnight when Jack finally reached his destination. He knocked softly on the familiar door. When no one answered, he knocked again, more firmly this time. Shortly the door cracked open and a weathered face peeked out. The owner's eyes widened and he opened the door just far enough to wave Jack in and then shut the door behind him.

"Hello, Pedro."

Pedro stood silent in apparent surprise, mouth agape, for a few moments before speaking. "Jack?"

Jack motioned to the tattered sofa. "Mind if I sit down?"

Pedro shook himself. "Uh, yes, sit. Please." He scurried to a nearby chair and plopped down, eyes focused on his guest.

In spite of his fatigue, Jack grinned. "It's good to see you again."

"Yes, well, hm..." Pedro stammered. "What are you doing here?" he finally blurted out.

Jack placed his backpack on the floor and leaned forward, elbows on knees. "I need a place to stay. At least until I can find a ride out to the desert."

Pedro leaned back and rubbed the day-old whiskers on his chin. He intently studied Jack's face, making him wonder what was going through the old man's mind. Finally he jerked a nod. "That's fine. You found what you were looking for?"

Jack nodded. "Now I need to get back."

Pedro nodded. He'd been part of the secret organization long enough that Jack didn't expect him to pry for further information. "I'm sure we can arrange that. For now, you look exhausted. Why don't you rest here," he pointed to the sofa, "and I'll see what I can do in the morning."

"Thank you. I appreciate it."

Pedro moved toward the kitchen. "D'you want any water?"

"No, I'm fine." Jack's leg ached and his feet were sore. He just wanted to lay down. He never heard Pedro reply. Within moments of closing his eyes, he had fallen into the slumber of an exhausted man.

The click of the front door jolted Jack from his sleep. He sat up, heart pounding, and for a moment couldn't remember where he was. Disoriented, he stared at the two men standing just inside the door. Within a moment, everything came rushing back and with relief he recognized the friendly faces.

Behind Pedro stood Joshua, hands on his hips.

"Look at you." Joshua shook his head. "Pedro told me you were here and I thought I'd better come see how your leg was doing."

Jack threw a concerned glance at Pedro.

"Don't worry." Pedro waved his hands in protest. "I arranged for your ride and then stopped to get Joshua. You've been sleeping for hours. After the way you looked last night, I wanted to make sure you're okay."

"That bad, huh?" Jack scrubbed his hands on his face.

"How are you feeling?" Joshua's voice had adopted that clinical tone used by almost all medical professionals worldwide.

"Terrible," Jack confided. "But I'm okay. Just tired."

"How's the leg?"

Jack sat on the edge of the couch and stretched it out straight. He flexed the muscle in his thigh, then tried not to wince at the pain that followed. "It's okay. The wound has healed well. It just seems to tire easily."

Joshua nodded. "That's to be expected." He rubbed the back of his neck. "Sounds about normal. How's the rest of you? You didn't get yourself shot again, did you?" He settled down in the side chair, a wry grin stretched across his face. Pedro disappeared down the hallway.

Jack shook his head and leaned back. "Not hardly." After the past several days, it was a relief to just sit with a friend in a safe place and relax. And yet, Jack knew in the back of his mind that all too soon, he'd be out there on the street again, running for his life.

But then again, they didn't have anything to say, anything to talk about. Everything that came to mind was something he didn't dare tell Joshua. And Joshua didn't pry. It hadn't taken him long to learn the rules of the underground. The less said, the better.

Joshua broke the silence. "Will you be here long?"

"Nah. I'll be leaving as soon as Pedro says it's time."

"And that time would be in about two hours." Pedro carried a handful of papers over to his little desk.

Once again, Jack's thoughts drifted back to Amber and the unending ache he felt inside. Sure, Clare had suggested that Amber might still be alive, but he found that hard to believe. However, looking over at Joshua, he thought he might as well ask.

"Joshua," he crossed his arms over his chest, "let me ask you something."

Joshua raised his eyebrows inquisitively and waited.

"If someone was shot and fell to the ground bleeding profusely, what are the chances they would survive?"

Joshua leaned back and interlocked his fingers behind his head. "Well, it all depends on where they were shot and how quickly they were treated. Why do you ask?"

"Just curious. I heard of a similar instance recently and it made me wonder."

Joshua looked at him doubtfully. "And this 'instance' you heard of, do you know where the person was shot?"

Jack looked at the ground and then back up. "I'm not sure. In the torso somewhere, I think."

Joshua grimaced. "That could be bad."

"You said 'could.' Does that mean there's a chance they could survive even though they lost a lot of blood quickly?"

Joshua nodded. "Not likely, but, yes, it's possible."

Jack lapsed into silence. Ever since Clare had raised the possibility that maybe Amber hadn't died, he had not been able to leave the thought alone. *No*, he told himself. *She's gone—I just know it.* He rubbed one hand over his eyes. So much blood.

"Hey, are you okay?"

Jack looked up and forced a smile. "Yeah, thanks. I'm fine. Just tired."

Joshua continued to watch him, a slight frown across his forehead. After a minute or so of awkward silence, he stood. "Well, I should get going." He reached out and shook hands with Jack. "I just wanted to check up on you and make sure you're okay. I've been praying for you, Jack."

"Thanks." Jack stood as well. "I really appreciate that. Thanks for coming by." He clapped Joshua on the shoulder. "I'm sure I'll be back sooner or later."

"Sounds good. Okay, then. Take care." Joshua let himself out.

After the door clicked shut, Pedro said, "He is a good man, this Joshua."

Pedro's comment brought a smile to Jack's face. "Yes, yes, he is."

❖

Within a couple of hours, Jack's ride arrived to pick him up. This time, the same older man he had ridden with before was the one to ferry him to the little desert town. When they reached Maria's, the old man spoke before Jack got out.

"Young man," he said, "you need to know something. There's a reason for everything. The Creator knows you. He's watching you, guiding you, using you to accomplish his purposes. He loves you."

Jack stared at the man for a second, then thanked him politely and got out. But inside, his thoughts were troubled. *Yeah, right. If the Creator of everything loves me, he sure has a strange way of showing it.*

Though surprised to see him, Jose agreed to drive him out to the lab. The day was already heating up and the sun was hot. Jack wished he had a hat to shield his eyes from the bright sunlight.

The truck lurched as it plunged through another pothole in its race across the desert floor. Jack wondered if Jose purposefully aimed for every dip and bump in front of them, but then again, the narrow trail they followed didn't leave much room for negotiation.

After another hour or so, the familiar landscape came into view and they pulled up to the loading bay door nestled into the hillside. Jack looked forward to a good rest, free from the fear of looking over his shoulder, even if only for a little while.

The truck pulled into the cool of the garage and the door closed behind them, shutting out the harsh sunlight. The vehicle slowed to a stop and Jack hauled himself out and slung his backpack over his shoulder. It seemed every muscle in his body ached. With effort, he tugged the hall door open and stepped into the artificially lit passageway. He made his way to the lab where Stan typically could be found. As usual, Stan was working, hunched over the workbench. Jack rapped on the door and Stan glanced up, a smile brightening his face when he saw his son. Stan held up his hand, fingers splayed, signifying he would be out in five minutes. Jack nodded and motioned that he'd be farther down the hall. Although it was only mid-afternoon, with any luck he'd find some kind of food available in the kitchen.

And he did. An apple and a nutrition bar would tide him over until dinner. Dumping his pack on one of the small tables, he plopped down in a chair and bit into the piece of fruit. With a satisfying crunch, juice trickled into his mouth and he licked the red skin before it dripped onto the table.

He was just nibbling the rest of the fruit from around the core when Stan walked in.

"Hey, Jack! You made it." He clapped his son on the shoulder and sat down across from him. "How'd the trip go?"

Jack swallowed the last of the fruit and tossed the core into a nearby trash can. "Not good, unfortunately."

"You must be exhausted," Stan said calmly, but Jack could see eagerness in his eyes, probably anticipating whatever information Jack brought with him. Jack hoped he wouldn't be disappointed. He didn't have much to offer.

"Yeah." He unwrapped the nutrition bar and took a bite. The chewy oats mixed with sweet honey tasted so good that Jack hoped one portion would be enough for now.

Stan tapped his fingers on the table, then leaned forward and folded his hands in front of him. "Want to talk about it?"

Jack sighed and his mind took a quick survey of his recent experiences. Much of it he would keep to himself. At least for now. Meanwhile, he might as well give Stan the information he was obviously anticipating.

He told his father of his arrest and how Robert had threatened him with execution.

"But get this," Jack said. "Robert told me that the solution they use for lethal injections...," he paused for dramatic effect, "is the same solution that will repair one's DNA and grant a soul."

Stan's jaw dropped as he just stared at Jack and considered the implications.

"I'm sorry I couldn't bring a sample with me. I tried..." Jack's voice trailed off. He wasn't ready to talk about the events surrounding his leaving it behind. About Amber.

And yet, as he spoke, a smile broke out across Stan's face. "That's okay, Jack. I know you did your best. The solution would have been helpful, but knowing its ingredients might be enough."

Jack tipped his chair back and looked away. Amber had tried so hard to get him that sample. He hoped she hadn't given her life for nothing.

"You okay?" Stan regarded him with a worried expression.

"Yeah." Jack let the front legs of the chair drop back to the floor. "I just need some time alone for a bit."

Stan nodded. "I see. Well, I suppose that's understandable. I'll get back to work then and see what I can do with this new information." Before disappearing through the doorway, he looked back over his shoulder. "Thank you, Jack. And good job on the communicator." And with a smile, he passed from view.

Jack was glad the devices worked, but at this point, the success paled in comparison to everything else running through his tortured mind. He made his way to the bunk room and stretched out on one of the beds. Resting one arm across closed eyes, he tried to push the painful thoughts aside and willed himself to sleep. It wasn't long before everything faded into a restless slumber.

"Eh, Jack."

A nudge on Jack's arm jogged him from sleep. He blinked several times, squinting against the light, eyes somewhat focused on the face that belonged to the voice. Jack thought he remembered the man had something to do with cars. "Wha..."

"You hungry?"

That's right, Jack remembered. *This is the mechanic. At the Mojave lab. Right...that's where I am.* Jack groaned and sat up painfully. "What time is it?"

"Ees six o'clock. Señor Stan said you might want dinner."

"Yeah." Jack scrubbed his eyes with the heels of his hands. "I'm starved. Thanks."

With a jerk of his head, the man disappeared down the hallway. What was his name? Jack racked his brain. It'd come to him eventually. He took a deep breath and tried to shake the sleep fog from his brain.

Hungrier than an ox, Jack sat in a corner of the dining room and shoveled down a healthy portion of some kind of ham and potato hash. As long as it tasted half good, he didn't really care what it was. He was too hungry to be picky. On his way out, Jack acknowledged those who greeted him with a wave, then stumbled back to bed and crashed.

The next thing he knew, it was morning. Not that he could see the sun in this underground facility, but according to the clock it was morning. Realizing he'd slept in his clothes, he made a half-hearted attempt to smooth out the rumples. Still numb and exhausted, he went through the motions of brushing his teeth. An aching knot of fatigue lay in the back of his head and he wondered if he should go back to bed. But he wasn't sleepy.

He shuffled down to The Cave and retrieved his handheld. It flashed to life and Jack stared at the screen, trying to remember what he had been planning to do. Whatever it was, he thought, must not've been important. With a sigh, he turned it off and poked around at the equipment on his workbench. He'd wanted to organize it better for some time, but by the time he'd finished rearranging the tools, they ended up pretty much back where they started.

Maybe some fresh air would help, he thought. Outside, he walked a short distance to nearby crags and climbed up just far enough to see down the culvert a ways. He hugged his knees to his chest and, resting forehead to knees, his mind traveled back. He knew down inside he should be busy working on a new project, but nothing came to mind. And his mind kept replaying images from his recent experiences again and again. *Capture. Amber. Blood. Failure. Amber. Blood. Failure. It should have been me bleeding out on the floor, not her.*

He groaned, feeling the need to somehow make restitution for her death. But to whom could he apologize? *If there is a God up there,* he thought, *please help me make it right.*

Then, in his fog, he thought of Amber's parents. Surely Robert had been bluffing—or were they really in custody? If not, they likely knew by now that Amber had been shot, but he wondered if they knew the truth. Or had they been fed a lie about how she died? Suddenly, he knew he had to find out, to set the story straight if need be.

And yet, he felt like a yo-yo going from the city to the lab and back again. Stan didn't know about Amber and Jack wasn't ready to share. It was still too painful to talk about. He chewed on his lip, trying to think of some good reason he could go back. Maybe to fetch supplies? *That might work,* he thought.

As the morning passed, the sun grew hotter and hotter until it began to beat down on his back. When he broke out into a sweat, Jack pushed up to his feet and returned to the facility. He tugged on the door handle, already hot to the touch. He stepped inside and the cool air washed over him, instant relief from the heat of the harsh sun.

He wandered aimlessly down the hall until he stopped outside the window looking into the lab. He snorted a half-grin. Stan, hunched over the counter in the lab, surrounded by equipment Jack could only guess at the purpose of. His father glanced up and Jack knew that had he been able to see under the mask, he would find a wide smile stretched across his face. As it was, the corners of his eyes crinkled and the brightness in his eyes let Jack know something was going well. The scientist gestured for Jack to enter.

Jack selected a disposable gown and face mask from the rack outside and put them on. Once inside, he eased the door shut with a click.

"I'm glad you're here," came his dad's muffled voice from under his mask. "I want to show you something." His voice was bright with excitement. "See this?" Stan pointed at a set of angular images on a computer screen in front of him.

"Uh-huh." To Jack it looked like a jumble of blobs and sticks.

"This is what happens when I dilute the formula to a lesser strength. I don't know why I didn't think of this before. It's so elementary."

"O...kay..."

Stan looked straight into Jack's eyes. "It works, Jack. It completes the tail end of the DNA, pieces it together—exactly what I've been trying to do."

Stan turned back to the screen and moved the camera's focus to another part of the dish. "I have to get this to the city," he muttered. "Since Clare's still there, maybe she could test it. I don't want to test it on humans until I know it can achieve the desired effect. And I don't have the equipment here to do that."

Jack had to grin. "I'll take it."

His dad nodded. "I was hoping you'd say that. You're the only one who knows where to find her." After a pause, he continued. "First I need to stabilize it and prepare it for transport. Can you leave tomorrow?"

Jack agreed. *Maybe there is a God smiling down on me after all,* he thought.

The next morning, he tucked the items in his pack that he'd need. A change of clothes and nutrition bars mostly. His dad gently handed him a black box just larger than the size of his hand and about five centimeters thick.

"This is padded pretty well. There are two samples inside, just in case something happens to one, but still—please be careful. If I'm not mistaken, each vial should equal one dosage for a gen."

Jack placed it in the pack, carefully wedging it between his spare shirt and pants.

"I haven't written anything down, just in case it falls into the wrong hands, but I pray it doesn't. Tell Clare what I told you and she will know what to do with it."

Jack nodded, zipped up his pack, and shouldered one strap. Stan walked him out to the truck. He climbed in next to Enrique. His dad stood off to one side, hands in his pockets.

With a turn of the key, the engine roared to life. As the vehicle edged toward the garage bay door, Stan called out after him, "I'll be praying for you, Jack."

"Maybe it'll work this time." Jack knew his voice sounded cynical, but so far, he still had no proof whether there was a God or if he even cared.

Bouncing across the desert, then all the way back to the city, Jack pondered what he could do. What he *should* do. And yet down inside, he knew that to him, Amber's family took precedence over the precious box he carried. Even after striving so long to make this moment happen, the emotional wounds he felt were so deep, so raw, his sense of restitution so strong that he needed to find relief. To make a difference.

He knew where her parents lived. It wouldn't be that far out of the way to stop by their place on the way to Clare's. *It would be an easier trip that way,* he reasoned. *I wouldn't have to backtrack later.*

Jack glanced over at the man driving, his face creased into worry lines, his gaze constantly shifting around them, presumably scanning for trouble.

He doesn't need to know where I'm going, Jack thought. *No one needs to know.*

He looked out the window as the dry hillsides began to transition into houses. As they entered the city, Jack's heart began to pound. He directed the man where to drop him off, and shortly they had arrived at the intersection Jack had indicated. He climbed out, thanked the man, and watched him drive away. He hitched his pack up onto his shoulder and began walking, heading for Amber's parents. Hopefully Robert had lied about them being in custody. Hopefully they wouldn't hate him. Hopefully they wouldn't turn him in.

Chapter 18

Jack stood on the sidewalk looking up the driveway at the house. In the dusk of evening, lights shone softly in the four windows that could be seen from the street. A dozen paces from where he stood, two short, square pillars flanked the drive, each topped with a glowing post lamp. Each stood at the end of a chest-high hedge that formed a perimeter between the street and the front yard. To the left, a large tree behind the hedge hid at least half of the house, and another tree on the right also hid a good-sized portion.

His mouth suddenly dry, he moistened his lips and regarded the front door, which was set within an alcove flanked by round pillars that supported a small balcony above. Jack wasn't certain whether the door's red paint was a welcome or a warning. He took a deep breath, rearranged the backpack's strap on his left shoulder, and strode up the middle of the concrete driveway. Best get this over with.

Stepping into the alcove under the balcony, he eyed the doorbell, then rapped on the door instead. Somehow, it seemed less intrusive that way. He waited for several seconds, his hands growing damp, then knocked again.

Soon he heard the *click, click* of footsteps approaching, then a pause. Jack tried to consciously smooth his face to be as pleasant and nonthreatening as possible for whoever was peeking through the peephole. Shortly, he heard a *rasp* as the occupant unlocked the door and then opened it slowly. An older woman with short silvery blonde hair looked up at him.

"Yes?" Her eyebrows raised inquisitively, voice refined. She looked into his golden eyes distrustfully.

"Mrs. Stroud, I don't know if you remember me. I'm Jack Metcalfe, a friend of Amber's."

At the mention of her daughter's name, Leigh Stroud's eyes grew sad and yet her defensiveness remained. "How do you know her?"

"We...we met some time ago." Jack fumbled for words. "We've been friends for a while."

Mrs. Stroud seemed to relax a bit. "Well, any friend of Amber's is welcome here." She stepped aside and opened the door a bit farther. "Won't you come in?"

Jack wondered if she would have felt the same way had she known the entire story. He swallowed and stopped just inside the door. No matter how much he had rehearsed what to say, nothing seemed right. "Mrs. Stroud...I just want to say that I'm sorry for your loss."

"My loss?" She shut the door with a click of the latch. "I'm not sure where you got your information, but we haven't lost her. Well, not yet anyway."

"What? She didn't die?" Something sprang up inside Jack that he hadn't felt in a long time. Hope.

Mrs. Leigh Stroud shook her head slowly. "No." The word was drawn out soft and low. "But she's still in the hospital."

Jack ran his hand across his mouth and sighed. "I...um, is there any way I could see her?"

"Well, you could see her, but I'm not sure what good it will do."

Jack's newfound surge of hope sputtered. "What do you mean? Why not?"

"You don't know? Amber is in a coma."

The sun beat down on Jack's head. He looked once again at the paper in his hand, reconfirming his destination. He didn't trust his memory. Ever since Mrs. Stroud had revealed that Amber was in a coma, it seemed he was surrounded by fog, his thoughts fuzzy and confused. He didn't know if he should be glad that she hadn't died or sad that she might never awaken.

He watched the cab that Mrs. Stroud had rented for him pull away. She had told him where to find Amber, but cautioned that she didn't know whether he would be able to see her. At least one guard hovered outside her door twenty-four hours a day.

Somehow I have to get past that guard. I have to see her one more time, to know that she's still alive.

Maybe there was some way, he reasoned against hope, that she might awaken and then he could help her escape. If nothing else, he had to talk to her, to apologize for all of this, even if she couldn't hear him.

He walked through the hospital's main doors and, keeping his eyes downcast, headed for the elevator. Maybe if he could hide his eyes, no one would stop him. The elevator arrived and he stepped on alone. He pushed the button for the fourth floor and the elevator lurched into motion. At the fourth floor, it coasted to a stop and, hitching his backpack farther up onto his shoulder, Jack waited impatiently for the doors to open. When they finally did, he stepped out. The antiseptic smell of a recent cleaning assaulted his nostrils.

One hallway stretched in front of him while another ran to the left and the right. A placard at the corner of the wall declared that room 404, Amber's room, lay straight ahead.

Jack strolled down the hallway in the direction indicated. Ahead lay a nurses' station, beyond which, a guard leaned up against the wall, just outside a doorway. That must be it.

When he reached the nurses' station he turned left and followed another hallway out of sight of the guard. He ducked inside a bathroom, locked the door behind him, leaned against the closed door, and sighed in relief that he had gotten this far without detection. Somehow, he had to get past that guard. Collecting his nerve, Jack stepped outside the bathroom. Just down the hallway, a directory was mounted to the wall. He stopped to study it, to see where all of the exits were in case he needed a quick getaway.

Out of the corner of his eye, the guard stepped around the corner. Jack's heart beat a tad faster and he hoped the man wasn't coming after him. Then the man stopped at the nurses' station, drawing a shallow sigh of relief from Jack.

"Hey, Carmen."

"Hm?" A pretty blonde nurse looked up.

"Would you mind keeping an eye open? I need to use the restroom." He tipped his head in Jack's direction, toward the restroom behind him.

"Sure. Go ahead."

With a thank you, the guard sauntered closer. Jack held his breath and pretended to study the map in front of him. With barely a glance toward Jack, the man stepped into the restroom and locked the door behind him. Jack sighed in relief. He'd rather take his chances with the nurse than the guard.

For maybe thirty seconds, the nurse busied herself at her station, then something beeped at the monitors behind her and she walked over to check on them, her back facing the hallway where Amber's room was located. Nonchalantly, Jack turned and walked past the station right up to Room 404 and ducked inside.

The room lay quiet as death itself. Jack paused just inside the doorway. Amber lay on her back as if sleeping peacefully and unaware of the tumult that surrounded her. Of the threat that she would face should she awaken. In a way, he wished she wouldn't awaken and have to face a trial and possible execution.

He stepped into the room. A rustle came from the shadows in the corner to his left.

"Jack?" The woman's voice was barely more than a whisper but filled with disbelief.

Startled, Jack flinched and shot a glance toward the corner. A woman rose from a chair and stepped into the light.

"Mother?"

Eva rushed forward and wrapped her arms around him, head on his chest. Jack returned the embrace and held her tight. He felt her shudder in a sob.

"I didn't think I'd see you again." Her voice cracked with emotion.

Jack gently disentangled himself and held her at arm's length. "What are you doing here?" he whispered and glanced toward the door, expecting the guard to return any minute.

Eva sniffed and wiped away a tear trickling down her cheek.

Jack slowly pulled her back into the shadows, out of view from the doorway.

"Amber's mother and I have been taking turns sitting with her in case she awakens."

"But how did you know she was here?"

"After you were arrested, Amber came by the house and told me what she knew. She was afraid and told me that if anything happened and she didn't come back to my house over the weekend that I was to contact her parents. She came by faithfully every weekend the whole time you were gone. But when she didn't show up by Monday, I went to the address she had given me and found her parents. Her mother told me she was here. The guard has allowed us to come in one at a time to sit with her."

Jack brushed away another tear from Eva's cheek.

"Did you know they've already passed a sentence on her?" Eva whispered.

Jack closed his eyes as dread crept in.

"She's been stripped of her soul and is to be executed."

The look in her eyes expressed grief of the worst kind imaginable, an emotion so intense it touched Jack's heart. Something inside Jack whispered that she was right. To be executed was one thing. But to be executed with no hope of eternal life was the worst fate imaginable. And it was his fault. But then the seed of an idea sprouted in the back of his mind.

Eva looked into Jack's eyes, probing the depths as if she could find answers there. "Jack, I know that look. What are you going to do?" Worry settled on her brow and she wrung her hands together.

"I'm sorry, Mom." He shot her a look of apology. "I can't explain right now." If his new plan was to work, he had to hurry. He plunked his backpack on the chair and tugged at the zipper.

Jack wanted to stay, to explain everything to his mom, but there was no time. If he got caught, his plan would fail and Eva would be in danger. He pulled the black box out of his pack and cautiously opened the lid. The two vials lay nestled inside just as Stan had left them. He hoped his father would forgive him, but he'd rather risk the man's anger than see Amber die without hope.

He gently removed one vial. Holding it in his hand, he then closed the box and returned it to his pack. He rushed to Amber's bedside. So beautiful. He stroked her cheek with one hand, then removed the vial's stopper with his teeth. He eased her jaw open until her lips parted and poured the solution into her mouth. Then he brushed her forehead with his lips. "Be well, my love," he whispered.

"Jack," Eva said with alarm. "What was that?"

"I'm trying to give her a fighting chance, Mom." He stuffed the empty vial in his pocket. Hopefully it would work and they wouldn't discover what he had done. He gave his mother a quick hug and kiss on the cheek, then scooped up his pack and slung it onto his shoulder. "I love you, Mom. I promise I'll be in touch and will explain everything then." He peeked out the door. Still no guard. The whole thing had only taken a couple of minutes. He flashed his mom a grim smile and stepped out into the hallway.

Hands in his pockets and head down, Jack headed down the hallway as quickly as he dared without drawing suspicion, hoping he wouldn't run into the guard on his way out. And yet, his heart remained behind with Amber and he breathed a prayer for her safety, hoping he had done the right thing.

Chapter 19

Clare's eyes shot daggers at Jack. The black box lay open on the table between them, one slot nestling a glass vial, the other glaringly empty. "Where's the other one?"

Still standing, Jack returned her glare. He had no regrets. "I used it."

"Used it?" Clare's voice grew in intensity.

Jack didn't reply. He just clamped his jaw shut and stared at her.

"Oh no." She shook her head slowly. "You didn't. You used it on a live person, didn't you?"

Jack's silence gave her all she needed to know.

Clare stood and paced, running her fingers through her hair. "But we still don't know what it will do!" She stopped and leaned across the table, weight on her fists. "Do you realize you might have just sentenced that person to death?"

"There was no harm in trying. She was already as good as dead."

With an exasperated sigh, Clare paced again. "Furthermore, you don't understand how science works, do you? Jack, I need a control."

It was true. Jack hadn't known that. "Well, can't you just split that one in half?"

Still fuming, Clare's lips stretched into a tight, thin line, eyebrows scrunched into a frown. "It would be nothing short of a miracle if that works, but it might be possible."

Jack attempted a weak smile, but she just shook her finger in his face. "You better hope this works, mister. If it doesn't, many people's lives and years of research might be all wasted."

Jack gulped. He hoped that wasn't the case, and yet he knew down deep inside that given the chance, he'd do the same thing again.

Parcel delivered, Jack excused himself and headed for the door. Clare called after him, "I need to know who received the therapy! They need to be monitored." But he kept walking.

"I'll be in touch," he said and scooted out the door. The sooner he escaped the glare of her anger, the better.

Besides, there was no time to waste. He had one more stop to make.

Jack stood at the edge of the human quarter and gazed into the gen's destitute neighborhood. After having been in human territories for so long, this part of town looked worse than ever. *I never knew it was this bad,* he thought.

Jack made use of the dusky light of approaching evening and stayed in the shadows as much as he could. Probably too early for street toughs to be out, but it never hurt to be careful.

He paused for a split second when he saw their house. It seemed like eons ago when he had last been here. He went around to the back door, eased it open, and stepped inside.

"Hello?" Eva's voice came from the other room. "Who's there?" She came around the corner and an expression of joy crossed her face, her eyes grew wide and sparkling. "Jack!" She reached out and drew him into a hug that might have even been tighter than the one in the hospital, if that was possible. "You said you'd come, but I didn't know if you'd be able to."

She clasped Jack's hands in her own. "I have to tell you about Amber!" Her eyes shone and the corners of her mouth rose in a wide smile. "She's awake!"

"What?" Could it really be true?

Eva nodded. "After you left, I was sitting with her, holding her hand and praying for her. Leigh was to arrive any minute. Then all of a sudden, she moaned and opened her eyes ever so slightly. Slowly she came around. When Leigh arrived, I had to leave, of course, but not before I got to talk to Amber."

"You talked to her?"

"I did. And Jack," she looked at him meaningfully, eyebrows raised, "she asked about you."

Jack felt a goofy grin cross his face, but he didn't care.

"She said to tell you, 'I'm okay. I know the truth. Tell Jack he's doing the right thing.'"

Jack chewed the inside of his lip, pondering her words. He flicked a glance up at Eva. "So...did she say anything else?"

Eva shook her head. "No, that's all. After Leigh came, she wouldn't say anymore." She grabbed a saucepan from the stovetop, filled it with water, and placed it on the stove. She lit a match and held it to the burner as she turned on the gas. "You know, Jack, she looked so tired. But she looked different. More...peaceful, maybe."

Jack sat at the table and leaned back, crossing his arms. If only he had more information. That wasn't much to go on. *Well, regardless,* he thought, *she's awake and doing well. I guess that counts for something.*

Eva finished brewing the tea, weak enough to barely flavor the water, but strong enough to be called tea. She always made the leaves last as long as possible. Jack accepted the cup, placed it on the table, and rubbed his brow as he leaned over the steaming brew.

"Is everything okay, Jack?"

He jerked a nod but continued to stare into his tea. He couldn't help but think of how ironic it was that out in the desert, in the middle of nowhere, they had tea. Real tea. Here in the capitol, where Eva was supposed to be better off, she had barely flavored water. Old anger that had built over many years threatened to come back now that he saw once again the poverty in which his mother lived. But she hadn't known about Stan for this long and Jack wasn't going to tell her just yet. It wouldn't do any good; she wouldn't feel better and it wouldn't bring food to their door.

Eva interrupted his thoughts. "You are staying here, aren't you?"

"Hm?" Lost in his thoughts, Jack barely heard her. "Here? Um, well."

"Jack," she developed that motherly tone he knew so well. "You have to have somewhere to sleep. I don't know where you've been sleeping." She took a deep breath. "In fact, I'm not sure I want to know, but you certainly don't look any better for it. You need some rest."

Jack frowned. "But what if they come here looking for me?"

She raised her eyebrows and tipped her head sideways. "Whether or not you're here won't stop them from coming to look for you." Then her face lit up. "I know, we can make a hiding place for you. Then if—"

"When..."

She glared at him. "If," she emphasized the single word, "they come, we can hide you."

Jack had to admit her excitement was a bit contagious, but he still wasn't sure the plan would work. But neither did he want to extinguish the flicker of hope in her eyes. Besides, she was right about one thing. He needed rest. "Mom, I can't build any kind of permanent hiding place tonight, but I'll stay tonight. If they come, I'll try to slip out the window."

Eva ran her finger along the chipped cup's handle. "Okay. But you'll stay at least one night, right?"

"Yeah, Mom. I'll stay at least one night."

With a half-grin, she stood and began to bustle around the kitchen. "You haven't had anything to eat, have you?"

No matter what he answered, Jack knew she would prepare whatever already was in her mind. Besides, he was a bit hungry. "I could use a bite to eat."

With a satisfied nod of her head, Eva continued her preparations. Within a short time, she placed a sliced apple and a couple of slices of bread on the table, along with a small pot of honey. Jack smiled. She only brought out the honey on special occasions.

After they ate, Eva encouraged Jack to get some rest. Grateful, he walked the short trip down the hall to his room. He stood in the doorway and looked around. She had straightened up the room and made the bed. That alone told him that he had been on her mind.

"Is everything okay, dear?" she called from the kitchen.

"Yeah, Mom." He grinned. "Everything's fine." He stretched out on the bed and within minutes was asleep.

Jack sat next to Amber on the cool grassy hillside, watching puffy clouds float across a deep blue sky. She turned toward him, took his hand, and opened her mouth to say something. Then the scene faded to black and reality began to creep in as Jack woke. He kept his eyes closed, trying to go back to sleep, to drift once again into the blissful dream, but sleep refused to come.

With a groan, he scrubbed at his eyes and sat up. He shuffled down to the bathroom and then checked the time. Mid-morning already? He wandered down the hallway.

"Mom?" No answer. In the kitchen he found tea on the stove and griddlecakes under a cotton towel, butter nearby—and the pot of honey. He smiled. She must have gone to the hospital. He marveled at how she always had the needs of others in mind.

After he ate, he dug the handheld out of his backpack and flipped it on. He flopped down on the couch and settled in, but before he had a chance to actually start anything, the back door creaked open, then snapped shut.

"Jack?" Eva called.

"In here."

A few quick footsteps and Eva walked into the front room. She sat next to Jack and smoothed down the skirt of her worn yellow dress. Jack looked up and was surprised to see her face creased in a frown.

Jack's heart skipped a beat. "What's wrong?"

Eva closed her eyes for a couple of moments. "Amber's gone. I went to the hospital and her room was already tidied up with no trace she had even been there. But one of the nurses had a note for me." She handed Jack a folded paper.

He took it hesitantly, afraid of what he'd find.

Eva: The police came and took Amber in the night. They wouldn't say where they were going, but I'm afraid. Please pray. My husband will try to find out what's happened. I'll call you. Leigh

Jack read the note again, then handed it back. "Isn't Mr. Stroud a lawyer?"

Eva nodded. "I guess he knows a lot of people. If anyone can find out where she is, Benjamin can."

Jack leaned back and sighed, tired of this roller coaster of events. He wondered if it would ever end.

Later that afternoon, a knock sounded on the door. Eva rushed in the front room and started to shoo Jack out, but he didn't need encouragement. He was already headed for his room. He scrambled under the bed, and as he lay on the floor, hardly daring to breathe, he heard the front door creak open.

"Hello, Eva." Footsteps paced leisurely through the door and scuffled to a stop. Jack would know that voice anywhere. "How are you today?"

"What do you want, Robert?" Eva's voice had a hard edge to it, but she also sounded uneasy.

"I just thought I'd check in on you." The sound of footsteps circled the room.

"I'm sure that's not the only reason you're here."

"So perceptive, as always." Robert's oily voice filtered down the hallway. Jack could hear him clearly. "It just so happens you're right." After a pause, he continued. "I heard you were at the hospital today checking up on a mutual friend of ours. Or at least trying to check up on her."

"What have you done with her?" Eva spoke in quiet anger.

"Always so suspicious. Well, it just so happens that this time you're right. Now that she's awake, we needed to get her to a more...secure location. She's been charged with crimes against the state, you know."

In the ensuing silence, Jack could just imagine the look on his mother's face, the cloud of anger beginning to show.

"And her health seems to be improving at a miraculous pace. We suspect someone gave her something, some kind of medical therapy that is causing her recovery, and we'd like to know what it was." The footsteps stopped. "You wouldn't know anything about that, would you?"

Silence.

"I see. Then let me ask this. You haven't seen Jack recently, have you?"

"Isn't he in your custody?" she asked dryly.

Robert chuckled. "I think you know that he isn't. In fact, I think you know where he is. Is he here?"

Jack had trouble hearing her quiet reply. "No."

"Mm-hm. Well, maybe you can give him a message for me." Robert's voice grew louder and Jack cringed. Robert probably meant for him to hear what he had to say. "If he plans to see Amber again, he can forget it. She's a very important test subject now and we're keeping a very close eye on her. She's a medical marvel now, you know." After a few more footsteps, the door creaked open. "You tell him that for me, would you?"

The door clicked shut, and after a minute or so, Eva's feet appeared in the doorway of his bedroom.

"Jack?" she whispered. "Where are you? I think it's safe now."

Jack scooted out from under the bed and sat on the edge. "This is a disaster."

"I take it you heard?"

He nodded.

"We'll get through this, Jack. I'm sure her father will find her."

He studied his mom's eyes. "How can you be so sure?"

Eva's lips tightened into a grim line. "I'm trusting that God will take care of her."

Jack snorted and shook his head. "I guess we'll find out, won't we? Meanwhile, I need to talk to her father."

Eva frowned. "I don't think it's safe for you to go out."

"Mom!" The exasperation inside Jack built. "I'm not safe here. You heard him. He knows I'm here."

"But if you leave the house, they'll arrest you!"

"That's just a chance I'll have to take. If it will make you feel better, I'll wait a couple of hours until after dark."

Jack spent the rest of the day in frustrated silence. He paced the house, lay down, knowing it would be a long night. Then he paced again.

After darkness had fallen, he told Eva he was leaving and slipped out the door. Cautiously peering into the night, he looked for the enemy, but saw no one. For once, he was glad there were no streetlights here.

He walked down a side street toward the human quarter, taking a different route than normal, just in case they had the main road staked out. Once he was a few blocks over the border, he headed for a street that was not too deserted but not too busy. He found an older car and stood behind it, then waved at the next vehicle, trying to flag it down. It would take a couple of hours to reach the Strouds' house if he were to walk the entire way. On the fourth try, the vehicle slowed and pulled to one side. The window slid down a bit. Jack leaned over, trying to stay just far enough away that hopefully they wouldn't see the golden color of his eyes.

"Excuse me, sir, but my car broke down." He gestured at the car next to him. "I'm wondering if you would be so kind as to give me a ride home."

A burly man inside pursed his lips. "Where ya going'?"

"Just a couple of miles, up near Country Club Lane."

"Hm. Well, I guess so. That's not too far out of my way." He waved his hand. "Get in."

The door popped open, and with a thank you, Jack climbed in, careful to keep his gaze focused ahead of them.

Jack had the man drop him off a few houses away from the Strouds. He walked the short distance and knocked on the red door. When nobody came, he rang the bell. A series of chimes sounded inside the house, and within a minute or so, Leigh opened the door. When she saw Jack, she raised her eyebrows in surprise.

"Hello, Jack. Come in."

Jack thanked her and stepped inside.

She closed the door behind him. "What can I do for you?"

"I'm wondering if Mr. Stroud is in."

"Yes." She drew the word out slowly with an inflection at the end that indicated her curiosity. "Come with me." She turned and walked through the foyer, slippers padding softly on the marble floor tiles. "I believe he's in his office," she said over her shoulder. They turned left, skirting along the edge of a formal living room, the likes of which Jack had never seen. A giant wool rug covered the center of the floor, framing a pair of brocade-upholstered couches and offset by a wing chair in burgundy velvet. On the back wall, a large window extended from floor to ceiling and Jack was sure that had it not been dark, the view outside those windows would have been just as spectacular.

Just beyond a grand staircase that circled up to the second floor, a pair of double doors opened into an office paneled in what must have been mahogany. Seated at a desk inside was a distinguished-looking gentleman, roughly sixty years old. A full head of silver-gray hair framed a stern face with dark eyebrows and a strong jawline. He looked up from his work.

"Dear," Mrs. Stroud stopped just inside the doorway. "This is Jack, one of Amber's school friends. He asked to see you."

Benjamin Stroud studied Jack for just a minute, then leaned back in his chair. "Come in, Jack. Please, sit." He gestured to a guest chair off to one side of the desk. Leigh excused herself and left the two of them alone.

Surprised to be treated with even a modicum of respect, Jack quickly took a seat.

"What can I do for you, Jack?"

Jack licked his lips nervously. He had a feeling that he would never be able to hide anything from the man. Might as well be up-front. He took a deep breath. "First of all, sir, I want you to know that Amber and I did not attend school together."

Benjamin leaned forward, forearms on the desk, hands clasped in front of him. "I appreciate your honesty."

Jack gulped. "You knew?"

He nodded. "I know quite a bit about you, Jack. It's my job to know things."

Jack had the feeling this wasn't unusual.

"I also understand my wife met your mother while Amber was in the hospital."

"Yes, sir." Jack paused, collecting his thoughts. "I came to talk with you about Amber."

Mr. Stroud sat unmoving, waiting for Jack to go on.

"As you know, Amber is no longer in the hospital. Now that I've met you, I see it's possible that you may already know the details, but the reason I came was to help if I can."

"And how would you help?"

"I know who took her. Robert Bradley."

"As in Father Robert Bradley?" he said somewhat incredulously.

"Yes, sir." Jack loosely interlaced his fingers, hands in his lap. "Robert is my half-brother."

The older man studied his hands as Jack continued.

"He came to our house today. Told my mother that he has Amber under lock down so they can study her medical...situation."

Benjamin looked up, his eyes full of fire. "He told you this." It was more of a statement than a question.

"Not me directly, sir. But I could hear him talking to my mother."

"And where were you?"

Jack would have done practically anything to not be the target of Mr. Stroud's fierce gaze. "I...I was hiding." Jack looked down. "You might as well know that there's a warrant out for my arrest."

"Yes. I hear there's a price on your head as well," he said dryly.

That Jack did not know. He turned his head to one side, chewing on the inside of his cheek.

"Why do they want you in custody so badly?"

Jack wasn't sure if this was a trick question or if the man truly did not know. He collected his thoughts before deciding how much to reveal and still remain trustworthy. "For one thing, I saw Amber get shot."

For the merest instant, Benjamin's eyes widened slightly and Jack knew this was new information to him.

"I'm afraid it was my fault, sir," Jack said in a near whisper.

"And why do you think that, Jack?"

"Because I...stole something from the government labs. They arrested me." Thoughts of Amber's betrayal flashed through his mind, but he quickly pushed them aside. "And Amber was trying to..." Jack searched for the right word but finally blurted out, "take it for me."

"To steal it, you mean."

Jack bit his lip, then said in little more than a whisper, "Yes, sir."

"And what was this thing? Does it have something to do with your father, Stan?"

Jack flicked a glance up, took a deep breath and ran one hand through his hair. Time to come clean. "Yes, sir. If you know that much, I'm sure you know everything about my father there is to know." Jack gathered his courage and looked straight into the lawyer's eyes. "My father has developed an antidote that might complete the gen's DNA and give them a soul." Having already said that much, Jack rushed on. "My mother said they had already stripped Amber's soul from her. I had some of the antidote with me and so I gave her a dosage."

Benjamin leaned back, arms crossed over his chest. "It would appear that this medication your father has created also possesses the ability to effect rapid healing."

Jack nodded. "I think that's why they want to study her. They don't know what she was given."

"So they don't have a sample of this antidote?"

Jack shook his head no.

"Hmph." Benjamin sat in thought for several moments. "I suspect, young man," he finally said, "that it is not your fault Amber landed in the hospital. She made her own choice." He gave a sad smile. "She always did have a heart for the underdog."

Jack waited in silence, not wanting to break the man's reverie.

"Well." Benjamin took a deep breath and then re-focused on Jack. "Do you know where they're holding her?"

"No, sir."

"Hm. Well, I have a few ideas, but this will have to go through the courts." A look of fierce determination crossed the man's face again. "And the courts are something that I know very well."

He stood, signifying the interview was over, so Jack stood as well. Benjamin Stroud extended a hand, and for a second, Jack just blinked at it. He couldn't recall any human ever offering him a handshake. Then, with a smile, Jack accepted the gesture with a firm grip.

"Thank you, Jack, for coming. This information will be very helpful in our quest to gain Amber's freedom."

Jack turned to go, but the man called him back.

"Jack, if you need anything, try to get word to me. Meanwhile, you should stay hidden. I appreciate what you're trying to do. Amber never realized it, but I knew of her clandestine activities. And I would have supported her had she come to me. As it is, I believe it to be a worthy cause. I've always respected your father. He's a good man."

At hearing this new information, Jack wasn't quite sure what to say. But he did manage to mumble a quick thank you.

"Now, I want to arrange for a car to take you home. You've been most helpful."

"Thank you, sir," Jack repeated. He followed Mr. Stroud out to the foyer.

"Wait here," the gentleman directed. "I'll be right back."

He continued down the hallway, then returned within a couple of minutes.

"My gardener lives in a cottage behind the house. He will drive you home." He opened the front door for Jack. "He'll be around with the car shortly." He shook Jack's hand again. "Thank you again. I'll be in touch through your mom," he said, and closed the door, leaving Jack on the front steps awaiting his driver.

Jack eyed the red door in a new light. It hadn't been a warning but a welcome after all.

Chapter 20

"Jack!" Eva called out as she swept into the back door.

"In here," Jack replied from the front room. He quickly set aside his handheld and turned around, leaning on the back of the couch toward the sound of her voice. She rushed in from the kitchen, her eyes bright with excitement.

"Jack, I talked with Leigh!"

Jack froze hoping his mother had found out what happened when Mr. Stroud met with the judge. From her disposition, it must be good news.

Eva perched on the edge of a tattered armchair, hands clasped in her lap.

"Well? What happened?" he asked.

"You know I was to meet Leigh at the courthouse, right?"

"Uh-huh." Jack nodded.

"Well, I did. When I found her, she was still waiting for Benjamin to come out of the judge's chambers." She leaned forward on her elbows. "Finally he came out. And he said it looks really good. It turns out that Benjamin actually knows Pope Cyriacus—the head of the North American Orthodox Church—and had been in contact with him, explaining the whole situation with Amber. Benjamin wasn't able to get a final decision from the pope, but he said the Holy Father seemed sympathetic toward Amber's circumstances and anticipates a positive decision soon. As you know, the pope has final authority to offer clemency. As the supreme authority in the government, no one can overturn his decision once his mind's made up."

Jack could hardly believe it. It seemed too good to be true.

But within a week, Pope Cyriacus ordered that Amber be released and a full pardon issued.

Once Jack got the word, he decided to stay in New Santiago, anxious to see Amber as soon as she was released.

Knock, knock, knock.

Eva shooed Jack into a back room before answering the door. But he didn't need any encouragement. The fewer people who knew his whereabouts, the better.

Jack heard Eva open the door and heard the murmur of two voices, but they were so low he couldn't make out what they were saying. Curiosity overcoming his sense of danger, he crept into the short hallway, easing toward the entrance to the front room until he could make out the conversation.

Then Jack smiled. He would know that voice anywhere. He stepped into the doorway and his eyes drank in the sight of the young woman.

Amber's eyes grew wide and a smile spread across her face. "Jack!" She rushed across the room, wrapped her arms around him, and laid her head on his chest.

Jack returned her embrace and kissed the top of her head. The soft scent that was Amber drifted up to his nose and he drank in her presence.

After several quiet moments of just holding each other, Jack pushed back slightly, holding Amber at arm's length.

"So exactly why are you here? You don't look like you were just in the hospital a short time ago, fighting for your life."

"Well, I was, but now I'm feeling much better, thanks to you. I couldn't wait to see you again." She smiled. "Besides, Pope Cyriacus wants to meet you."

"What?" Jack could hardly believe his ears. Surely she was joking. "You're not serious."

But Amber nodded, eyebrows raised. "Dead serious."

Taking him by the hand, she led him over to the couch. She sat sideways, one leg tucked up under her, her arm resting on the back of the couch. Jack sat next to her.

"After I woke up, I started feeling pretty good within just a few days. They took me out of the hospital and to some kind of lockdown facility. They put me in a room that was much like a hospital room—just for observation, they told me. But it wasn't more than a week and a half later that a guard came to get me." She ran her fingers through her hair and took a deep breath. "They took me to the Ministry offices. I asked where we were going, but no one answered. They took me through some big double doors and led me into this really nice office. It was gorgeous, Jack. The furniture, the carpets..."

Jack motioned good-naturedly for her to get back to her story.

"Right. Anyways, I was beginning to wonder if these were the papal apartments. I wasn't sure exactly where they were but I knew we were close. Before you know it, there I am. Standing in front of the pope himself."

Jack tipped his head sideways and studied her face, trying to figure out if this was a joke.

"Seriously, Jack. I'm telling the truth. I told him what happened when I was in the hospital—"

"Wait. What happened?"

"Oh yeah." Amber sighed and looked up at the ceiling. "So much has happened. Let me back up a bit." She paused, and when she spoke, her voice was very soft and serious. "Jack, when I was laying in the hospital bed just after I got shot, a doctor I'd never seen before came in the room. He had on a white lab coat and was looking at my records. He asked how I was feeling and all that, just like the other doctors. I told him that my side hurt pretty bad where I got shot. He pulled back the bandage and took a look, then covered it back up, smoothed over it with his hand, and told me it should heal pretty quickly." She met Jack's eyes with an intense gaze. "Then he said I was pretty lucky, that the wound would have killed most people. And he told me that God must be watching over me. That he must have something special for me to do. Now here's the weird part." She rested her hand on his leg. "After that doctor left, I thought about what he said and I decided that the next time he came in, I would ask him what he meant by that. Except I never saw him again. The next doctor I saw was the same one I had been seeing before. I asked him where the other doctor was..." She paused.

"Yeah?" Jack prompted.

"I was told that there wasn't any other doctor. I said, no, someone else had been there. So the hospital doctor got all nervous and questioned all the nurses, but everyone he talked to insisted that they hadn't seen anyone matching that description. Ever. That other doctor just touched my wound—through the bandage. And when the nurse came later to check on me, she pulled off the bandage and the wound had closed. Completely. New skin and all."

Jack looked away. Her earnestness spoke to the fact that she truly believed someone had visited her in the hospital, someone that nobody else had ever seen.

Eva joined them and eased herself down into a chair, eyes riveted on Amber. "So what happened when you told this to the pope?"

"Oh, right. When I told Pope Cyriacus, he thought about it for a minute, and then he asked me if I believe in angels. He thinks that the doctor might have been an angel. Jack," she placed a hand on his arm, "your mom told me what you did, that you gave me something when I was out. The doctors said they were surprised I had even woken up. That in itself was amazing, but they also said that the wound never should have healed so quickly. Then they ran some tests and found traces of some kind of medication in my system. Apparently, the effects of the DNA modification they had given me had been reversed. When Father Robert came in, he was really mad and demanded more tests. When the second set of test results came back the same as the first, he demanded I be taken to a secure facility for observation."

Jack was having trouble following Amber's story. It sounded too fantastic to be true. "So you told all this to the pope?"

Amber nodded. "Then he wanted to know if I had been given some medicine by someone other than the medical staff. When I said yes, he wanted to know who it was. I told him," she swallowed nervously and her voice dropped to a near whisper, "that it was you."

"You told him about me?" Jack didn't know if he was honored or horrified.

"It's okay, Jack," Amber reassured him quickly. "I felt like it would be okay to tell him. It just felt right. Then I thought that since he was helping me that maybe he could help you too."

"And?" Jack sucked in a deep breath and wondered if Amber had just signed his death warrant. "I'm still a wanted man, you know."

"I know, Jack. But he wants to meet you. He asked if I knew where you were. I told him I might. He said that if I would deliver his wish to see you, he'd greatly appreciate that. So I came here."

Now that her story was done, silence descended on the room. Thoughts swirled through Jack's mind like a tornado. Should he run? Would it even do any good? The police would probably find him anyway. Or maybe Amber was right and he should agree to meet Pope Cyriacus. He couldn't run forever.

"Jack," Amber drew his attention back to her. "I've been thinking about it and I think that maybe God has had his hand on you too. Maybe he's been protecting you so you could help the gens."

Old anger rose up inside Jack at her comment. He rose and stalked several steps away from the couch. "Amber, if that's the case, if God really had his hand on me, why'd he let me go through all of that? I almost died! I've been beaten, starved, shot, and near death more than once. That doesn't seem much like protection to me." Jack's feet itched to stalk out the door, but something in Amber's eyes made him pause.

"But you didn't die, Jack," she replied. "Think about it. Because of everything you'd been through, you had nowhere else to go, so you went to find your dad. Because of that you found the solution that we were looking for. You got the antidote." Amber rose and walked to where Jack stood, placing her hand on his arm. "I really believe that God used you to save my life. And now that you've brought the antidote, you just might be responsible for saving hundreds, maybe thousands of lives. All of whom might now have a chance to experience eternity."

Jack sighed and turned away, crossing his arms. He hated to admit it, but she was almost making sense.

"That never could have happened if you hadn't been captured in the first place."

Jack headed for the door. He didn't want to hear any more. No matter if the police were looking for him. He had to get out. As he pulled the door open, he heard Amber's quiet voice behind him.

"Just think about it, okay?"

But Jack just clenched his jaw and stepped out the door. Once outside, his sense of caution returned. It probably was stupid to come out here in the open like this, he thought to himself. But there's no way he was going back in there. Not yet.

Jack pulled up his collar and shoved his hands in his pockets. He wished he had brought his hat. Keeping a careful eye, he started walking, heading away from the house. The harder he tried to forget Amber's words, the more they lodged in his head. He just couldn't believe that any God who was supposed to be all about love would let him go through such pain and misery.

After a time, Jack found himself at the edge of Gen Town. Compared to the distances he had walked lately, it didn't seem that far. Passing the last building, the Grove caught his eye, the place where gens came to worship the nature gods. *How can anyone know for certain?,* he thought, *who the true gods are?*

He walked up to the edge of the trees and sat on one of the rocks arranged in a ring around the standing stone. There in the center, at the foot of the stone, lay offerings of fruit, flowers, even a few coins, which no one dared to take and thus risk angering the gods. He stilled himself and focused his thoughts on the gods, the way everyone said you were supposed to. "They'll speak to you if you're quiet enough," he had been told. So he focused, opened his mind to them...and felt...nothing.

Instead, thoughts of his mother's God filled his open mind. Then he remembered Robert. Such a wicked man—and a respected priest of the church.

But Robert is not God.

The unbidden thought drifted into his mind. He didn't want to admit it, but down inside, he knew that even though a priest might be evil, that didn't make the church evil. That thought he chose to push aside.

There's only one way to find out where Pope Cyriacus' heart is, Jack thought. *If he wants to meet me so badly, I'll go, just to see his weaknesses for myself. Then I'll prove that their God doesn't exist either.*

Returning to the house, he found Amber still there, hoping he'd return soon. He told her of his decision to go with her to the papal offices. In response, she scooped up her bag and took him by the hand.

"What?" It was more of a statement than a question. "Now?"

Amber nodded, eyes bright. "Pope Cyriacus said to come as soon as possible. Besides, we should go before Robert or his henchmen come back here looking for you again."

Jack sighed. Might as well get it over with.

They hiked to the edge of the gen quarter and Amber called the ANN center for a car. Soon a vehicle bearing the insignia of the ANN Public Transportation System pulled up to the curb in front of them. Before long, they had arrived at their destination, climbed out of the car, and were approaching the gate guarded by Ministry guards. Amber dug in her purse, emerging with a small, yellow sheet of paper, which she showed to the guard.

Jack regarded her with surprise. "You have a pass?"

Amber flashed him a grin. "One of the benefits of absolution, I guess."

Jack shook his head. But despite his cynicism, the closer he got to their destination, the more nervous he became.

Amber led him resolutely through the main halls and eventually they stopped in front of a young priest. He sat behind an ornately carved desk that was really more of a library table than a desk. A small computer—a Spektrum 501, Jack noticed—stood on one corner of the table, its back toward them. Jack tried to still the nervous thoughts racing through his mind. He planted both feet firmly on the floor, held his hands behind his back, and forced himself not to fidget.

The priest looked up, and seeing Amber, his eyes flickered with recognition.

"Miss Stroud. It's good to see you again. Please have a seat." He gestured toward a pair of overstuffed chairs covered in an ornate red and gold fabric. "I'll inform His Holiness that you're here."

Amber thanked the man and they took a seat, as directed. Jack couldn't help but run his hands over a small portion of the chair's arms, covered in a velvet that was the softest fabric he had ever felt. His feet rested on plush carpet rich with intricate patterns, heavy velvet drapes trimmed with gold cord fringe served as window coverings, and every inch of the walls were painted in frescoes of Biblical scenes—most likely painted by the best artists. Directly across from them was a painting of a regal-looking man in robes of white, wearing a golden crown and carrying a long scepter, and standing at the top of a set of wide stairs. He was surrounded by men, some watching the noble figure with awe, others talking with each other in various animated discussions. But Jack had only a short minute to take it all in.

"He will see you now."

Jack started at the voice interrupting his examination of the painting's lifelike depiction of the reverent scene. He and Amber followed the black-robed man, their feet not making a sound on the thick rugs. The priest showed them through a pair of heavy, gold-trimmed doors carved with the image of Christ sitting under a spreading tree, surrounded by smiling children, one of whom sat perched on the Savior's knee.

The interior matched that of the previous room, and like the other, a faint scent of incense hovered in the air. A white-haired man sat on a surprisingly simple, upholstered chair. When he saw them, he smiled warmly.

As Jack entered the room, a certain calmness that he couldn't explain settled over him and his heart inexplicably filled with respect for the old man.

"Amber," the pope's voice was as kind as his eyes. "It's so good to see you again."

She bowed her head respectfully. "Your Grace."

"I take it this is Jack?"

Jack drew back. Although he knew Amber had mentioned him to Pope Cyriacus, he was surprised the man remembered his name. He figured the venerable man would have forgotten such a seemingly insignificant person as himself by now.

"Sir." Jack tipped his head slightly in deference, knowing that more obeisance was probably customary, but determined not to be intimidated by this person who was a mere man like any other. Amber darted a warning glance his way at his casual action that bordered on disrespect.

Cyriacus chuckled. "You are your own man, I see. There's nothing wrong with that. Each man must find his own way."

Jack had no idea what this old man was babbling about, but he did understand when the man offered them a seat.

"Amber tells me that you are the one who saved her life."

"Uh..." That was the last thing Jack had expected to hear and he found himself speechless, his angry retorts dissipating in the face of the pope's direct honesty. "I'm actually not sure," he managed. Inside, Jack berated himself for such a weak response, and yet somehow, the man's manner put him at ease nonetheless.

"That was a very brave thing to do, my son." He paused and looked from Jack to Amber and back again. "You must care deeply for her to risk so much."

Jack chewed on his lip and looked down, uncertain where this conversation was headed.

"Tell me, my son, why did you do such a thing?"

"Because..." Jack faltered, "I care for her." He looked sideways at Amber and she grinned in response. "And she didn't deserve to die."

"Ah. So you have a compassionate heart as well. Tell me," he continued in a fatherly tone, "is this something you would have done for anyone?"

Jack looked back at the man and searched his mind for a truthful answer. Come to think of it, he truly didn't know.

"Let me ask you another way. Do I understand correctly that you have labored to help your fellows, to improve their lives?"

Now here was something Jack could talk about. He nodded. "That's because the gens have no hope...sir."

"What do you mean by 'no hope'?"

Jack sighed in frustration. Was this man really so out of touch that he didn't see their segregated society for what it was? "When gens die, they die. You say that your God loves man, that he wants them to spend eternity with him. But what about the gens? Doesn't he care for them?"

The pope's lips pressed into a thin line. "A worthy question. I have thought much on this issue myself of late." He paused and looked deep into Jack's eyes, grasping the arms of his chair firmly. "And I think you might be right."

Jack sat up straight and sucked in a breath of surprise at the unexpected reply.

"And yet I fear that the traditions of society, the prejudice held so deeply by man, is not something that I can change by myself. As you have seen, this intolerance for the gens—whom humans depend upon to support their lifestyles—this hypocrisy exists even among the people's spiritual leaders." His face took on a look of sadness. "And yet, I hang my head in shame because you have proven that a single person can make a difference. I fear I have not done enough."

Jack sat in shocked silence. Pope Cyriacus folded his hands in his lap, absentmindedly rubbing his thumbs together.

"You, Jack, have done something that I could not do. Your actions were yours alone. And yet, I can't help but think that this medicine you used to save Amber's life certainly was not something you created on your own."

A sense of caution rose in Jack. Perhaps he was right after all. Maybe this was all a show in order to get him to reveal the underground and their secrets.

"Can you tell me more about it?"

"You mean, will I tell you my secrets and betray my friends?" Jack knew his words were bitter, but he didn't care. He was too angry at this man and his apparent manipulation of Amber's feelings, how he apparently convinced her to get Jack to reveal himself to the authorities.

Amber laid her hand on his arm. "It's okay, Jack. It's not what you think. I trust him. Do you remember our conversation? Please give him a chance. Maybe, just maybe, God has guided you through all of this."

Jack huffed. "Amber, don't you see what is happening here?"

"My son. Jack."

At the mention of his name, Jack looked back at the pope, and when their eyes met, somehow his anger abated a tiny bit. The calmness the man exuded was uncanny.

"I can understand your anger. You have been through much. Suffered much injustice. I wish I could undo all of that, but I can't. What I can do is try to further your efforts. Your people deserve equality. They deserve a chance to choose for themselves whether they want to spend eternity with God. Please, Jack. Let me help you."

Jack regarded the man distrustfully, unable to believe him completely. And yet, he could not deny the look of earnestness the man offered. "So what do you want from me?"

"In order to bring the gens a chance to hope, we need to make this antidote available to them. Jack, we need the antidote."

"I...will...not...betray my friends." Jack's words were drawn out and adamant.

"And I do not ask you to do so. But you have been through much and I will give you what I can. I will protect you. I can do that. There are enough good men in the church that my word will stand. And...I can offer protection to others involved in the effort. Contrary to what you may think, I am not so completely out of touch. I know enough to suspect who your sources are. And yet, I will not force you to reveal their locations or secrets. But if they come to me, I will help." Cyriacus leaned back in his chair. "Regardless of what you decide, you will personally still have my protection. I promise you this."

Jack grunted. "For that, I thank you. As for the rest, I will have to think on it."

The pope nodded. "That is well. I know you are a resolute man or you would not have gotten this far. But I will pray you do not wait too long. Every day we wait delays the hope we can offer to the gens."

In the silence that ensued, it was clear their audience was over. Jack rose, once again acknowledging the man with a slight nod, and left. Behind him, he heard Amber paying more customary respects. Before long, she was at his elbow.

They rode back to Jack's house in silence, Jack debating in his mind whether to accept the pope's offer to help the resistance or to ignore his possibly insincere offer and continue helping the underground to further its efforts. By the time they reached their destination, Jack knew one thing. He needed to talk to his father. This was not a decision to be made on his own.

In the face of Jack's silence, Amber said her goodbyes to both him and Eva and left. Jack retrieved his communicator prototype and headed for the edge of town. Once there, he placed a call to his father.

He didn't have to wait long.

"Jack! Is that you?"

Jack relayed his conversation with Pope Cyriacus, ending with the holy man's desire to obtain the antidote Stan had spent so many years developing, and the man's offer of absolution to himself, Stan, and any others involved in the process to develop the therapy. When he finished, the line fell silent.

"Stan? Dad? Are you there?"

"Um, yeah." He sounded uncertain, his speech faltering. "I think I'm missing something. Why were you speaking with the pope? What happened?"

Jack cringed at the explanation he owed his father. He told him of how he had used a dose on Amber and how tests showed the damage to her DNA had been repaired.

This time, Stan's voice was incredulous. "You used your friend as a guinea pig?" He went on, not giving Jack a chance to respond. "How could you do that?"

In reply, Jack offered a feeble excuse. "I left the other vial with Clare."

"But what if it's not enough for testing?"

"But..." Jack offered, "medical tests showed it works! Your therapy works!"

Stan fell into silence for a time, then finally, he spoke. "Amazing. And absolution, huh?"

"That's what he said, but I don't know if he's to be trusted. I knew I had to call you."

"You were right to do so." Stan's voice softened. "Cyriacus is a good man. If that's what he said, I trust him."

"How can you know that?"

"Once we were friends. I knew him before he became the Cosmopolitan of North America."

Confusion filled Jack's mind. "If that's the case, why did you run?"

"I did try to talk with him before I left New Santiago." Stan's voice was apologetic. "But I couldn't. He was new in his position and out of town on a world tour. I couldn't get a message to him. The police were on my tail and there was little hope of surviving if I stayed in town much longer—and no hope of using the material I had risked so much to obtain if I stayed." After a long, pregnant pause, Stan gave his decision. "If my old friend has promised protection, I will come. Will you go with me to visit him?"

"Yes, I'll go." Jack reluctantly agreed, but inside, his thoughts whirled in confusion. "Dad, I've gotta go."

"Wait, Jack. Do me a favor and don't tell your mother I'm coming. I don't want her to get her hopes up and then have things go bad. I don't want to risk hurting her. And I want to tell her myself. Just keep your communicator close. When I get there, I'll contact you."

Jack needed to think. In light of Amber's conversion to the church, Stan's revelations and then his surprising decision to visit the pope, Jack's world had just turned upside down. The Grove was not far away so he headed that direction. Even though he was now convinced that the place had no divine connection, it was still a quiet place to think. And he definitely had a lot to think about.

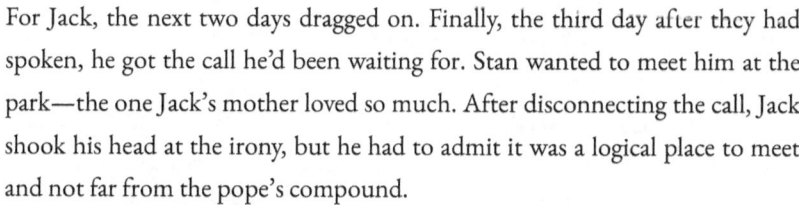

For Jack, the next two days dragged on. Finally, the third day after they had spoken, he got the call he'd been waiting for. Stan wanted to meet him at the park—the one Jack's mother loved so much. After disconnecting the call, Jack shook his head at the irony, but he had to admit it was a logical place to meet and not far from the pope's compound.

By the time Jack arrived at the park, Stan was already there waiting for him. Together, they headed toward the papal compound.

Once at the gate, Jack showed the guard an old ID card he had brought with him, hoping his name had been added to the list of approved visitors. The guard checked his records and with a nod, opened the gate. Jack still couldn't get used to the idea that after running for so long, he was free to come and go. He had half expected to be hauled away in cuffs. Surprisingly, Stan was also cleared for entry.

After they checked in with the priest outside the papal apartments, they waited for about five minutes, which seemed to stretch on forever.

The priest finally returned. "His Holiness will see you now."

Stan and Jack walked into the reception area and when Pope Cyriacus saw Stan, he held his arms open wide at the sight of his old friend. For Jack, the entire thing was a surreal experience and he wondered more than once if he was dreaming.

"Please, please sit," the pope urged.

Jack and Stan took seats in guest chairs and the pope sat across from them. After a brief silence, Stan cleared his throat. He flicked at an imaginary piece of lint on the arm of the chair he sat in.

"I hear you want to help the gens," he said to the pope.

Here was the part Jack had been waiting for. Time to get down to business.

Pope Cyriacus nodded slowly. "I hear you've been busy." He paused and turned a kind gaze on Jack. "So has your son."

"So I've heard," Stan said and eyed Jack.

"Don't be too hard on him," the holy man urged. "Have you met the girl, Amber?"

Stan shook his head.

"Hm. I hope you do soon. Her recovery has been quite remarkable. And without your son's efforts," he gestured at Jack, "we still wouldn't know whether you had achieved your goal."

Stan spent the next several moments in quiet contemplation. "Yes, so I hear," he said in a near whisper, then fixed his gaze on Cyriacus. "So what made you change your mind? Why do you want to help the gens? I didn't think you cared."

"At one time I didn't. But I was wrong, Stan. Please forgive me."

Hearing the pope's readmission of his guilt, a crack formed in the wall of anger Jack had erected around his heart. For the first time, he began to consider that true change—and not just another set of lies—could be on the horizon.

"I'm sure your son has told you that I have offered absolution and freedom from prosecution in exchange for your helping the gens."

Stan nodded. Jack could have sworn he saw his dad's eyes glisten with unshed tears.

"I would also like to offer you a laboratory at the federal facilities where you can continue your research and create everything the gens will need."

Stan's jaw dropped. "I...this is more than I could ever have hoped for. This will allow us to move ahead so much more quickly."

And as for Jack, he could only sit and gape. Finally, their goals would be realized.

A wide grin stretched across Cyriacus' face. "So does that sound acceptable?"

"Oh, yes." Stan nodded vigorously. "Definitely."

"Good. Draw up a list of what you need and I will make sure it gets to the right parties so we can get you set up as soon as possible. However," his expression grew serious, "I'm sure you realize that changing people's minds won't be easy. But Jack has shown me that one has to start somewhere. And this is where we will start to usher in a new era for the gens."

Stan rose and grasped one of his friend's hands in both of his own. "Thank you so much, Cyriacus. You won't regret this."

"I'm sure I won't. After all, what are old friends for?"

With another thank you, Stan and Cyriacus said their goodbyes. Jack followed his father out to the waiting area and toward the courtyard.

"Can you believe it, Jack?" Stan exclaimed as they burst out the door into the warm sunshine. "This is more than I ever..."

He stopped and his voice trailed off, eyes riveted on the sight that met his eyes. There, Amber and Eva stood arm in arm. When Eva saw her husband, a smile spread across her face and tears of joy spilled down her cheeks.

"Eva," Stan whispered, his voice husky with emotion. "Is it really you?"

Without a word, Eva rushed into Stan's arms and clung to her long-lost husband, eyes closed. Stan's frame racked in a sob.

"I'm so sorry, Eva. I didn't mean to hurt you."

"Shh, it's okay," she soothed. "You're back and that's all that matters."

"How did you know I was here?" Stan still held her tight, apparently unwilling to let her go.

"Jack told me you were coming."

Stan regarded his son with raised brows. Jack shrugged and offered a guilty grin. "I didn't think it was right to not tell her."

"Then, when I found out you had arrived and were here, I couldn't wait another moment. Amber offered to bring me and here we are."

Jack wrapped his arm around Amber and kissed the top of her head. "Thank you," he said in a throaty whisper. He didn't think he'd ever get tired of seeing his parents hugging each other like young lovers. Then he remembered. "Amber, Cyriacus offered my father his own lab where he can continue his research so he can create all the therapeutics needed to help the gens."

Amber gasped and looked up at Jack. "Really?"

Jack nodded. "Really. I never thought I'd see this day come. You know, I think you were right after all. I think God's hand has been guiding events, bringing everything together, just like you said."

"I'm glad to hear you say that." She beamed up at him. "So you admit there is a God?"

"How can there not be?" Jack chuckled. "It's a new day. A new era has begun."

Acknowledgments

Jack's story came to me one day when I had a "what-if" moment. What if it were possible to remove someone's soul? From there, the story mostly wrote itself. But no story can live on without its readers. For that, I want to thank my incredible readers. I truly appreciate all the wonderful reviews, feedback, word-of-mouth endorsements, and interaction via email and social media.

I heard it said once that every writer needs a good editor. There is much truth in that statement. Thank you to Denise Harmer, copyeditor extraordinaire, for helping me to wrangle this manuscript closer to perfection. Any errors that remain are mine alone.

There's a good chance Jack's story wouldn't exist in published form without my amazing critique partners, who encouraged me to get this story to market. Many thanks to Joanne Bischoff, Beverly Nault, and Ashley Ludwig for your input. It took a few years, but I finally made it!

Thank you to my beta readers who helped me check for errors and offer feedback. If you'd like to be part of my pre-pub street team for my next book, email me at: dona@donawatson.com.

Thank you to cover artist Kirk DouPonce for the stunning cover art that helps bring Jack to life! Your talents are amazing and truly appreciated.

Many thanks to my family for putting up with me and my quirky writer's habits. Special thanks to Kris, who drew early sketches of Amber so I could keep her pictured in my mind as I was writing. Many thanks also to Gavin for answering all my questions about computer hacking, networking, and pharmaceutical laboratory procedures.

Most importantly, I want to thank my Lord and Savior Jesus Christ, who has sustained me on my journey. Without Him, I would be nothing.

About the Author

Dona Watson fell in love with fantasy in high school when she found an old copy of *Sword at Sunset* by Rosemary Sutcliff in a used bookstore. From there it was a short jump to discovering the joys of science fiction. She earned a Bachelor's in English from Vanguard University and has worked for most of her adult life as a full time writer and editor. These days she can be found tucked away at her home in Middle Tennessee, creating new worlds filled with magic or technology that hasn't yet seen the light of day.

Download for FREE three flash fiction stories and hear about new releases by going to https://www.donawatson.com/free-stories.

Web site: www.donawatson.com
Email: dona@donawatson.com
Facebook: https://www.facebook.com/dona.watson
Instagram: https://www.instagram.com/donawatson/
Amazon Author Page: https://amazon.com/author/donawatson
The Dona Watson Show devotional podcast can be found on all major podcast platforms or at TheDonaWatsonShow.buzzsprout.com

I enjoy hearing from my readers, so please feel free to reach out with questions and comments. I also greatly appreciate book reviews and word-of-mouth promotion. If you enjoyed Soul Designers, please consider taking a few minutes to leave a review on Amazon, Goodreads, or your favorite online bookseller. Thank you so much!

Also by Dona Watson